James

Sandy Loyd

Published by Sandy Loyd
Copyright 2012 Sandy Loyd
Cover design by Kelli Ann Morgan
Interior layout: Judi Fennell at www.formatting4U.com

For more information on the author and her works, please see www.SandyLoyd.com

This book is also available in electronic form from some online retailers.

Chapter 1

"Get a good look, buddy!" Samantha Collins wanted to shout when she caught the guy's interested gaze taking a trip to the front of her blouse. And here she thought he was being polite, opening the door for her.

She made eye contact. He had the grace to flush and murmured a quick apology before his eyes darted straight ahead and his feet followed. He obviously didn't find her boring, she thought, glancing down at the blouse she'd unbuttoned in an act of defiance just minutes before entering the noisy, trendy hangout. Shaking her head in disgust and working to clear the haze of pain from her brain, she muttered, "What is it with guys? We all have to be half-undressed, otherwise they'll think we're uninteresting?"

She charged in the direction of the bar and perched on a stool with one goal. She needed a drink.

"What'll it be, sweet thing?" The bartender halted in front of her and wiped the bar in swift, easy movements.

She eyed the lanky, attractive man. Would he have called her *sweet thing* if her blouse had been fastened at its usual top button? *Probably not.*

"A shot of tequila," she said, going for something with a kick. She normally drank wine, but this abnormal situation definitely warranted Mexican courage. Her special dinner had ended in a disaster. She'd expected a proposal from the man of her dreams, not a verbal attack concerning her personality quirks.

A shot glass filled with clear liquid appeared in front of her as Charles' concerns replayed in her mind. How could he think their relationship was predictable and unexciting?

He thought she was boring? Sam slumped forward. Maybe she was.

He hadn't actually said boring, she reminded herself. *He might as well have*, she argued back. "Sedate" and "settled" amounted to pretty much the same thing. The way he'd spoken the two words, like she was suffering from a contagious disease, really stung.

Of course she was sedate and settled. She was also precise and determined. Knew exactly what she wanted. Had her life outlined better than any AAA road map. Her trip to success began at the age of sixteen, and since then she'd spent a lot of time and effort to become someone. Someone worthy of marrying a successful man like Charles Winthrope III. Marriage to a man like him meant everything to her and, in three years' time, she'd hoped to be the mother of Charles Winthrope IV. She and Charles loved each other, for heaven's sake. Yet, he found their relationship lacking. He found *her* lacking.

Where had she gone wrong?

She downed the tequila in one swallow and blinked back tears, as more of their earlier conversation filtered through her consciousness. He'd called their relationship "tedious."

Tedious!

How could he think that? She wasn't tedious. She was an architect. A talented businesswoman. She could understand him saying they needed to spend more time together, but he'd asked for a break to think about his future. What about *her* future?

Just then the bartender stood in front of her.

"I was expecting to celebrate my engagement tonight," she offered, when his eyebrows lifted.

She cast her eyes down and stared at her empty shot glass, remembering Charles' serious expression as he'd delivered his news. At that moment, she'd kissed the thought of finding a diamond ring in her tiramisu good-bye. She might never get a ring from him.

Sam glanced up and noted a touch of sympathy in the bartender's eyes. "Do I look rigid?"

"No way." He filled a glass of beer from the tap.

Yeah, she thought, now becoming angry. How dare *he* call her *rigid*? Not a man whose bedtime routine included flossing between each tooth twice, and he counted for twenty seconds while brushing each part of his mouth to make sure he followed his dentist's advice. That was pretty damned rigid, if you asked her.

His every minute was scheduled. Just like hers. They understood each other completely. How could he now view their stable relationship as tedious? She'd even given him an opportunity to back down by reminding him of their shared values.

And his reply? She shook her head. He'd like more spontaneity. Apparently, Lucinda Thomas was spontaneous.

"I think he's got the hots for his new co-worker," she whispered. The spots of color that had hit Charles' cheeks confirmed her assumption when she'd asked him outright about the perky woman who'd never hidden her interest in Charles.

Yet, Sam had always thought he was immune to such temptation because they were so well matched. That thought set her back a bit. Maybe they were tedious together.

She nodded toward the empty shot glass. "I need another."

In moments, a second shot appeared.

So Mary Ann was right. Hadn't she warned about complacency in relationships? According to her best friend, men were vulnerable to feminine tactics, especially right before they actually committed to one specific woman. Sam hated to admit that she might have been a little too confident, a little too accepting, in just assuming everything would work out. After all, he was her perfect match, the stable dream man she'd always yearned for. They were perfect for each other. Unfortunately, an impulsive, bubbly loan officer could mar that perfection.

She wouldn't let that happen. Maybe Charles had a valid point. If their relationship needed a little spontaneity, she could do spontaneous. How hard could it be?

"Hey, Collins."

She groaned, rolling her eyes skyward. "Please, Lord, don't let it be Morrison," she said under her breath. She knew without glancing up, prayer did no good. No one called her Collins but him. She turned toward the voice and sighed.

Just what she needed to make her night a total bust—James Morrison, one of her partners in the architectural firm of Morrison, Morgan, Stone and Collins—and the last person she wanted to witness her attempt at drowning her relationship sorrows in tequila. He was the one with the relationship problems, not her.

Why oh why had she claimed, and quite smugly she might add, that she was practically engaged? The memory of her boastful conversation with James flashed through her mind as he walked up to her.

She shrugged, then swallowed the second shot. *Who cares? He'll have to get used to the new Samantha Collins along with Charles.*

She pasted her best fake smile on her face and nodded to the guy who grabbed the stool next to her as if he owned the place. Of course, the move was so like him. The man had a smooth confidence. Had a way with the ladies, too. She was immune to his early Robert Redford appeal, the same look immortalized in *Butch Cassidy and the Sundance Kid.* Those baby blues and streaked blond hair did nothing for her. She was into Charles' classic, dark looks, and he was too much of a gentleman to have a reputation. She snorted. *Until now!*

"I'd ask what you were doing here without Winthrope, but I can see for myself."

"Oh? What would that be?" She captured the bartender's notice and held up her empty glass.

"Getting drunk."

He chuckled. Ignoring the fuming glare she sent him, he took the glass out of her hand and sniffed. "What are you drinking? Looks like tequila. I never took you for a tequila kind of gal, Collins."

"Yeah? And what kind of gal do you see when you look at me?" They had a great working relationship, but he probably thought she was boring too. She definitely didn't fit the mold of women he usually dated, which was fine by her.

His hands went up in mock surrender. "That's a loaded question, and one I can't answer without matching you drink for drink."

Her aggravation vanished as an uncontrollable giggle burst free. James might be a guy who'd dated enough women since she'd met him to fill a small city's phone book, but despite her embarrassment of the situation, he did make a darned good friend. "There's the bartender. I'm sure he'll fix you right up."

"I'll pass. I still have to drive." He aimed his narrowed gaze on her. "What about you? You're not driving, are you?"

Sam shook her head. "Don't have my car. I can grab a taxi. I left Charles at Angelo's," she said, indicating a fancy restaurant a block away. "I needed air, so I walked."

"Lover's quarrel?"

She shrugged. "Something like that."

His attention moved to a spot beyond her shoulder. She watched as his eyebrows shot up and a smile covered the bottom half of his face. He nodded in the direction his eyes were focused. "Don't look now, but Charles is at seven o'clock, stalking this way. He doesn't look too happy."

Her smile faded. She straightened and swiveled around, grabbing on to the bar to steady herself. "I'm not the one who wanted a break."

"Ouch. Sounds serious."

"Nothing I can't handle."

Charles slowed to a stop in front of her. Even in the darkened bar, his face appeared flushed. "Samantha. I don't understand your behavior."

"What didn't you understand?" She tried hard not to slur her speech. "I thought I was quite clear. I read your remarks like the morning paper. You find me boring and want to break up."

"No," he blurted out. "I'm sorry I made a mess of things. My goal was to improve our relationship, not end it. I just wanted a little time to think."

Sam blew her bangs in exasperation, not really caring that her control had slipped and she was now arguing with Charles in front of Morrison. Besides, why bother hiding the truth? Their relationship did need improving. One lunch, and she'd be telling James everything anyway, only this time she'd be asking for his advice, not the other way around.

"How much time?" She met Charles' gaze and watched him fidget under her narrow-eyed scrutiny. *Let him squirm.* No way, she would make this easy on him. She noticed the hint of pink snaking up his face and smiled. "This isn't middle school, Charles. You should be mature enough to know your mind after three years and not act like an eighth grader."

He cleared his throat and looked at James.

"Don't look at Morrison. He's never progressed past high school so he can't help you." She ignored James' disgruntled, "Hey, careful with the verbal jabs," and added, "You started this. How much time do you need? A month? Two months? A year?"

"A week or so," Charles squeaked out. "I realize now it was a stupid idea."

"No. Don't back down now." She kept her unwavering gaze on him. Eventually he glanced at the bar and studied her empty shot glass for too many seconds. She sighed. "If you need time to be sure of me, then take it. I certainly don't want you rushing into something." Oh no, she wouldn't push him, but she wouldn't let this go without giving it her best shot, either. A few weeks ought to do it. She was good at reinventing herself. If Charles wanted spontaneity, then she'd become as free spirited as a leaf blowing in the wind. "Now go away."

"Go away?" he sputtered. "I can't leave you in a bar. Come on. I'll take you home."

The bartender placed her third shot in front of her. She was starting to see double, but she had her pride. Sam wasn't going anywhere with Charles tonight. She'd walk first. She picked up her drink. "I'm not ready to leave yet and I'm still too angry with you to let you stay, so go away."

"Now who's acting like an eighth grader?"

She shrugged and downed the contents, then slammed the glass on the bar. "Answer me this. Is an eighth grader sedate and settled?"

"What?" He pushed his glasses to the bridge of his nose. The lenses magnified his soulful brown eyes, exaggerating his stunned expression.

Unwilling to let that gaze affect her, she said, "Just answer the damn question."

He cleared his throat. "I would think not."

"Then it's an improvement, isn't it?" Oh yeah. This was just the beginning. He asked for it. He'd never know what hit him, once she was done with him after three weeks.

"I'll make sure she gets home, Winthrope," James said, interrupting her gleeful thoughts.

Sam smiled at him and giggled. "You will?"

He nodded.

She patted Charles' cheek. "See? No need to worry. I'm perfectly safe. My friend, and colleague, is taking me home."

Charles looked as if he were going to argue. Then, he sighed. "Fine. I wish I hadn't said anything. I'll call you tomorrow."

"Don't bother." She leaned back and almost lost her balance. She grabbed the bar just in time. "I don't expect to hear from you for at least three weeks."

His back went ramrod. His entire body tensed. Even his smile was stiff, but he didn't make a scene. Good old Charles, she thought, watching him. She wondered briefly if he could handle what she had in store when he got exactly what he'd asked for in the short term. Maybe this was for the better. After all, marriage did need spicing up now and then. She'd have to put that into her plans for their second anniversary.

"You're right about our relationship suffering from tedium. A break can only help us, but I guess we can talk on the phone," she said, taking pity on him.

She held out her cheek, careful not to lean too far, and he bent to kiss her.

He glanced at James. "I appreciate your seeing her home." Then, muttering something about women, he pivoted and walked out of the bar, holding his head high without looking back.

"That was interesting." James turned to her. "So, I take it you're not planning your wedding?"

A frown replaced her smile. Her mood went south in a hurry. "Silly me. I thought for sure Charles was going to propose tonight. Instead, he called me rigid. Said our relationship is tedious and I'm too predictable."

"You can be a bit predictable." When she stiffened and opened her mouth to disagree, he amended, "Except where your work is concerned."

Sam shut her mouth and stared at him in silence for a long moment, noting only sincerity in his eyes. James cared about her and he would never lord it over her about this, not like she'd secretly done with him and his relationship problems. Maybe she'd been a tad judgmental.

"It's more than that," she finally said, losing the rest of her bravado. "I told you Charles has been acting funny for weeks, just assumed his behavior was related to nerves over asking me to marry him, but I left out the part about his new loan officer. Mary Ann says the timing's not a coincidence. Now that he asked for a break, I see her point. He says he likes her spontaneity. What if he likes more about her? She's gorgeous. What am I going to do?"

She'd never given her nondescript looks much thought. Primping was beneath Sam. So was makeup. Besides, what could Sam do to improve upon brown hair and brown eyes, other than become someone she wasn't? No, she wasn't a beauty by anyone's standards, but she had good bone structure, as her grandmother had always said. Since college, airheads with nothing but looks going for them certainly hadn't threatened her—until now.

"She's everything I'm not. What if I can't compete?" This was like high school all over again.

"Where's the Collins I know and love? What've you done with her?" James teased and pretended to search around her. "You're a creative artist and you're the woman Charles loves."

"He shouldn't have concerns. Not after three years. I've always thought we were in sync with each other. Obviously, he thinks differently."

"Maybe you match him too perfectly. He's a man. We men are simple creatures who only want to be needed. Of course, if you throw in a woman who's exciting in the bedroom, you'll have a slave for life."

"Leave it to you to make this about sex."

"I'll let you in on a little secret, Collins. Sex pretty much works on most guys."

"All I want is reliability in a mate, someone I can count on, who's stable enough to offer security." Her expression turned wistful. "It's all I've ever wanted." The memory of her bleak childhood flashed through her mind. She'd never had stability. She'd never had anyone to count on. She'd never known her dad, and her mom would never make Mother of the Year. Sam had decided early on to live her life differently and recoup everything her childhood lacked. From the first moment they started dating, she'd always been able to count on Charles. Until now.

"Well, cheer up, I'm here to help."

"You're joking, right?"

"Never been more serious in my life. Have you eaten?"

Sam ignored his question about eating, as her lips curled in disbelief. "How can a person who changes partners as often as you change your sheets help me fix my problems with Charles?"

"Ouch. You know you're exaggerating. What's more, you shouldn't offend me. I just might tell Brad and Russell we made a mistake and revoke your partnership."

She snorted. "Yeah, right." She'd made full partner only months earlier. Since her talent added a perfect mix to the firm, his threat held no more weight than a feather. Plus, their relationship had started out from the very beginning as friends, despite his penchant to go through women. In the four years she'd worked for the firm, he'd never been anything but a friend and an excellent mentor. James had also introduced her to Charles. "The only way you can help is to let me get drunk in peace."

"And that answers my question about eating." When she glared at him, willing him to leave, he only grinned. "I've never seen this side of you. Are you always this prickly when someone riles you?"

"Just being honest. I've been with Charles for three years. Your longest relationship in that time was—what? Four months?"

"Yep. Definitely hungry when you start insulting one of your peers without provocation. You shouldn't drink on an empty stomach." He stood, threw thirty dollars on the bar, and grabbed her hand to pull her off her perch. "Come on. I'll buy you dinner."

"Wait. I'm not ready to leave yet." Dizziness assaulted her as she reached for her purse and almost toppled.

"Yes, you are."

"No, I'm not." Thank God he held her hand firmly, making it easier to maintain her dignity.

"My image needs a major overhaul. I'm throwing out the old Sam and becoming more spontaneous. I plan to start by drinking a lot more tonight."

"Then we'll buy a bottle of tequila and go to my place, so you can finish. That way I can join you."

"It's Friday night. I'm sure you have better things to do than babysit me."

"Not a thing," James said, leading her to the door.

Her wobbly legs were slow to follow her brain's signals. Simply placing one foot in front of the other required intense concentration. "What happened to Veronica?"

"Same old, same old."

"Too bad. She seemed nice."

He shrugged, still tugging her along.

Unsteady, she barely kept up, thankful he still had a strong grasp on her hand, otherwise she might have embarrassed herself. She'd die before she'd let him know it. She'd also die before she'd let him know how much Charles' honesty hurt, or how that little voice in the back of her brain piped up again after a ten-year hiatus to tell her she didn't measure up. With all her success, the voice should be silenced for good. Since her pain hadn't abated, she wasn't near drunk enough. The thought of continuing at his house sounded much more appealing than going home to an empty apartment too sober, so she was glad his plans with Veronica had changed. She lived within walking distance, in the same San Mateo, California, neighborhood. Neither would have to drive.

~

James and Sam walked in silence through the parking lot to his Toyota Sequoia. He helped her inside the SUV.

"This really isn't a chick magnet. Someone like you should drive a sportier, sleeker car," she said, slurring her words, once he climbed in beside her and started the engine. "Why don't you?"

He bit the inside of his cheek to keep from laughing. "You know, Collins, I'll admit I have commitment issues, but I'm not that shallow."

"Sorry." Sam giggled. "Must be tough to go through so many women and not find one keeper in there somewhere."

James gave up the struggle to hold on to his laugh. "You're being a pain, you know? So I've had a problem finding the one? Is that a crime?" Usually, she was more understanding and less outspoken. But not tonight. The tequila had totally obliterated her normal restraint. He decided he liked her this way. He'd always liked her and felt comfortable around her. Never felt attracted to her, though. Which was a good thing because, as she'd often pointed out, his track record with women was shitty. Beyond shitty. He made a much better friend than long-term partner. Besides, she was too set in her ways—too serious, too single-minded for his taste. He liked his women softer, especially for a lover. She was a terrific friend, even when she was being too honest. "If you continue to insult me, I'm not going to help you."

"Fine." Another giggle escaped. "I still say you should drive a sportier car."

"Why? I like this car."

"Really?"

"Yeah. It's big enough with plenty of horsepower."

"Ah! The truth finally comes out."

"What truth?" He ignored the surge of irritation her comment brought forth, put the car in gear, and backed out of the space. "I like having ample power to use the four-wheel drive for going skiing in Tahoe, and being able to haul four adults and luggage is an added bonus." He spared her a glance after turning onto the main road.

"Enough about cars. Let's talk about you and Charles."

"Spoilsport."

"We're not here to poke fun at my mode of transportation," he said, braking for a red light. When the car came to a stop, he gave her his full attention. "Do you want my help or not?"

"Sure. My problem is simple." She made a face. "I'm too rigid. I doubt talking will do much."

"Talking always helps put things in perspective."

"I already have perspective. Charles is concerned about our relationship. He called it tedious...said he wants more spontaneity...that I'm too predictable."

When he didn't respond, her chin shot up and she glared at him. Her entire body straightened into one tight board. "I am not predictable."

"Of course not." He shook his head, stifling a grin at her outraged denial. In his opinion, Samantha Collins was someone he could set a clock to, she was so regimented. "Let's see. Monday you wear brown, Tuesday navy. Wednesday and Thursday you mix it up a bit with either brown, navy, or gray, but Fridays are always black."

"So, what are you? The clothes police? I happen to like those colors."

Of course she did. He rolled his eyes. "You know you could vary your pattern, go a little crazy and wear black on Monday."

"I'm organized." She broke off, considering his assessment. "And I'm a professional. I have to act the part."

"And you do—too much."

"What do you mean?" Some of the stiffness left her spine.

"I mean it wouldn't hurt to throw a little femininity into the mix. Those business suits you always wear make a guy wonder if there's really a female underneath."

"Just because I poked fun at your car doesn't mean you have to retaliate."

"I thought we were being honest. Don't think I've ever seen you in anything that shows off your feminine side. Red would look great on you." The look she sent him was priceless. "Trust me. I haven't lost any marbles. While you're at it, you should learn to relax. Enjoy life. You take everyday shit much too seriously."

When she stiffened up once more, he added quickly, not giving her a chance to interject, "When's the last time you left work early to do something frivolous?" The light turned green and he resumed driving. A half a block later, he added, "And your routine never varies. Every morning you come into the office at exactly seven forty-five with your usual cup of black Starbucks coffee and an apple. God forbid, you should ever eat an orange or drink a Coke."

"I guess I have become a little rigid in my quest for success." She leaned back into her seat and sighed. "Thank God I have three weeks to change and be more flexible." She remained silent until he turned into the Burger King parking lot. "Why are we stopping here? I thought we were going to dinner."

"It won't kill you to eat fast food."

"Yes, it will."

"Live a little. Think of this as your first exercise in flexibility."

"Studies have shown—"

"Quit reading the studies," he said. "Besides, you're in no condition to wait hours for a restaurant table, which is what it would take this time of night on a Friday." When she opened her mouth to complain, he put his finger over her lips. "Ah, ah, ah. You're being rigid. Three weeks isn't a lot of time." He grinned at her fuming glare—a glare so hot, he was sure he saw steam rising from the top of her brown hair that was tightly pulled back and held in place with its usual clip.

"I don't get what all those women see in you. You're obnoxious and pushy."

"It's my temperamental side, the artist in me. Can I help it if women love it?" He broke off and nodded toward the menu at the side of the car, ignoring her snort of disagreement. "Pick out something. FYI, I see a few nutritious items listed up there."

She told him and he ordered when the box outside his window squawked.

"See? Now was that so difficult?" he asked twenty minutes later, watching her wolf down the burger and fries like she was inhaling air, as they sat picnic style on a blanket in the living room of his San Mateo home. One thing about Collins, he thought, his gaze fixed on her as he polished off his margarita. He was always comfortable in her company. He could relax—be himself. He may give her a hard time about her inflexibility, but she was okay. Mainly because he could be an inflexible bastard at times, so they shared something in common.

"If I didn't know better, I'd say you like fast food more than you let on." He shook the frozen contents in the blender pitcher before topping off her drink, and then adding to his own.

"I guess I was hungry. I love BK Whoppers."

"Then why avoid them?" Her answer was a lift of her shoulders, which didn't satisfy his curiosity. "You don't have a weight problem, so what's wrong with enjoying a burger every now and then?"

"I'm not worried about gaining weight. I promised myself a long time ago I wouldn't do stupid things that weren't beneficial to living the best life I can. Since fast food's unhealthy, I don't eat it."

He considered her response while taking a sip of his margarita, wondering why she had this need to control her environment. Except in her designs. She gave her creativity full rein when she worked, never ceasing to amaze him with her fantastic ideas. Those two facets of her personality intrigued him. If he was going to help her with Winthrope, he needed to get her to push past that control, get her to lighten up.

He grinned. He'd bet a month's pay Collins was even controlled while making love. He mentally rolled his eyes. Not his problem. Like he had room to make judgments. He knew he was going through some kind of weird cycle right now, especially since he'd called it off with Veronica. He sighed. He didn't want to think of that either. He shoved his errant thoughts aside and teased, "I only know of one other woman who can eat like that and never gain an ounce."

"I've seen the women you date. Most look like they've never eaten a full meal in their life, much less enjoyed it."

"You know, you just might hurt my feelings."

When she snorted and said, "Fat chance," he chuckled. Sam always gave him a hard time about his choices in women. Which was why he'd been ultra-picky with Veronica and so sure a relationship with her would be different. Yet, somehow she'd bitten the dust, just as too many others had before her, and right now he was tired of the whole dating game.

"I was talking about Kate," he said, mentioning his sister-in-law.

"How're she and the baby?" Sam grinned, paying no attention to his affronted tone. "It's been a while since I last saw her."

"Both are doing great. My godchild is six months old tomorrow."

"Spoken like a true uncle."

"Kids are fun." All teasing left his demeanor. He shook his drink and studied the contents, working to understand his unsettled mood. Was he a selfish, self-absorbed bastard who couldn't commit, as Kate had accused right before they'd broken up? She hadn't pulled any verbal punches back then, had even claimed everything in his life had come too easy, especially women.

Of course, he'd denied it. Hell, he wasn't selfish. Nor was everything handed to him. True, women did seem to find him appealing, but so what? He always put his friendships first and he gave regularly to charity. Both time and money. He just wasn't good in the relationship department. He had to admit, commitment scared him. What if he made a mistake? At times, like right now, Kate's remarks echoed in his mind and he wondered if they didn't hold too much truth. He certainly didn't want to be that type of person. He took a sip. "I can see the allure of fatherhood. Paul took to it like he was born for the role."

"Do I denote a hint of dissatisfaction?"

He shrugged, and said honestly, "Maybe."

She didn't say anything for the longest time. He was beginning to think she'd dropped the subject until she asked softly, "Do you ever wish it had been different?" When his eyebrows rose in question, she added, "That it had been you instead of Paul?"

"Sometimes I wish I had what they have." His gaze moved to the picture window, overlooking the San Francisco Bay. A blanket of fog rolled in, slowly covering the bay like a carpet. He stared through holes left in the white, billowy patches, as if what he saw held the answers to love and happiness. He just didn't think he had it in him to commit to a woman.

"I loved her but I was never in love with her," he said, of his one and only long-term relationship. He'd dated Kate for so long without committing, their prior relationship had become a running joke among his family with Paul as the main instigator. Now his brother was happily married to her.

A sigh escaped.

Yeah. He'd love to experience with someone what they had found. After seeing Paul and Kate together, he realized the emotion he'd felt for Kate had been hollow compared to what his brother felt. He was well into his thirties and had dated a broad range of women without succumbing to anything close to what he assumed love entailed. He'd tried, especially in the last three years. He simply reached a certain level in his relationships and lost interest without understanding why, yet fully understanding the consequences. Love, marriage, and fatherhood simply weren't in his future. Maybe Kate's observations weren't so far off the mark after all.

"She was easy and there. And like the bastard I am, I took advantage of it." He broke off and grunted. "Nice try, but it won't work. We're supposed to be figuring out a way to help you with Winthrope, not dissecting my failures."

"Do we have to? Thinking about him and what he said just depresses me. Mostly because he's right." Sam swirled her frozen drink, put the glass to her lips, and downed the contents in one long gulp. "You know, when you promised me tequila, margaritas weren't exactly what I had in mind."

"I happen to like my margaritas. Besides, you got your tequila."

"Yeah, but the ice and lime juice dilute it too much. Earlier, I was drinking shots and the tipsiness has worn off. Discussing failures requires more liquid courage. Unfortunately, after one of these, I'm still too sober." She held up her glass. "This is for lightweights."

"Lightweights, huh?" When she nodded, he grinned. "Can't have that." He got up and headed toward his kitchen.

"So, what're we going to do?" she asked, following. "Drink it straight out of the bottle?"

"Never let it be said that James Morrison is a lightweight. My ego won't allow it."

She leaned against the doorjamb while he picked up the knife lying on the black granite countertop and rinsed it off. He reached for a lime.

"Real limes? How impressive."

"Yeah? Stick with me, kiddo, and I'll impress the hell out of you."

"You already do."

He began cutting the lime and ignored the way her approval slid over his back, much like a warm blanket. He also tried to ignore the way her blouse stretched, outlining a pair of well-proportioned breasts as she propped her back against the doorjamb with her hands behind her.

Quit looking at her. He concentrated on cutting, but his gaze wouldn't cooperate with his brain's signal and kept moving in the direction of the open *V* of her shirt.

Funny how he'd never noticed before. He did now. Samantha Collins had a damned fine body.

Get your mind out of the gutter, Morrison. She's off-limits. Not only is she a colleague, she's a friend who's practically engaged to a nice guy—a man you know socially. Just because he's being an idiot, doesn't mean you should be a bigger idiot and take advantage.

He sighed and went back to cutting, forcing his head down so his eyes stayed focused on the limes. When done, he handed her the salt and two shot glasses. Then he grabbed the plate of limes and bottle of tequila. "Come on. We have some serious drinking to do."

~

"**O**kay." Sam trailed after him, as he strode from the kitchen in the direction of the sofa. He set the limes and bottle on the coffee table and relieved her of the salt and glasses.

She watched him line up the ingredients in single file in front of him and pour tequila into the glasses, before both got comfortable sitting Indian style next to each other in the space between the sofa and coffee table.

"So, what do I do first?" Excitement filled her. "Limes, salt, and tequila. I had friends who used to do this in college."

"You've never done shots of tequila before tonight?" When she shook her head, he grinned. "You really need to let loose more."

"Isn't that what I'm doing?"

"I give you an *A* for effort. Here's to fun." He held up the shot glass.

She copied his movements…licking the salt, downing the shot, and sucking on the lime.

"Whew. That's powerful."

"I aim to satisfy. You got a double shot. Can't have you calling me a lightweight."

She giggled. "I wasn't referring to you when I made the comment."

"Oh?" His eyebrows shot up; he clearly expecting her to continue.

"Yeah. I was talking about myself. I just want to make sure I do it right because I've never been drunk before."

"So, how is it you're twenty-nine and still a virgin?"

He grinned when she shot him a surprised, "What?"

"You've never had a hangover, right?" His startling blue eyes danced, drawing a desire to join him in the steps. She couldn't take her gaze off his amused smile as she tilted her head to the side. He really was charm personified.

"See! A mere virgin if you've never experienced a hangover. It's a rite of passage. So, answer my question."

"What question?" She picked up the bottle, ignoring a sudden urge to grin, and poured the next round.

He chuckled. "For a virgin, you're a natural. I'm not dropping the subject. How did you survive college without at least one hangover?"

"I couldn't risk drinking then." Her thoughts drifted to her college days—a lifetime ago. Back then, she'd had too much riding on her scholarship to ever let loose and have a good time like all her friends, who thought of college as one big party. Doing well in college was a stepping-stone to a better life and she couldn't risk screwing it up with something as stupid as drinking. Times had certainly changed since then, she realized, after her best-laid plans had veered so far off course. In fact, she'd use tonight as a catalyst to a new, spontaneous Sam. "But I'm all for it now."

"I should warn you. The side effects can be brutal."

"Oh? I think I'll survive."

"Yeah, you will, but you're going to hate me in the morning for luring you into temptation."

"You have it backward. I led you. You'll probably hate me."

"I doubt it." He tossed out another chuckle then picked up his shot glass.

"I know why I want to get drunk. I'm just not sure why you do."

"I need a reason?" He saluted her with his glass, saying, "Cheers," and followed the ritual.

"It's so unlike you." She grinned. "Come to think of it, I've never seen you drink more than two glasses of wine. So…why are you letting me lure you into temptation on a Friday when you could be with Veronica instead of me? What happened with her?"

"Does it matter?"

Her grin stretched. "Call me curious."

He shrugged. "Beats the hell out of me." Then, after a long pause, he sighed. "I felt like I was going through the motions with her, and I wasn't in the mood to do it tonight. I'm glad I found you.

This is a lot more fun. The headache will be worth it."

The smile he sent made her think he really meant the sentiment, and she felt the same way. She was having the time of her life. A headache would be a small inconvenience in exchange.

Sam wasn't sure how many shots she drank; she only knew she was feeling no pain. They never did get around to talking about Charles and her inflexibility, which was fine by her.

She didn't think she could laugh any harder when James relayed the story of how his brother and sister-in-law, who were sworn enemies at the time, got together after a snowstorm stranded them for several days in Lake Tahoe.

"I want you to know, I made sure Paul suffered for stealing my girl."

"Was she?" His eyebrows rose, and she answered his implied question honestly. "Seems to me, if she'd been yours, he wouldn't have stood a chance." She needed to take her own advice. If Charles was truly hers, his loan officer didn't stand a chance either.

"Maybe. If I had thought of her as mine, I wouldn't have let him steal her. That's probably the same reason why I never seriously pursued the only other woman I've ever been totally attracted to. After getting to know her, I'd lost my chance. By the time I realized her allure, she belonged to someone else."

"No?" His comments about someone he'd never mentioned before brought her out of her thoughts and, giggling, she slapped his knee. "You mean someone actually stole your heart? Who was she?" Oh yeah. She was definitely feeling no pain when she could make such personal jokes about his love life. That he was responding in kind meant he was just as far-gone.

"No one. Just a fond memory of what might have been…" He sighed, staring wistfully at the full shot of tequila he held. "Oh, the things we do for friends," he said softly, before he finally downed the liquid and placed the glass on the table.

~

James touched her head as Sam reached across the table. She straightened abruptly, glancing at him with a question in her eyes.

"You know, if you let your hair down once in a while, it'd help." His words slurred a bit, which meant he was far too wasted, but by that point he didn't care. "Make you appear softer."

He released the clip from its usual tight grip, creating a startling effect. He couldn't take his gaze off her. He stilled the urge to run his hands through the thick, lush halo of silky softness that surrounded her face. Those lovely tresses highlighted expressive brown eyes, giving her an almost innocent appearance. She was quite pretty when she wasn't being so serious.

"I don't want to be softer. I'm fine the way I am." With an unsteady movement, she yanked her clip out of his hand, and bent to pull her long hair together.

"Charles might like you softer."

"Really?" Sam dropped her hands and drew her eyebrows together while her hair fell around her face again.

"All men do," he said, nodding. "Men want women to be women." He smiled. She looked so hopeful…so adorable…so irresistible…and, God help him, so kissable.

"Why are you looking at me like that?" Her voice came out in breathy wisps of air.

"I must be drunk." He shook his head to clear it. "All of a sudden I had an urge to kiss you."

She giggled. In seconds, her giggle erupted into uncontrollable laughter.

Though he knew she was as wasted as he, irritation swept over him as he stiffened. "You find the thought of kissing me funny?" He moved in closer. For some reason, he couldn't ignore her reaction.

"No." Her laughter died as quickly as it sprang to life. Her expression turned solemn.

Sam leaned against the sofa and ran her tongue nervously along her mouth before she bit her bottom lip, while studying him with huge, beautiful doe eyes. Her actions did nothing to ease his desire to smother her with kisses, in fact drew his attention to those pouty lips. Why had he never noticed before how perfect they were for kissing?

Whoa, back up, Morrison. This is Collins you're lusting after.

Despite the fact that her inclined position gave him an unobstructed view of a rounded, ample breast, he forced all sexual thoughts out of his brain. Yet, when she cleared her throat, sat up straight, and said too convincingly, "I'm immune to you, is all," they snuck back in and wouldn't budge. Especially after she added, "I'm not a gullible female who'll fall for a pretty face."

Her statement rankled, and his mind wouldn't let go of her implied challenge.

James had drunk too much tequila, and he knew damned well he should let her comments pass. He should stay on his course of helping her with Winthrope…he should remember they were friends. Hell, he should definitely ignore the heat now pooling in his groin at what a tempting sight she made, sprawled out next to him half exposed, with those generous, full lips begging to be kissed. Too late, he realized his biggest mistake. He should never have gotten drunk with her. Not tonight.

"So, you're immune to me?" He leaned in closer and smiled smugly at the doubt now shrouding her overconfident expression. "That's bullshit," he whispered as his mouth hovered over hers. Giving into impulse after pushing all sanity aside, he lowered his head and captured those lips. Once he leapt into craziness, Sam surprised the hell out of him. She wrapped her arms around him, pulled him closer, and inhaled his tongue in a wholly unpredictable way, sucking him in further. Nothing of her actions reminded him of his straight-laced friend, but he was too caught up in his own unexpected reaction to care.

He deepened the kiss. Savored what she offered with her tongue and mouth.

Of their own volition, his hands found her breasts. He took in the citrus scent of the limes mixed with the perfume she always wore. He'd never thought about it before, but her smell was intoxicatingly sexy, just like the feel of her. Eventually, he traced her bottom lip with his tongue. Tasted salt. Her loud moan floated somewhere above him, inciting a hunger he'd never experienced before this moment.

Stop, his mind screamed. *Before your need for her veers completely out of control and you ruin a friendship. Even you aren't that much of a selfish bastard.* Somehow, James found the strength to pull away, but he teetered on the edge of absolute insanity.

With his head mere inches above hers, he studied her expression. Her eyes were closed and a serene smile rested on her lips. How could such an unremarkable face elicit more desire, which still strummed at a fevered pace through his veins? Every cell in his body vibrated with yearning. He shouldn't want her, but he did.

Sam chose that moment to open her eyes, and the warmth spilling from them did nothing to ease his fight to stay motionless and not succumb to the lust pumping in his bloodstream.

"That was nice."

Nice…nice? "That's all you have to say? It was nice?" He'd never been so insulted. She'd given him one of the hottest kisses he'd ever had, and the only descriptive term she could use was nice?

"Okay, so you know how to kiss." She slurred the words. "I never doubted that." Her voice trailed off and her head slumped back. It took him a moment to realize she'd passed out.

Chapter 2

The pounding woke him. Pain reverberated inside his head and left him with no idea of where sound began and the headache left off. The dull, throbbing thuds also reminded him why he never drank more than a few glasses of wine in one sitting. His mouth tasted putrid—something he supposed a small, dead animal might taste like after a night of decomposition.

Hangovers were a bitch.

More pounding vibrated through his teeth, and the jackhammers inside his head went off again.

Who the hell was knocking his door off its hinges this early on a Saturday morning? He glanced at the clock and groaned. *Amend that. Saturday afternoon.*

James rose and his focus landed on Collins. She appeared so peaceful on the other side of his king-sized bed. A calm sight before an emotional storm, he thought, wondering how she'd feel about spending the night with him. It was definitely a spontaneous move. On his part, not hers.

Hell, he couldn't just leave her passed out in his living room. Since he loathed the idea of placing her in his guest room, he carried her to bed with him. Somehow, last night it seemed right. Now, in the light of day while stone-cold sober, he wasn't so sure.

Another reason to never get shitfaced again. God, my head hurts.

He held his head and moved at a quick pace toward the front door to cease the pounding before his brain exploded.

He yanked the door open. "What?" he said, as heatedly as he could and still get the word out without creating more pain.

Kate Morrison, his sister-in-law, handed him the carryall containing his sleeping nephew, then pushed past him into the room.

"Don't you ever call?" He anchored Nick to his side, held the carryall with a firm grip, and followed Kate. He stilled a wave of nausea that threatened at the same time the sinking feeling hit in the pit of his stomach, making him think he was being pulled in two directions.

The sensation intensified when he glanced at Kate's face. Something about her expression didn't bode well. He knew that determined look…he'd spent eight years trying to dodge it. He really regretted last night now.

"Call? Why would I call?" Her smile brightened. "I just dropped Paul off at the airport and you knew I was coming. You promised a week ago you'd watch Nicky this afternoon while Judith and I play. We're getting the works. Hair, manicures, then doing an early dinner after shopping."

"Damn." He closed his eyes, fighting misery. *How stupid of me to forget.* He never turned down an opportunity to babysit Nicholas. He opened his eyes, trying to focus on her as she paused, did a full three-sixty, and took in the remnants of the night before.

Her eyebrows shot up. "I didn't interrupt anything, did I?"

"No." His denial came out too rushed. He set the carryall in a playpen he kept in the corner of the room and started cleaning up.

Collins chose the next moment to appear in the doorway, looking like death in a body that moved, all color gone from her cheeks, her hair sticking out, and her clothes a total mess.

"I think I'm going to be sick." She charged for his bathroom.

"You slept with Samantha Collins?" Kate stretched her five-foot-two-inch frame into something that looked like a mother bear defending a cub and raged indignantly, "What the hell is wrong with you?"

"I didn't sleep with her," he growled, not liking the accusation flashing in her eyes. Even though he technically did sleep with her, he hadn't *slept* with her. Thank God. "Back off. My head hurts and I haven't had a cup of coffee." With an empty tequila bottle and two shot glasses in hand, he stormed to his kitchen to remedy his lack of caffeine, saying over his shoulder as he went, "Can you give me a few minutes?"

He looked toward the heavens. *Please, Lord; don't let her leave without giving me a chance to shower so I can at least feel human.*

"No problem. I've got time before I have to pick up Judith in the city." Kate came up behind him and pushed him out of the way as he filled the pot with water. "Here, I'll even take pity on you and make coffee." She relieved him of the pot, then poured the contents into the right slot, and grabbed a filter. "In the meantime, you can fill me in on last night."

Seconds later, she began to grind coffee beans. The whine of the grinder, along with the pitch of her voice, ricocheted through his brain. He closed his eyes, working to still the hammering. Would he ever feel normal again? He yanked the cupboard open and groped for the aspirin bottle. He shook out six extra-strength tablets, and popped three into his mouth, not waiting for water. He left three on the counter for Collins.

"You need fluids." Kate placed a full glass of water in his hand. "Drink this."

James hadn't even heard the faucet, but he thankfully downed the water to wash the aspirins' acidy aftertaste away. The minute he put the glass on the counter, she stuck another in his hand.

"Drink."

He was too weak to disobey the firm tone she'd often used on her son, and swallowed it down in seconds.

"So, what the hell happened last night?"

"Nothing happened last night."

"I see." There was a long pause before she said, "Let me reword my question. What the hell was Samantha Collins doing coming out of your bedroom?"

"It's really none of your business."

Her back straightened. She eyed him skeptically, letting one brow rise. She waited.

He hated that look. He's spent enough time with her to know she'd never back down. He sighed and surrendered to her mental thumbscrews. "We got a little carried away doing shots of tequila. God, just the thought of tequila now makes me want to puke."

"Shots of tequila? You and Samantha Collins got drunk together? And nothing happened?"

"Yes."

"Why? What's going on? You seriously can't expect me to buy such a lame explanation."

"Okay…okay…you win. Quit with the interrogation." The incredulous tone of her voice hurt his skull. She'd only gotten better at the game since becoming a mother. "I was being a friend." He left out the part about the kissing. He wasn't quite sure what he thought about that. Not when his head was about to explode. Besides, she didn't need to know everything. "I found her at the Pit Stop and couldn't leave her there. Charles is being an ass. From what I gathered, Winthrope has a burr up his butt about their relationship becoming predictable. Can you believe it?"

"You're kidding." Kate's response brought out the first real desire to smile since he woke up. He gave in to the impulse and his lips curled. "The guy's totally nuts, if he thinks Collins is more predictable than he is. Theirs is a match made in heaven. Only an idiot would let her get away. She's perfect for him."

Which was the very reason he introduced the two in the first place. Collins might have a few quirks, but she was genuine. He was damned lucky she'd passed out, he realized. Otherwise, he might have done something stupid. Something that might have ruined their friendship.

James sighed and took the cup of coffee Kate offered. He inhaled deeply, letting the rich aroma infiltrate his body. Finally, he took a sip. The warm liquid eased part of his misery. Thank God for coffee, he thought, as he watched Kate pour two more cups without waiting for the entire pot to brew.

"I don't think I've ever felt so bad," came the croaky voice from the direction of the doorway.

"You don't look good, Sam," Kate said, clucking and looking past his shoulder.

He glanced over and pressed his lips tightly together to keep a straight face. For some reason he couldn't fathom, it helped to see someone who was in worse shape. Samantha Collins appeared to be suffering much more than he. *Yep! Misery definitely loves company.*

"Told you, you'd hate me today."

"Hate is too mild a word." When her gaze took in the coffee, he saw a spark of life touch her eyes. "Hi, Kate. Is that for me? Please tell me yes. I really need a cup of coffee right now." She moved very slowly into the room, holding her head as she walked. "I never knew hair could hurt so much."

Kate handed her a glass of water. Her nod indicated the aspirin. "You might want to take those and drink this first. Fluids help."

She groped for the pills, flashing thanks with her eyes.

"You know, Collins, seeing you like this makes up for my own pain."

Without moving a muscle, irritation flared in those brown eyes, extinguishing all gratitude.

He grinned. "Remember the right of passage. A person can't go through life without experiencing at least one hangover."

"I can't believe you let me drink so much, knowing how I'd feel this morning. That's got to be the most sadistic thing you've ever done."

"Actually, I'd forgotten how bad they can be, so don't go painting me as the devil," he said, chuckling, only too glad she seemed to be taking their kiss in stride. "You were well on your way to a hangover before I even got to you."

He turned to Kate who was watching their conversation with too much interest.

"What? You weren't there, so keep quiet. I was drinking margaritas. I'm not the one who forced her to do shots." He turned back to replenish his coffee. "Give me ten minutes to shower before you take off, will you?" Relieved to have the excuse to exit, he grabbed his cup and headed for the bathroom before Kate could ask any more questions about last night.

~

Samantha took a long drink of coffee and watched him go. Parts of their evening floated back in a foggy haze. She wondered if she'd imagined their kiss. Or was it a drunken stupor and wishful thinking? She mentally groaned as flashes of those wonderful, magical feelings flared to life, overlapping the pain. The kiss wasn't a delusion. Surely she hadn't kissed him so boldly? Was her memory skewed? What about James? He didn't look fazed this morning. No, it had to be the alcohol. Charles never kissed her like that. Maybe the spontaneity their relationship needed could be found in a few shots of tequila.

"So, you spent the night with James?"

Kate's question pulled Sam's attention. Her voice and expression held concern along with curiosity. Sam smiled as much as her face would let her while her hair hurt so much.

"The evening is still hazy. I'm sure James was just being nice, letting me sleep in his bed."

"Really? You slept in his bed?" Kate pushed away from the counter she'd been leaning against and grabbed the coffeepot. She refilled Sam's cup first, then her own. "Drink up." She picked up her cup, studying it thoroughly.

They spent a few minutes in companionable silence before

Kate's speculative voice interrupted Sam's thoughts again. "You know, James never lets women spend the night here."

Sam shrugged. "So? What was he going to do, kick me out after I passed out like a log in his living room?"

"Interesting," Kate murmured, then took a drink. She gave a satisfied nod and added in a louder voice, "James says Charles is being an ass. Last I heard, you two were almost engaged. What happened?"

"James is only half right. He *is* being an ass, but it's for the right reason. Our relationship has become a little staid and he wants more spontaneity. Seems his new co-worker is spontaneous." She spent a moment updating Kate on what happened, ending with, "My friend thinks Lucinda, that's her name, is out to lure him away from me." She shrugged. "I doubt that'll happen. I mean, I trust Charles, but I don't want to be overconfident either."

That wouldn't help their relationship. After all, hadn't she thought everything was moving in the right direction before last night, only to be totally wrong? "Anyway, she's gorgeous. I'm not, so I'm thinking of doing something drastic. You know, like reinventing myself so he'll see what's right in front of his nose," Sam added, half joking. Unfortunately, there was too much truth to her remarks to laugh.

"What'd you have in mind?"

"I have no idea. I only know I've got three weeks to do it." She sighed and brought her cup to her lips. "I always thought our relationship was perfect. Until last night. Why do we go to such extremes for love?"

"I can think of a few good reasons." Kate's eyebrows shot up and down. "In the end, men are worth whatever we put into the relationship."

"Maybe, but I'm not sure they're worth a hangover. I'm not cut out to drink."

Kate chuckled. "Makes you wonder why there are so many alcoholics, huh?" She broke off, clearly thinking. After a long pause, she said, "I'm meeting Judith McAllister in the city. Why don't you make a day of it and come with us? We'll help you reinvent yourself. I'm sure Maurice will squeeze you in for a hair appointment."

Sam eyed the elegantly clad woman, who, like her, had brown hair and eyes. That's where the similarities ended. All of a sudden, she felt lacking and insignificant. Oh, not exactly like in high school. Kate didn't have a mean bone in her body. Not with her bubbly personality. And, Judith was married to James' best friend, Dev McAllister. She'd known the two for as long as she'd worked at Morrison, Morgan, Stone and Collins, and in that time, both women had never been anything but warm and caring. Still, Sam always felt a little in awe around them and right now she didn't need more reasons to beat herself up.

"I don't think so." She scrunched her nose. She wasn't in their league. She'd never seen either woman look anything less than glossy and put together, like a page from a fashion magazine. She was anything but. "You don't need a third wheel messing up your plans for the day. Besides, I can't think right now. I only want to go home and figure out a way to spice up my relationship with Charles."

"This is perfect. What better way to put your plan into action? Be spontaneous and get a complete makeover. You'll feel great. A makeover will definitely get Charles' attention, don't you think?"

Sam was about to decline again when Kate clapped her hands and cut her off, saying, "You'll see. We'll start with hair, nails, and makeup, then move on to shopping. We'll hit Nordstrom's and Union Square."

"I don't think so." She shook her head. "I'm just not into girly-girl stuff."

"Oh, come on. All women are into looking better. Say yes." Kate laughed, and all but jumped up and down in excitement. "I won't let you say no."

"I wouldn't enjoy it." She didn't add that shopping wasn't high up there on her to-do list. A root canal sounded more appealing. "I feel like dog poop right now."

"Not a good enough excuse. Remember, if you want to be spontaneous, you have to just do things on the spur of the moment. We'll drop by your place so you can shower and change."

Kate's enthusiasm was contagious. Plus, she presented a good argument. How would Sam ever accomplish her goal if she weren't willing to try something new? Suddenly, shopping and getting her hair done sounded perfect. They might be just the spice she needed to feel better about herself. "What about James?"

"He's done showering. The water shut off five minutes ago."

James strode out, blond hair still damp and face clean-shaven, with a towel around his neck, looking much more refreshed. "Thanks for waiting. I feel human now and the headache's just a dull thud."

"Well then, our day of fun awaits. Sam's joining us." Kate winked at Sam, before she turned and kissed James' cheek. She strode over to the playpen and observed her sleeping son. "He's still out. Should be for at least another hour. Everything you need is in the bag." Then, she headed for the front door, grabbing Sam's hand along the way. "We'll be back," she said, giving a good Arnold Schwarzenegger impression.

Samantha followed her out with the notion that despite feeling so wretched, she was embarking on the adventure of a lifetime. Funny. Never in a million years would she believe she'd ever think of shopping and makeovers as adventurous. Torturous, maybe…but not adventurous.

~

"You're sure Judith won't mind me tagging along," Sam asked forty-five minutes later, as Kate sped up the car to merge onto I-280, the main interstate heading north to San Francisco. She'd showered, changed, and at Kate's urging, had a bowl of cereal. Though not one hundred percent herself, she did feel better, but she was having second thoughts about the day.

"Why would she mind?"

"I'm horning in on your plans." Why had she agreed? She had a million things she could be doing.

"Oh, please. Nothing could be further from the truth. Maurice is a genius. His help, along with a good makeup artist, will work wonders. Trust me. Seeing what they accomplish is much more fun and exciting than having the same old cut."

"I hope you're not disappointed." Sam sighed and looked out the window, wishing she wasn't so plain. "I'm not convinced the afternoon will generate the results you want."

Kate only grinned and said in a smug voice, "You'll see."

"Sam's joining us today," Kate said twenty minutes later when Judith opened the car door after they'd pulled into her driveway and honked. "I told her you wouldn't mind."

Judith climbed inside. "Why would you think I'd mind? The more, the merrier."

"I found her at James' house when I dropped off Nicky. She ended up in bed with him."

"Don't tell her that," Sam shrieked at the same time Judith paused in the middle of putting on her seat belt and looked up. "Really? This I've got to hear."

"Why? It's true." Kate shifted into reverse.

She backed out of the driveway as Sam said, "She'll get the wrong idea about what happened."

"Not if you tell me exactly what happened." Judith snapped her belt into place with a final click and grinned. "Now, I'm dying to know."

"There's nothing to tell." Sam crossed her arms and glanced out the window.

Kate's snort said otherwise.

Sam leaned her head against the seat and blew her bangs, reaching for patience, before she turned to meet Judith's speculative gaze. "Nothing happened."

"Nothing happened," Judith mouthed to Kate in the rearview mirror. She shook her head slightly and added, still mouthing, "Something happened."

"Please!" Sam sighed in exasperation. "This is James we're discussing."

Judith shrugged. "She's got a point."

"No." Kate waved a dismissive hand, shaking her head as she drove. "I know James. He never lets a female invade his space. He was even guarded about it when I dated him. This means something."

"Will you two stop." Sam giggled. "Charles and I had an argument last night and James just happened to be in the right place at the right time to take me under his wing. End of story."

"He's good at that, isn't he, Kate?"

Kate nodded. "Yeah. James can't commit to a woman, but he's always there when you need him. Still, I wonder what got into him. It's so unlike him to let a woman stay at his house."

"Tequila got into him. And he *was* there when I needed him." Sam paused, still smiling. "I'm glad you twisted my arm into coming today, Kate. I think I needed this, too."

"Kate can be persuasive, not to mention tenacious, when she gets something in her mind. She *is* the same woman who spent eight years working to bring James to the altar, so run with it," Judith said good-naturedly.

"Can I help it if James is dense in the relationship department? Thank God, Paul saved me from myself. This is a great plan of attack." The mischievous smile Kate flashed sent a wave of apprehension over Sam, the sensation strengthening with her next sentence. "Charles won't know what hit him when we're done."

"I hope so." Lord, did Sam hope so. Not only for Charles' reaction, but she certainly didn't want to disappoint these two.

"Sam has no clue about what's in store, does she?"

"Hush, Judith, you're scaring her." Kate patted Sam's hand, reminding her of a gesture someone might make when trying to calm a frightened child going in for surgery. "You won't be sorry. Maurice is really good and worth every penny."

More uncertainty tightened in her stomach. However, she had no more time for concerns. Within ten minutes, the trio walked into the salon on Union Street. Shortly after that, her self-consciousness disappeared, replaced with a sense of fun and excitement. No one could feel awkward amid Judith's easy charm or Kate's enthusiasm. Not only were both gorgeous opposites—Judith's tall, willowy, blonde, green-eyed loveliness, against Kate's energetic, petite, brown-eyed beauty—they were two of the nicest women Sam had ever met. Definitely not mean girls.

Even Maurice's *tsks*, *ooohs*, and *ahs* as he lifted her hair and examined the brown strands with a speculative gleam in his eye, like she was some kind of experimental monster to his Dr. Frankenstein, didn't faze her newfound confidence. So what if she was plain? She had other assets. Assets that had attracted Charles in the first place.

"Such rich color and so thick. Where have you been all my life?" Maurice teased. "When I get done with you, you'll be mine forever."

He turned, snapped his fingers, and gave a few terse orders. Next thing Sam knew, he had her in a chair, wrapped in a plastic sheet secured with Velcro at her neck while he gripped a pair of shears.

What have I gotten myself into? Now he really does resemble Dr. Frankenstein.

Sam marveled over her calm demeanor as he chopped. She'd never liked having people mess with her hair, had only had it cut a handful of times in twenty-nine years. She loved the length, even if the color was a little dull. As each dark strand fell to the floor, she pretended that it was someone else's hair, not hers.

An hour later, Sam spied her reflection in the mirror and smiled.

The world had surely tilted on its axis. Wired for sound with foil while a manicurist filed her nails, her reaction amazed her. Not only had she allowed everything with dignity, she now relished the idea of being waited on like royalty.

Soon it was all over and they were ready to leave.

"Come on, we're not done, yet," Kate said, half dragging her toward the door of the salon, just after Sam had paid Maurice and promised to be back in six weeks for a trim.

"And remember. No hair clips," he shouted from the back of the shop.

Sam grinned, shook her head, and caught her reflection in the mirror she passed.

My goodness. I've become a girly girl. The woman staring back was not plain. Not any longer. *Is that really my hair?* It was still long, which seemed impossible judging from the amount of hair left behind, but the style somehow highlighted her face and made her eyes more noticeable. She couldn't get over what he'd accomplished in two hours.

Anxious to find out what else Kate and Judith had in store, Sam quickened her steps as they headed for the car. Once inside, Kate started the engine, then wound her way downtown before finally pulling up to a valet station.

"Ooh, valet parking." Judith grinned. She turned to Sam and winked. "She's splurging today. Usually, you can't get her to part with a dollar."

"We have Sam with us and this is a special occasion."

"She rates and I don't? Aren't I special too?"

"We have legs and can walk from self-parking. Can I help it if I'm frugal?"

"I put myself through school, so I understand frugality," Sam interjected, trying to be helpful.

"See?" Kate jammed the gearshift into park. "She understands."

They all climbed out of the car and started for the glass doors.

"So, you paid for college yourself?" Kate asked as they walked into Nordstrom's. "Must've been rough."

"Scholarships mostly." Sam gave a negligent lift to her shoulders. "The rest I earned working as a waitress. The job had fringe benefits. All I could eat when I worked which allowed me to survive on next to nothing. I didn't want loans hanging over my head when I graduated."

"Wow. I never realized how lucky I was to have my parents pay for my education."

"Me neither," Judith chimed in.

"Now you know the biggest reason why I'm not into the girly-girl thing."

Judith laughed. "Girly-girl thing?"

"You know…beauty. Beauty costs money, money I never had to spend when I was younger. Plus, I've never felt the need."

Until now. So why did she feel the need to do it now? Was it to impress Charles? Shouldn't he love her for what was on the inside? She should be doing this for herself, not him. Otherwise, wouldn't she be selling out her values? That thought brought her up short. Was any man really worth so much effort? On the other hand, this was Charles, not just any man, she reasoned. Still, the nagging thoughts continued, which concerned her. She couldn't be having second thoughts. Not about him.

"Maybe, but it's also fun to play." Kate's voice drew her out of her thoughts as the women halted in front of an aisle leading to ten similar cosmetic counters, each promoting a different company's line. Kate turned to Sam. "What do you do to play?"

"Play?"

"Yeah. You know, enjoyment…fun."

"I never had the luxury of doing something for fun." She shrugged, feeling as uninteresting as dirt just then. "I've been too busy trying to get ahead and planning my life so I don't end up like my mother." Heck, her explanation sounded pitiful, even to her ears.

"How'd she end up?" Judith asked in a soft voice.

Sam cleared her throat, wishing she could take it back. She rarely talked about her poverty-stricken childhood; in fact, she pretended those years belonged to someone other than her. "Too poor, with one too many mouths to feed." She caught the look Kate and Judith sent each other and quickly added, "It's in the past and not a big deal. I'm lucky. I've got brains and talent. So far, it's worked." She sighed. Now she sounded even more boring. "I guess I could use a little fun. Maybe that's what Charles thinks is missing." She placed a warm smile on her face and looked expectantly, first at Kate then at Judith. "You two are exactly what I needed today. Thanks, Kate, for insisting I do this."

"That's what friends are for." Kate grabbed her hand and pulled her up to an empty chair at a brand-name cosmetic counter and commanded, "Sit." She then nodded to the perky assistant, who, judging from her skillfully made-up face, looked like she got a discount on the merchandise. "She needs a makeover."

Sam complied with her demand to sit, then cautioned, "I don't want to look like a clown." When both Judith and Kate dissolved into gales of laughter, she backed down. "Okay. I trust you two. Just go easy on me. I'm a virgin at this."

"Careful. It's habit forming," Kate teased. "Just like sex."

Sam didn't add to the comment because to her the act was anything but habit forming. Sex with Charles was okay. She enjoyed it on occasion, but not enough to make it a daily routine. She even caught herself making excuses to avoid it.

"You're not laughing." Kate studied her with eyes that appeared to miss nothing. "Don't tell us. You think sex is overrated."

"It *is* overrated." Heat stole up her face and Sam didn't need to look into the mirror in front of her to know her cheeks were red. Thankfully, Dory, identifiable by the name on her lab coat, was covering Sam's face with foundation. "My sex life just needs a shot in the arm. We'll be fine."

"Can you believe it?" Kate gave Judith an incredulous look. "She's as bad off as we used to be."

Judith laughed. "Since you've inadvertently let us in on a few of your little secrets, it's only fair to tell you a couple of ours. Though, they're really not all so secret. Both Kate and I were idiots before we each met the love of our life."

While Dory worked on Sam, transforming her into someone she barely recognized, Judith entertained her with the story of how she and her husband, Dev McAllister, got together. Even Dory would stop every now and then to ask a question, proving she listened intently to the tale about the college party Judith and Kate attended where the fated couple met.

"I was wildly attracted to Dev. Given what happened that night, he was too. Yet, what did I know?" Judith snorted. "I was a scared, seventeen-year-old virgin who'd never had a boyfriend, so I ran. Took him ten years to catch me, but I didn't make it easy."

"That was before I took Paul away from her," Kate chimed in.

"Wait. I'm lost." Sam stared at Judith, her gaze narrowing. "You and Paul were an item too? Before Kate and Paul?" she asked, clarifying in her mind exactly who was dating whom at the time.

"Paul and I are old friends." Judith nodded. "But never a true couple. He was waiting for me to realize I loved him. Unfortunately, I only loved him as a friend." When Sam whispered, "Incredible," Judith added, "I've known the Morrisons for as long as I can remember. Our parents went to school together." She scrunched up her nose in distaste. "Never could stomach James, though. Until he helped me avoid Dev. Then, we got to be friends too."

"Yeah. Judith attracts Morrisons. Paul grew up loving her before I stole him and she had James after her at the same time his best friend was making his move." Kate chuckled. "We should write a soap opera."

"James had a thing for Judith? Our James?"

"Yeah," Judith said. "You could say that, but it never really developed past friendship because I had Dev to deal with and James understood."

Interesting, Sam thought, opening her eyes and glancing over at the two women, now that Dory was finished with her eyelids. It was amazing what could be learned while having hair and makeup done. She'd known these people for years and never realized their pasts intertwined so closely. James had certainly never mentioned it.

"I never thought I'd say this, given how much I disliked James for the way he treated Kate, but if it wasn't for Dev, who knows?" Judith winked at Kate. "I see why you spent eight years chasing him."

Kate stuck out her tongue at Judith. "See, I told you back then James was okay. I will admit, we were never meant to be, but I wouldn't give up the idea. He simply needs to meet the right woman."

"You guys are too unbelievable for daytime TV." Sam smiled with her chin held high while Dory added the finishing touches to her cheekbones.

Then, Dory handed her the mirror and she sucked in a breath. "Wow." She looked like herself, yet she wasn't. Samantha Collins still stared back, but plain no longer described her. It was as if she'd taken an exclamation point and emphasized her face somehow. "Wow," Sam said again. No other word worked.

"Doesn't look like a clown to me. What about you?" Kate asked, turning to Judith. "Do you see a clown?"

Sam ignored their teasing and looked hopefully at Dory. "Will I be able to do this?"

"It's not hard. You don't need much, just a little foundation underneath, a bit of liner, shadow and mascara for the eyes, and blush to complete the look. Use more for night. Gives a more dramatic look. You might feel like a clown at first, but you get used to it," she said, grinning. Dory spent a moment going over the basics, just as Maurice had done.

When she left the counter carrying a bag filled with cosmetics, Sam wondered how she'd ever lived so long without them. She also wondered how she'd lived so long without fun. And *fun* described her day.

Her best friend, Mary Ann Murphy, was forever trying to get her to do things with her and her family, but Sam always had an excuse. In her mind, having fun served no purpose other than to waste resources better used to improving her situation. The life she'd mapped out never included something so frivolous. Suddenly, Charles' remarks took on a new meaning. Boring and predictable did seem to sum up Sam and her life. But no more.

"Now for something to eat, then we shop." Kate nodded toward the curved escalators.

Sam obediently followed. These two women obviously had done this before and had a plan of attack. Lucinda Thomas was history. If the new Samantha Collins didn't put spots of color in Charles' cheeks with today's results, then the man was a fool.

Chapter 3

Monday morning Sam pulled into a parking space at her usual time. Before opening the door, she turned to grab her usual *venti* coffee from Starbucks, along with her laptop. When she spied the apple she'd tossed on the seat earlier, she stuffed it into her bag.

Screw Morrison. I like my Starbucks coffee black and I like apples. It doesn't mean anything.

She climbed out of her car and slung the briefcase over her shoulder. Then, holding on to her morning ritual like a symbol of courage, she stormed into the building. Unfortunately, as she waited for the elevator doors to close, the very man she'd rather not see barreled into view at the last minute. He placed his hand in between the closing doors, forcing them open again.

"Wow!" he said, after giving her a cursory glance, halting in mid-look. A smile tugged at the edges of his lips, while his gaze took a slow journey up one side of her and down the other. "I'd say Kate and Judith knew what they were doing." His smile grew, showing off an expanse of white teeth. He nodded appreciatively. "I approve of that red concoction you're wearing. Looks good on you. You look…feminine."

Ignore the blatant admiration in his voice. He knows how to flirt—how to make a girl feel pretty. She took a deep breath to still her racing heart. Her chin went up. "I told you I was revamping my image."

"Aaah. Has Charles seen you yet?"

"No. I'm still getting used to it before I spring it on him. You don't think it's too much, do you?" Smoothing her skirt, she looked down at the bold color, before glancing anxiously back at him. As the doors closed, something in his expression reminded her of their shared kiss. The confined space of the elevator shrank in seconds. Her lungs malfunctioned and wouldn't expand so she could take in air. Her focus darted to the floor and she studied the patterns in the carpet.

"I want to apologize for that kiss," he said after a long pause, recapturing her attention. "I never got a chance."

"No need." She smiled brightly. "I understand. We were drunk and got carried away. It won't happen again." She wouldn't give him the satisfaction of letting him know how much the kiss bothered her. He didn't need to know she'd spent most of the weekend obsessing over it.

"So, it was the alcohol, nothing more?" He snared her gaze with an intense look, the heat of it melting her insides. "You're sure?"

"Of course. I haven't given it a second thought." A person could get lost in those eyes, but not her. She had more sense than to let him charm her. James Morrison was born to charm and she was born to resist all temptation.

His head tilted to the side and he grinned. "Liar," he whispered, taking a step closer. Her neck stretched away from his hand when he reached out to tuck an errant lock behind her ear. "I bet you've given it more than a second thought. I know I have."

Goose bumps of pleasure streaked up her back, making the chore of ignoring him more arduous. *Pay no attention to him, Sam. He's used to women melting at his feet.*

The entire time James towered next to her, crowding her, she couldn't breathe.

The elevator doors opened to break the spell, saving her from further distress.

Now that she could finally inhale, her wits returned and she was able to say with more conviction, "You're right." She patted his cheek, turning her smile up a notch. "I did enjoy the kiss. But, no need to worry—I have no designs on your body. I have all I can handle with Charles." She turned and sauntered off, still grinning.

If only she had a camera handy to capture the moment. She left him speechless, given his stunned expression, and she'd bet a year's salary it didn't happen very often.

Humming, she stepped into her office. Like the other architects' offices on the floor that housed the firm of Morrison, Morgan, Stone and Collins, hers was spacious and held similar furniture, including a stately mahogany desk across from her drafting table.

She set the coffee, apple, and briefcase on her desk and reached for her cell phone. She'd texted Mary Ann earlier with an overview of Friday night. Except for the kiss she'd shared with Morrison. She hadn't mentioned anything about locking lips with him. Once the haziness cleared, the memory was embedded in her brain, like the deep cuts in a Waterford crystal bowl. It wasn't one she could readily discuss. Not until she fully understood her emotions, so she'd procrastinated on having lunch with her friend, using weekend chores as an excuse, hoping to get that kiss out of her system first.

"Hey, Mar," she said, once the line was answered. "I just got your text about the game tomorrow afternoon. Is the offer still open?"

"You mean it?" Mary Ann shrieked into her ear, causing her to hold the phone out a bit. "You'll actually go? You'll take time off on a workday?"

Sam grinned. "Sure." Mary Ann's brother, Kevin, had Giants season tickets for four and was always inviting the pair. Weekends were usually reserved for Charles, who hated baseball, and Sam had never accepted during the week. Until now. Now, she was making a few changes.

Yesterday, she'd done more than run errands. Unable to ignore James' comment about lightening up, she'd reassessed her life. Did he really see her as an unbending person? After viewing things from his perspective, she hated to admit her answer. Before her makeover began, she was totally pathetic. In her efforts to control her rise to a better life, she *had* become boring and inflexible. Outside of her friendships with Mary Ann and a few work friends like James, Charles was her main focus, other than work. She vowed right then to change the flat line of her life. "A baseball game sounds like *fun.* I'll even spring for the hot dogs."

She hung up, swiveled her chair, and looked out the wall of windows that offered plenty of natural light every artist needed. The day was a gorgeous one. Not a cloud marred the crisp autumn sky, the startling color adding warmth to her already lifted spirits. Sam stuck her purse in her desk, picked up her laptop, and moved to her workstation, a drafting table spanning the wall opposite the windows. She pulled out her stool from underneath, plopped down, and got busy on her latest project, designing an office building.

While she worked, her thoughts remained on the new Sam Collins. What would Mary Ann think of her makeover? James' reaction during their elevator ride flitted through her mind and a thrill went through her. Yep. Considering the male appreciation she'd spotted in his interested gaze, she was making progress. She wondered what James would think if he knew her plans included leaving work early to attend a baseball game. Definite progress.

A small laugh escaped before she concentrated fully on the design in front of her.

Thirty hours later, Sam answered her apartment door to Mary Ann, who stared open-jawed for a long minute. "Oh…my…God! Look at you. You look fabulous," she gushed, hugging her. "Amazing what a little makeup and a good cut will do, isn't it?"

"I am different, but the same." Returning the smile, she patted her hair. "Can you imagine? Me spending money to be a girly girl?"

Mary Ann laughed and waited as she locked her door. They headed through the hallway toward the apartment building's main foyer. Once there, Sam shoved open the glass door and added, "I've got to tell you it feels good."

Mary Ann's brother climbed out of the parked car, but paused with his hand on the door handle and did a double take. His grin stretched from ear to ear as he ushered her inside the back seat. "Mar told me to expect a new Sammy, but she never told me you'd be stunning."

"What a sweet thing to say, Kevin."

"You should give up that deadbeat Winthrope and run away with me." He slid in beside her. "You can sit in the front seat," he said to Mary Ann, who'd shot him a *what are you doing* glance. "I'm riding next to Sam. That way, she won't feel neglected."

Sam laughed at his teasing, enjoying the attention. Kevin Murphy, with his arresting Irish black hair and blue eyes, had almost as easy a time capturing the ladies as Morrison did.

"Is that a new outfit?" he asked.

"Yes." She looked down at the clingy white shorts and frilly, ruffled red top, and her grin spread. "How'd you know?"

"It's about time you showed off some skin, Sammy. You've been hiding all those feminine assets for too long."

"Down, Kevin," Mary Ann piped in from the front seat, eyeing them from the rearview mirror. "She's practically engaged. What's more, she's like a sister to you, so quit hitting on her."

"Hey, that's right. Last Friday was supposed to be the big night. Winthrope's a lucky dog." He lifted her hand. His eyebrows furrowed in confusion. "Where's the ring?"

Damn, he would have to bring up Friday night. When would she learn to keep her big mouth shut? She didn't want to make a huge deal of what actually happened and said, "Charles had to reschedule, so our momentous date got postponed."

"Well, then," Kevin said smugly, nodding at Mary Ann in the mirror. "The last time I checked, we weren't related and until I see a ring, I'll flirt all I want." His gaze caught Sam's again and his eyebrows shot up and down as he added, "So, how about it? Want to run away with me? I'll marry you. Just name the date and I'm yours." His grin could only be called sexy.

Laughter bubbled up in the form of pure feminine delight. Normally he treated her like a kid sister, just as he did Mary Ann. She'd known him forever, had even bunked with the Murphys as a teen when life with her mom became unbearable. She couldn't remember another instance of him flirting with her and couldn't dismiss how wonderful it felt to be noticed.

During the twenty-minute ride to AT&T Park, Kevin kept up the charm and she ate up every word. She'd never realized how exhilarating something as frivolous as flirtatious bantering could be, especially with someone like him.

The parking lot was packed and they had to walk a distance, but Sam was laughing too hard to mind. "That's unbelievable," she said to Kevin when he relayed a story about an actress who'd paraded down Lombard Street in the city, drunk and half naked.

"No. It's true. I ran into her that same night at the Balboa Cafe." He winked. "Except she *wasn't* drunk. The tabloids never get their facts straight."

"Really?" She stared at him, thinking about their differences. Kevin was a successful manager with a tech firm, but he was also a player. He always had fun. Both Sam and Mary Ann were a year younger, and the two of them had shared a rental house with him during college. In all the time she'd known him, he never seemed to worry about tomorrow. Mary Ann wasn't the player he was, but she'd done her fair share of partying in college. Without her, Sam might add, having been too busy making up for what she lacked. Her mother loved to party and Sam wouldn't risk becoming a clone of a woman she disdained.

As they made their way to the stadium, Sam observed the pair more closely. Their parents were loving and their early lives stable.

Neither had to prove they belonged anywhere. They just belonged. Sam never felt as if she belonged, not if the right boxes weren't checked.

Wow. Where had that thought come from? She cleared her throat to push the disturbing notion aside and concentrated on wading through throngs of people all with the same goal, finding their seats before the game started.

"This is a perfect day for baseball," Sam said, once they'd gotten settled into their seats. The sun was still high enough on the horizon to add warmth to the September afternoon. Fall, the Bay Area's summer, was Sam's favorite time of year. The fog tended to burn off early and it rarely rained before the beginning of October. Today was no exception. It was a spectacular day.

"So, have you heard from Charles?" Mary Ann asked, the moment Kevin was out of earshot, having gone on a food run.

Sam shook her head. "No. I should call him. At this point, I have no clue what to say." She spent a moment going into more detail about Friday night and ended with, "As you can see, I'm trying to change my approach. Be more spontaneous. Feels pretty good so far."

"Yeah, but I can't believe he actually complained." Mary Ann's nose scrunched into distaste. "I mean, come on. He's not that damn spontaneous himself, and talk about inflexible? The guy could write a book on it." Just then, a player from the other team hit a line drive and the Giants' basemen ended it with quick action and two outs, adding to the first. They were now up at bat.

Mary Ann stood and shouted a long hoot, then sat back down and continued talking as if nothing had interrupted. "I've always admired how you put yourself through school, yet I've never understood how you've kept so driven all these years without a break. You've never even gone on a vacation that didn't involve work. Sam, James is right. It's time to reap the rewards and let loose a little bit."

Heavens, did Mary Ann think she was boring too? "I thought that's what I was doing."

"You are. I'm astounded at how quickly you're changing."

"I don't want to lose Charles."

"You shouldn't change just for him." She frowned. "Your spouse should accept you exactly as you are. Faults and all."

"He was just being honest."

"Yeah, but I can tell his honesty hurt you." She harrumphed loudly, her frown back in place. "Are you sure you want to spend the rest of your life with him?" Mary Ann glanced at her. "What if he's not *the one*?" When Sam's eyes narrowed, she went on. "A complacent relationship could be a warning flag. You have to admit, he's the only guy you've ever dated long term and the only guy you've ever slept with. What if there's someone else out there who'll like the new you better?"

"I'm not you," Sam said, holding eye contact. Mary Ann was the proverbial girl next door, everyone's darling who'd had several long-term relationships, but she also didn't have Sam's baggage, nor did she even care about the long term. "Charles is the only guy I've dated long term for a reason. We want the same things. Love and commitment."

Sam had dated a little in college, but those guys only wanted a good time back then, which usually included casual sex that she wasn't about to engage in. She had higher aspirations than to be anyone's good time when that's all her mother had been. Look where Vickie ended up. She refused to repeat her mother's mistakes and finally quit dating altogether. Once James introduced her to Charles and they connected, she felt like the luckiest woman on the planet.

"And Charles fell in love with the old me. He just wants me to be better. He wants *us* to be better."

Mary Ann nodded, but Sam caught the skepticism in her eyes that matched her tone of voice when she added, "I think you should go out more. Meet other guys before you take the plunge."

Sam sighed. Her friend had never liked her choice in men. Called him a stuffy moneybags who liked to work, which was Mary Ann's complete opposite. Money wasn't Mary Ann's be-all and end-all, not like it was hers.

Sam had never minded Mary Ann's sentiments before or felt she had to defend him or her relationship, mainly because she'd been guilty of the same. Work *was* all that mattered. So in that respect, she and Charles were well matched. Still, she couldn't help but feel the beginnings of dissatisfaction and, for the first time in three years, she started to doubt her reasons for her relationship. She quickly pushed all niggling doubt away, unwilling to think such heavy thoughts. She was determined to have fun if it killed her.

Soon, Kevin returned with their food and talk turned to other topics during a whirlwind game where the San Francisco Giants beat the San Diego Padres.

"Good night." Laughing, Sam waved to Mary Ann and Kevin before closing the outside door, once they'd dropped her off. Now completely alone with her thoughts, her smile died as she walked through the hallway to her apartment. She unlocked the door, slipped inside, and looked around. Her gaze swept her empty living room, roamed past a neat, color-coordinated dining area with a table and four chairs, and ended in her kitchen. All her doubts resurfaced along with thoughts of Morrison.

She kicked off her sandals and sorted through the mail she'd thrown on the coffee table earlier, hoping for a diversion, anything to detour her from thinking about that kiss. Her mind had already been stuck on it too often lately. Baseball and hot dogs had provided a perfect distraction to pause the continuous, endless video of Friday night that kept running through her mind's eye any time she didn't have something to do. New doubts about Charles formed and she felt every bit of her hard-won control slipping. This couldn't be happening.

For so long, her goals had been right in front of her and very attainable. At the moment, she was as confused as ever. She always thought that once she married Charles, her life would be perfect. Now, she realized life was never perfect. Even worse, she no longer had any idea of the answer to her self-imposed question. What the hell did she want?

No, no, no, no, no. She knew what she wanted. Charles and a life with him, yet that kiss and everything leading up to it flared to life in her mind once again, along with those sensations of bliss that Morrison had made her feel. Damn him.

Sighing, she headed for bed. She had a few weeks to figure a way to extract the same level of excitement from Charles' kisses. If she could do that, then everything would work out.

As she brushed her teeth, she examined the new Samantha Collins she saw in the mirror. *What will Charles think when he sees the new me? Will he be swept away? Then sweep* me *away? Enough so that I won't need tequila to feel like I felt in James' arms?* Of course, she would. Then, she would have everything that kid in high school didn't have. She would finally be somebody better than her mother. She would be Mrs. Charles Winthrope III. Confidence filled her. Sam rinsed her mouth and grinned, then hugged herself. Her plans for her future would work out. They just had to.

~

Friday morning, right before lunch, James paused at Collins' door and stood undetected for a moment watching her. She seemed so put together and competent. She'd ignored him all week. Yet, could he ignore her? Hell, no. Not anymore. Not when he knew how she kissed. Why did he have this sick need to get her to notice him? Was he really that self-absorbed? So selfish that he'd even consider ruining their friendship for sex?

He sighed. "Collins, you got a minute?" When she nodded, he added, "Can you come into my office, please?"

She grabbed a pen and notepad, jumped up, and followed.

"Shut the door." He watched her step inside the huge office with a wall of windows brandishing plenty of natural light, overlooking a drafting table at the far side.

She closed the door and turned back to him with questioning eyes.

He indicated one of the two plush chairs in front of his desk, and sat in his black leather chair with his hands together, his fingers touching his chin. His gaze never left her face.

"You wanted to see me?" she asked, after enduring long moments of his silent scrutiny.

"Are you avoiding me?" He hadn't meant to ask, but curiosity was eating a hole in his gut.

"No." The word came out too quickly for him to believe her denial. "Why would I avoid you?"

"You know why."

"I have no idea what you're talking about." She flipped her notebook open with crisp movements, then clicked her pen. Her eyebrows lifted and she met his gaze without blinking.

He grinned, now knowing full well he wasn't the only one bothered by what happened. "I don't believe you," he taunted. "You're avoiding me because of that kiss. Aren't you?"

"You're delusional."

"Am I?" Amusement flashed from his eyes and he sat back, still holding her gaze. "Then why change your schedule? Why haven't I caught so much as a glimpse of you in days? I've dropped by several times to see if you wanted to go to lunch, only to find you MIA. Why go to such lengths, if you're not avoiding me?"

"No," she said, dismissing his claims with the shake of her head. "You give yourself too much credit."

"So, you're not avoiding me?"

"No. I'm not."

"Good. Then you'll have dinner with me tonight."

"What?" Her gaze snapped back to his.

"We never discussed Charles last week and since I promised to come up with a way to help, I want to make good on it. We won't drink." A smile snuck across his face. "I promise."

"Oh no, you don't." Her back straightened. "I know what you're doing."

"You do?" Maybe she could tell him, so they'd both know.

"Yes, and I'm not some susceptible female who'll fall for your charming BS."

His smile died. "I thought we were friends. Is that how you really see me?" She shrugged, not agreeing or disagreeing. "The women I date are professionals with more going for them than looks." Why was he bothering to defend himself, and why did he have this impulsive need to wipe that unimpressed expression off her face?

"But, they don't seem to last long, do they?"

"And of course, you're perfect in the relationship department." The frosty look she gave him could freeze a fire. It certainly wasn't what he was after, even though he had no clue what that was. He was trying his damnedest to remember their friendship and not be a self-absorbed and selfish bastard in this instance, but she tempted him. Hell, she'd tempt a saint. "You know something?"

"What?" Her chin rose and those pouty lips tightened into a firm line.

A Grecian goddess in combat mode, ready for battle, defending her honor. That's what he caught just then…in her expression…in the tilt of her head…in the indignant sound of her voice…forcing him to take a closer inspection. Why had he never noticed her before? Sure, she'd had a makeover and was wearing a chic outfit, but as an artist, he should have looked past the props she used to hide herself from the world. He should have seen her hidden beauty underneath.

Suddenly the truth about *why* hit him. He *was* too self-centered to actually look. The thought unsettled him. He was even more unsettled to realize he now wanted to dig deeper—see what else she was hiding. He continued watching her, as more clarity struck. He wasn't unsettled enough not to pick up a shovel. Self-absorbed bastard or not, he couldn't refuse the challenge she threw out.

"Now I know damn well you're avoiding me. You're afraid of what went on when we kissed, aren't you?"

"Dream on." She laughed. Her chin rose another inch. "Your ego won't let you believe otherwise. I'm totally immune to you."

"Really?" He shouldn't let her comments goad him further, but somehow they were like a bullfighter waving a red flag in front of a bull.

"Yes."

The emphatic way she answered only rankled more. He knew he should just let it go but found himself saying instead, "Then it shouldn't matter if we have dinner, should it?" She seemed much too sure of herself, adding to his burgeoning desire to prove her wrong. "And since you're totally immune to me," he looked to her with eyebrows lifted, "do I have that right? Totally immune?" She nodded, only this time more warily. "Kissing will have no effect, and you'd never go to bed with me, right?"

"Of course not." She snorted. "I have no interest in you sexually."

"Okay, problem solved. I'll pick you up at seven."

"Having dinner together wouldn't be appropriate."

"Why?" There was no way he going to let her off easy. "We've had dinner together countless times before."

"I'm avoiding future problems. We've crossed the line. We're both partners in the same firm. How would it look to others?"

"This is a small company with only four partners, including you, and the last time I checked there were no rules that say partners can't date." He shrugged and added, "Besides, this has nothing to do with office rules, and you know it."

"Okay. But, I'm still not going out with you."

"Then you leave me no choice in the matter," he said, suddenly coming up with an idea.

"What do you mean?"

He sighed. "Now, I'm forced to resort to bribery." Using spur-of-the-moment bribery might not sit well with him, but he needed to do something drastic to get their friendship back on an even keel.

"You're kidding?" She threw out a derisive laugh. "Bribery won't work."

"Ah, ah, ah," he said, shaking his head. "Hear me out before you make such claims." He paused for effect, then grinned when she crossed her arms and glared.

"Well, I'm waiting."

Holding eye contact, he leaned forward. "The McAlpin project. You want it, it's yours." He knew she was dying to design the office building and would jump at such an offer. She'd mentioned it several times, lamenting the fact that McAlpin was his client and not hers. "Give me two weeks to test my theory and, no matter what happens, the project is yours." He refrained from telling her he'd asked her into his office to inform her the project was hers anyway, had been from the moment his client had stated what he wanted. Yet, she didn't need to know such details when she'd started this. He only intended to end it.

Indecision flitted over her face. "And all I have to do is go out with you, right?"

His smile returned. "No one ever called you stupid."

"And I get to design McAlpin's office building?"

"Yeah." He nodded. His smile faded. "I feel it only fair to warn you. My main objective is to get you into bed," he said, in an effort to throw her off-balance. "But, since you're totally immune to me—if I have my quote right—you have nothing to worry about. I don't see a problem. Two weeks."

She looked at him as if he'd lost his mind. Maybe he had. It did sound a little crazy, even if he had no intention of actually following through. He'd just go far enough to make his point, then they could both go back to their old easy friendship.

"What about Charles?" she finally asked. "You said you were going to help me with him. This sort of defeats the purpose."

"Sex with me will only add a spark to your relationship, don't you think? It certainly couldn't hurt." Oh yeah. His statement completely rattled her. Precisely the response he'd sought, he realized, looking into her concerned expression. He worked to maintain a straight face, immensely satisfied that she wasn't quite so immune to him now. She clearly thought he was serious, but she had nothing to fear. Not from him. After all, he wasn't a complete bastard. She was off-limits. Not only was she a good friend, she loved Charles who was also a friend. So, this would work with getting her to lighten up.

"You really think I'll fall for your famous Morrison charm?" she asked, no longer wary, so much so that her tone now sounded a bit incredulous, which sealed his determination.

Yet, he knew damn well she wouldn't fall for anything easily, Morrison charm or not. Collins could be stubborn when she wanted. He smiled deviously and mentally rubbed his hands together. So could he. "We'll never know unless I try, now will we?" James tossed back, mirroring her confidence.

She eyed him intently for a moment. Then her brow furrowed and her focus shifted lower. She studied the floor for so long he briefly reconsidered his plans.

"You know this might not be such a bad idea, Morrison," she said too triumphantly, meeting his gaze after a few more minutes of silence. "What a perfect solution."

He sat up straighter as a trickle of unease crawled up his spine.

Sam laughed. "Don't look so alarmed. I promise to be gentle, but you may want to rethink the next two weeks."

"I know that expression." His eyes narrowed. "What're you planning?"

"Nothing. I don't have to do a darn thing and I'll come out ahead. Because if I can withstand your attempts at seduction, yet bring you to heel, I know I can do the same for Charles." Her laughter increased. She definitely seemed pleased with herself. Too pleased for his comfort. "This is too rich. You're James Morrison, my buddy. I've watched you for years. I know all your moves."

Definitely a goddess preparing for battle, he thought. Though he was ready to throttle her, he watched her gloat, without moving a muscle, enjoying her amusement as she made a few more inane comments about his sexual prowess and her love for Charles…yada, yada, yada. She should have stopped while she was ahead. Yet, she had no sense. When she added, in such a taunting voice, "Never in a million years will your ploys work on me. *I am* totally immune to your charm," something inside him snapped. He couldn't let her comment pass without a small lesson in gloating.

He stood up, walked around the desk, and leaned against it, crossing both arms and legs.

"If you're immune to me, then it shouldn't matter."

Her smiled died and she cleared her throat, brushing a strand of hair behind her ear. "What shouldn't matter?" Chewing on her bottom lip, she peered up at him through a curious gaze, her expression not quite as confident as a moment ago.

"Whether we kiss."

"You wouldn't dare." Her shocked tone did nothing to deter him.

"Now, there's where you're wrong." Unbending, he leaned forward and placed a hand on each arm of her chair, halting inches from her. "I would dare, but I don't have to." He focused on her face and waited until she met his gaze. "You're going to kiss me."

Her eyes got rounder. "You're flipping crazy."

"Then, I'd say you're not as immune as you think you are." He smiled. "Only a kiss will prove otherwise."

Her wide-eyed stare moved lower to focus on his lips, as her jaw dropped an inch, leaving her mouth open. With a forefinger and thumb, he lifted her chin to close her mouth. "Well, how about it? Are you afraid to kiss me, or not?"

Her gaze darted to his before flitting away and her tongue traced her lips. The nervous gestures did nothing to change his mind, only reinforced his plans, as thoughts of having that tongue meet his wound their way into his brain.

She wrapped her hands around his neck, pulled him lower, and captured his lips with hers. Yet the entire time, she remained perfectly still, totally unresponsive.

He might as well kiss a cardboard box for all the emotion she put into it. He expected nothing less. Not from Sam. He broke the kiss, waited until she glanced at him again, and then whispered, "What's the matter, Collins? Afraid that famous control will snap?"

She stiffened and yanked him back. Her lips melded with his. Her tongue, flirting tentatively with his mouth in tiny thrusts, incited instant lust. Her mouth was soft and warm, and tasted exactly as he remembered. The scent he'd come to associate only with her filled his nostrils and added to his memory. A surge of heat rushed straight to his groin. When she moaned, he had to break away or risk losing his head. When she put her mind to the task, Samantha Collins knew how to kiss.

"Nothing to it," he said, fighting to sustain his even breathing. He moved away from her and grinned, as she slowly opened her eyes, then hurriedly vacated her seat once awareness hit. She practically flew for the exit.

"And Collins?"

She paused at the door to glance back.

"I'll pick you up at seven and we'll see who's immune to whom." He was positive he'd be a dead man if the daggers she sent with her eyes were real. Holding his grin in place, he watched her slam the door practically off the hinges and said under his breath, "Let the games begin."

Chapter 4

Samantha stormed out of James' office and raced in the direction of her own. Once there, she shut the door and sat in the chair behind her desk.

Questions swarmed in her mind, one right after the other. Why did he ask her to dinner and why did she agree to go? Sure, she wanted the McAlpin project, but why had she goaded him? Why hadn't she kept her mouth shut? Those questions concerned her, but not as much as the biggest one. Why did she like kissing him?

Why, why, why?

"It's his charm," she hissed, swiveling around to look out the window. Natural light poured into the room. She took no notice of the blue sky full of sunshine. Right now, her mood was blustery and tempestuous, not bright and sunny.

I miscalculated his appeal. Not good, Collins. Not good.

Somehow, in the course of the last ten minutes, James had introduced a new game, one that she sensed she had to play in order to work past her problem with Charles. No way she'd let him win.

Sam grabbed her running gear and went to change. She needed a few miles to figure out how best to proceed with this mess.

She headed out. After jogging a mile, she glanced up to see what looked to be Charles' car pulling up to the curb right outside their favorite restaurant. She slowed to a walk as a valet opened the passenger door. Charles climbed out of the driver's side at the same moment Lucinda Thomas allowed the attendant to help her out. Charles raced to her side, then bent to catch something she obviously said. He threw back his head and laughed.

Sam stopped, too stunned to do more than gape. From her vantage point, he looked amused, which was totally unlike the Charles she knew. The guy seldom laughed at jokes, was as serious as a heart attack, but there he stood, not more than a hundred feet in front of her, smiling warmly at his co-worker. Sam continued watching, not missing the spontaneity in their interactions as the two walked side by side toward the restaurant entrance.

Her gaze stayed fastened on the couple until they disappeared inside.

A pang of pain hit, as the thought of Charles taking Lucinda out to lunch at *their* favorite spot flashed like a neon sign inside her brain. He was laughing like a kid without any worries. How could he be having fun while she was obsessing? Was he sleeping with her? No. Charles was too honorable, but she'd never seen him so relaxed. He looked happy. She brushed away the tears that had slipped from her eyes and abruptly made an about-face, heading for her office. Oh, how she wished she hadn't witnessed the scene, because it just made Sam realize how lacking their relationship truly was. Charles was never like that with her.

As she hurried toward her building, she tried to rationalize the situation. *It doesn't mean anything. You don't even know what you saw.* On the other hand, what if it did? What if he liked her? What if he was in lust with her? Then he wouldn't stay interested in her for long. Sam knew that all too well, thanks to her mother. Passion, which was really unresolved lust, always faded once the man got what he wanted, and then he'd be gone. Charles surely understood that what they shared—a solid relationship built on mutual respect and trust—was better than lustful passion.

Unfortunately, Sam was beginning to want more.

Face it, Sam. You kissed Morrison and liked it. If Charles had kissed her like that, she knew damned well he wouldn't be laughing with Lucinda right now. He'd be laughing with her instead. What if Charles kissed Lucinda and liked it? The thought hurt, but not as much as the idea that she and Charles never laughed. She hadn't even realized the fact until a few minutes ago. Her dissatisfaction grew with every step she took. And the real kicker? A week ago, everything was perfect. Sam sensed her future was slipping out of her hands and she had no way to prevent it from happening.

She couldn't give up without a fight. Samantha Collins never gave up. If she had, she'd never have been able to claw her way out of an ugly childhood. Wasn't this just a different battle in the same war? So what if mean girls had always made her feel inferior. She was no longer that poor kid who'd never measured up to their idea of perfection. No, she was a survivor who deserved her dream man and, damn it all, she was willing to fight hard.

More thoughts of her mother emerged and blended with thoughts of her behavior with James.

Seven days ago, she'd been so close to achieving her goal of having what she'd perceived as love and happiness, which she'd always assumed would make up for her lousy childhood. For her entire adult life, all she'd ever wanted was the security and love a man like Charles could provide. Despite catching him laughing with the enemy, he was a good, stable man.

Good and stable? The thought stopped her cold. Geez, now she did sound boring. So what, she reasoned and continued to walk. They were necessary qualities for someone like her, given the instability and ugliness she'd endured as a kid. Every couple had problems. Charles had pointed out a few valid concerns, so if she addressed them, then everything would be fine. Yet, would it? More doubt crept in. She pushed it out, unwilling to dwell on the negatives.

Her pace increased, as her resolve stiffened. Soon, she was back to jogging. For the rest of her run, she dug deep to come up with a plan that would satisfy her newly recognized expectations. This thing with Morrison was lust, pure and simple. Her mom had experienced her share of lust. Hell, Vickie Collins went through losers like they were candy to her sweet tooth. She never got a damned thing to show for it, other than a lighter wallet and a broken heart, which had only added more ugliness to Sam's poverty-stricken beginning.

What if she could learn how to control lust? Then she could exploit it for her benefit. Who better a teacher than someone like James, who incited lust. Heck, she'd already agreed to go out with him and he was a good kisser. Why not use him to figure it out? Maybe he could teach her a few things, like how to incite a little lust of her own with Charles.

Yeah. She nodded and started running faster as excitement filled her. She liked the idea.

If she could practice on James and make him fall for her, then why wouldn't the same methods work on Charles? She had to believe Charles still loved her. They did have three years together and they shared the same basic values. Yet, as she'd already discovered, it wasn't enough in the ignorance-is-bliss kind of way. She'd never be satisfied until he kissed her like Morrison kissed her. If he did, she was positive he would never look at another woman again. Nor would she look at another man, Morrison included.

By the time she made it back to her office, confidence had replaced the sick feeling in the pit of her stomach. She hummed as she pushed the elevator button.

In minutes, she was back in her office. As she'd done so easily with other unpleasant experiences in the past, she pretended they didn't matter and dismissed all concerns from her mind. She moved to her drafting board and prepared to immerse herself in her one true passion—her designs. Within seconds, Charles Winthrope and James Morrison disappeared from her consciousness and she gave neither man another thought.

~

"Yellow roses?" Sam asked, after opening her door later that evening to James' jean-clad body holding a bouquet of the most beautiful roses she'd ever seen. He couldn't know roses were her favorite. She took them from him and tried not to notice how the snug fit of the faded, shrunken denim highlighted his firm, well-developed body better than any Sharpie. The navy pullover he wore *would* have to accentuate both the blue of his eyes and his blond good looks. "What happened to red? Yellow isn't exactly the color of romance."

"Yellow denotes friendship. I thought it appropriate to remind you how much you like me."

A bubble of laughter burst forth. "That's a little lame, don't you think?"

"Work with me, Collins. I have to take advantage of my edge here."

"You're nuts." She tried not to be charmed by those laughing eyes as they focused on her. *Remember, Sam. He's not charming.* She paid no attention to her mental warning and smiled. Even her toes wanted to smile. *Okay—the guy's charming.*

"Thanks. They really are lovely," she gushed. *Down, girl. Don't overdo it. The flowers are premeditated. Don't let his thoughtful, silly gesture get to you. His charm is an act.*

Still, if she didn't know better, she'd swear he found her more than interesting, given the way his gaze assessed her. She squelched the bit of elation the thought brought on and nodded, indicating his attire. "You're dressed fairly casual for a first date."

James shook his head. "Not date. How about…two friends going to dinner and spending time together?"

Her eyebrows shot up. "Is that how we're playing this out?"

"Why not? As friends we might have more fun."

"Sure. If it will make you feel better, fun has become my middle name." She stood aside and nodded toward her sofa. "Make yourself comfortable while I put these in water."

Sam headed for her small kitchen, an extended room off her combined living and dining room.

He followed in her wake and perched against the jamb, watching as she spent a few minutes filling a vase with water.

"Would you like something to drink?" She turned off the faucet and began arranging the flowers.

"No, we should get going. Even my charm has limits. We won't be necking on your couch for at least a few dates."

"What?" She stopped with a rose in the air, not sure she heard him correctly.

He grinned. "Gotcha. Just wanted to see if you were paying attention."

"You don't give yourself much time." She went back to adding the rest of the roses to the vase. "But it doesn't matter," she stated confidently. She picked up the vase, carried it to the table, and placed it in the center, before glancing back at James. "We won't be necking on my sofa at all."

"You're entitled to your opinion."

"And you're entitled to your overinflated ego. We will not be kissing." At least not until she decided they'd kiss.

James shrugged without answering. Her gaze stayed locked on his face. She scrutinized his expression, leery of his nonchalant confidence all of a sudden.

"What? Don't look so concerned," he countered. "When we neck, it will be your idea. I don't kiss women who don't want to kiss me back."

"My memory must be faulty. What about the macho scene in your office this afternoon? I don't remember asking you to kiss me then."

He snorted. "Goaded me, is more like it." He grabbed her jacket off the chair and held it out. "Come on, since we're not going to make out, let's get some pizza. I'm hungry."

When Sam hesitated, he grinned. "Surely that's not reluctance to be in my company? After all, I don't bite and even if I did, you're immune to me. Right?"

"Darn right." Her back straightened into a steel beam. Unwilling to let him know how much he affected her, she snatched her jacket and strode purposefully toward the door without looking back.

"Why are we heading into the city?" Sam asked ten minutes later, as he drove north on Highway 101.

"Being spontaneous. It's Friday night. You don't have to be home early, do you?"

She shook her head. No, she had no plans for the weekend now that she and Charles were taking a break from each other. They usually spent weekends together doing mundane chores neither had time for during the week.

"Good. There's a great pizza place Kate used to drag me to all the time. I haven't been there in months and thought it would be the perfect place to give you a taste of something you've never experienced."

"This may come as a shock, Morrison, but I've had pizza before."

"At Mario's?"

"No."

"Then you haven't had pizza."

She let the comment pass and turned to stare out the window. Soon, he exited the highway and drove north on Franklin Street.

"Look, I must be living right." James slowed the car after turning onto a side street ten minutes later. "We only have to walk a few blocks." He quickly backed into the space.

They climbed out of the car together.

"Just what I ordered." He grabbed her hand and pulled her along, striding with a purpose.

"What?" Sam had no clue what he was talking about. He seemed so pleased given his exuberant expression, like an excited kid heading into FAO Swartz with a hefty gift certificate.

"A brisk, cool night, perfect for walking. I can't take all the credit. San Francisco weather rarely changes even when the rainy season sets in. It's usually brisk and cool."

"Learn something every day." She rarely came to the city, so she never paid attention to the weather. Before last weekend with Kate and Judith, and the baseball game during the week with Mary Ann, she couldn't remember her last trip—at least six months ago. Maybe a year. San Francisco was too big and too unapproachable for her to feel comfortable driving in on her own. Charles didn't like the city. Too noisy and congested for him.

"Stick with me, kiddo, and you'll learn all kinds of things."

"That's what I was hoping." She laughed and hurried to keep up with his fast pace.

Wonderful scents of garlic and bread assaulted her nostrils when they entered the restaurant. It was a boisterous, crowded place alive with atmosphere, complete with checkered tablecloths and lit candles in straw-covered Chianti wine bottles on every table.

James ordered a pitcher of beer while they waited, standing at a table in the packed bar.

"I thought you said we wouldn't drink," Sam said, picking up the glass he'd just poured.

"Come on, Collins. Let loose a little, would you? You can't have a Mario's supreme without a couple of beers. It's like eating a hot fudge sundae without the ice cream. The hot fudge tastes the same no matter what, but ice cream adds to the mix, makes it a dessert. We'll walk it off afterward. I have the perfect destination in mind."

"Okay." She met his gaze and held up her glass for a toast. "Here's to friendship."

James' smile reached his eyes and he nodded. "Friendship. I'll drink to that." He took a sip.

When something more than amusement flashed in his eyes, and he added, "And here's to friends and lovers," she almost choked on her beer. But she didn't. Instead, her chin—as well as her eyebrows—went up a notch and she took a drink, keeping her focus on him. She wasn't about to let him know the heated look in his eyes, along the seductive tone of his voice, sent a flash of hot sensation from her center, spreading out to all her extremities. *Ignore the feeling, Collins. All part of his charm. He's only upping the pressure.* And of course, that played perfectly into her plans to discover every facet of how lust worked. *Note to self: Use the senses, especially eye contact and tone of voice.*

Luck was with them, as the usual hour-long wait was shortened substantially. Within fifteen minutes, a waitress led them through the cramped, narrow aisles of the crowded dining area to a small, intimate table for two.

Sam grabbed the menu the waitress handed her and sat in the chair James pulled out.

She wished she wasn't having so much fun. She found it hard to remember her purpose without constantly reminding herself that the guy across from her wasn't long term. Charles was. She wished it was Charles, not James, who'd introduced her to such a fun place, and she wished, more than anything, that James would quit smiling at her like she was special. She'd had too many dinners to count with him over the course of their friendship, but he'd never focused that boyish charm solely on her during them, not like he was doing tonight. And, it was damned distracting.

She focused on her menu, using the task to regain her equilibrium. Thankfully, after the waitress came and went with their food order, the noisy place offered lots of diversions from her thoughts. When their waitress finally plunked their order in the middle of the table, Sam laughed, happy to have eating to concentrate on now instead of James and his easy charm.

"I have to admit, it looks delicious," she said. The pizza was huge and loaded to the max, piping hot with an abundance of cheese. A whiff of garlic, peppers, mozzarella, and fragrant meats floated under her nose, and her stomach gurgled in response.

Mozzarella strings formed when James pulled apart the overstuffed slices, then plunked one on each plate and waited until she took her first bite.

"Well? Is it not the best pizza you've ever tasted?"

Her mouth was too full of the most scrumptious flavors to answer, but she couldn't contain the pleased giggle erupting at his earnest expression. "Okay," she was finally able to get out once she swallowed. "I'll give you that one, Morrison. *This*," she said, indicating the slice in her hand, "is worth the drive," before bringing it to her mouth for another bite.

Both the pizza and the beer went down fast. It was too good not to. James was right. Mario's was the perfect place for an informal, tasty meal.

While they ate, their talk turned to work, giving Sam even more of a breather. As always, the two shared an easy camaraderie concerning their mutual passion for their careers, and tonight was no different as they discussed a couple of current jobs.

"I never knew you guys struggled so much," she said after he made a comment about the lean, early days of the firm.

"What? You mean you thought Russell, Brad, and I started out in one of the most expensive office buildings in San Mateo? That we just lucked into it?" He laughed and took a drink of beer, then a bite of pizza, chewing thoughtfully. "No. Luck had no part in our success. We worked our butts off out of a small office in a strip mall and used one of those mailing services for a more prestigious address." He paused to take another sip and his smile grew more pensive. "Ah, the good old days. No troubles. No worries, just a drive to be independent and a quest for success. Sometimes I think we were happier back then. With our mix of talent, it didn't take long before our bids were taken seriously."

"Amazing what can be learned during an evening of pizza and beer," she said laughing.

"Yeah," he said, joining in. "We'd design anything and everything for a buck. Didn't even have set hours. Some of our best creations came out at three o'clock in the morning after an impromptu basketball game."

"Sounds like fun." Though they'd been friends for years, Sam never knew any of this. "And good memories," she added. By the time she came on the scene, the firm's business was booming, hence the need for her.

"It was. They are."

She nodded, surprised at the realization that even those with a wealthy background struggled to make their way in the world. James could be the boy next door, not a guy who hailed from a mansion in Woodside, California. She just assumed his silver spoon and family connections gave him the edge, not hard work and talent. After all, that's how Charles made his way. His father groomed him to take over the family business. His six-figure salary earned right out of college came more because of who he was, not what he'd accomplished, although to give him credit, Charles worked long hard hours. Just like she and James did.

"Now the firm's earned a decent reputation," James said, breaking into her thoughts. "We've become competition for the bigger companies, and thanks to our small size and talent we have more business than we can handle." He sighed and finished off his slice of pizza in one bite, washing it down with the last of his beer.

Noting his wistful stare, Sam traced a drop of condensation on her glass of beer with her finger, wishing she had a few fun memories to share. She'd climbed the ladder, but the early days weren't worth remembering because all she'd done was work, she suddenly realized. She never made time for fun. Lord, she really was boring. No wonder she and Charles didn't laugh together.

The conversation died while the waitress cleared their dishes, before setting the bill on the table.

"Come on." James stood after signing the charge slip. He grabbed her hand, pulling her with him. "The night is still young. We've only begun."

As they walked out into the night air, his excited boy-in-the-toy-store demeanor returned in full force and Sam was laughing once again, trying to match his stride, and enjoying every step. It seemed stupid at this point to keep taking mental notes. Why not just enjoy herself and have fun?

"We'll leave the car parked." He bought tickets from a machine located at the cable car stop at the bottom of the hill and handed her one. "Since it's evening and not tourist season, there's no wait. In summer, we'd have to go further up the hill and have exact change to get on. You can't get within a block of the ticket machine. Tourists must find it easier to charge the ride, rather than have dollar bills."

After jumping on the next car, they quickly found a seat in the almost empty trolley as it clanked along. Perched on a wooden bench, she took in the shadowy streets, lit with lights every few hundred feet. Everywhere she looked, life went on. Cars honked, people walked, and James pointed out interesting facts. They rode to the end of the line at Market Street, and stayed on as the cable car made a brief stop, then switched directions.

The ride back, made in relative darkness with the sounds and scenes from the city as a backdrop, was the most romantic half hour of her life. Again, the thought of wanting to share the moments with Charles flitted through her mind. She shook it off. Charles would never take the time to enjoy a cable car ride, nor would he eat pizza in a noisy, crowded restaurant. Her thoughts flashed to earlier that afternoon when she'd spotted him laughing with Lucinda. Maybe she'd misjudged him. Maybe he yearned for something like this too.

Or maybe Mary Ann was right and Charles' lack of spontaneity was part of their problem. After all, he never suggested they do anything fun. Maybe she had to be the instigator, in which case, two weeks with James would yield more than she anticipated. Maybe after experiencing life through James' eyes, she could get Charles to do the same. *All more food for thought.* Maybe… If only she wasn't enjoying herself quite so much.

Life should be fun. Don't feel guilty for enjoying the moment. "I've never done this before," she said, pushing guilt out of her mind.

"You're joking, right?" When she shook her head, he sighed and clucked his tongue. "I can't believe you live twenty minutes south of San Francisco and never experienced one of America's treasures from a tourist's point of view. You really have to get out more and live a little."

"I thought I was doing that," she said with a grin. He jumped off the car and turned to help her. When his hands grabbed on to her midriff, lifting her down, her breath caught in her throat and her pulse galloped.

She pulled the sweater under her jacket lower and smoothed her jeans, forcing herself to breathe. *Concentrate. Take one breath then another and another and another.*

"Now I know exactly how to spend the next two weeks."

"How?" she was finally able to get out a moment later, praying he couldn't hear the loud thumping of her heart.

"Playing tourist. Have you ever been to Pier 39?" When she shook her head, he frowned at her playfully. "How about Fisherman's Wharf?"

Again, the answer was a negative shake of her head. He sighed and pulled her along without giving her the slightest clue that he was aware of her inner turmoil. Every nerve in her body stood at attention, on full alert because of his touch. Lust. That's all it was.

"Come on. We're not done yet."

She laughed and followed, stilling her racing heart at the solid, warm connection of her hand in his. No wonder all those women went out with him. He was a lot of fun. She was definitely learning about lust. She felt alive. Not only that, it felt great to laugh.

They walked for blocks. She didn't mind. Adrenaline fueled the journey.

"Where are we going?" she asked after they'd walked close to a mile. He definitely had a purpose in mind.

"Coit Tower." He pointed to the lit tower, standing out of the darkness like a beacon. "Everyone says Lillie Coit wanted it built as a dedication to firefighters, but her main purpose was to add beauty to the city she'd always loved."

"How do you know so much about San Francisco?"

"My sister-in-law. When I dated her, Kate lived in the Marina District and she loved discovering what she called the city's treasure trove of interesting facts and places. She'd get after me because I was one of those who lived within driving distance and had no clue about what the city offered." His look told her she was now one of those.

She laughed. "Guilty as charged. I'm sure during the next two weeks you're planning on rectifying that."

"Of course. I'd be remiss in my duty if I didn't pass on what I learned." After they made their original destination, he led her through another maze of streets. By this point, her legs felt like Jell-O, but she was having too much fun to say anything. Every now and then, he'd slow and point out a park or a building.

"We can cut over to Lombard Street from here. You can't visit San Francisco and not walk down the most crooked street in the world, only we're going to walk up it."

The night was quiet, adding a romantic quality to their hike. She followed him until they finally made it to the top of the hill entrance of the winding street. *Thank God.*

"Eight turns in all. Great view, huh? It's better by daylight, more impressive. On a clear, sunny day you can see for miles."

"It's beautiful." And worth the hike, she added silently, looking out over the bay spreading like a purple carpet surrounded by dark shadows of blue with lights twinkling in the foreground and background. Again, Sam wondered why she felt such a connection with James while taking in the spectacular, romantic sight. A moment like this should have been shared with Charles, not James. Sadly, Charles would never have hiked for an hour in the dark, so she'd never share something like this with him. Did she now crave the impossible? Staring into such breathtaking beauty, she couldn't believe…no, she wouldn't believe it. She spent more time just peering into the darkness and said honestly, because the moment seemed to require it, "Makes me feel part of something greater."

"Yeah, I know exactly what you mean." James smiled, then grabbed her hand and they headed back in comfortable silence. As they walked on, he continued holding her hand. For some reason, it just felt right. When the two neared James' parked car, the connection she'd felt on top of Lombard Street still enveloped them.

He unlocked and opened her door. She bent to climb in, but his hand on her arm stopped her.

"Wait."

Sam straightened and turned with a question in her eyes.

James grinned. Her hair whipped around her face in the steady breeze. She watched, too stunned to move, as his fingers brushed blowing strands behind her ear. Blood rushed to her head and her mind went blank. Her lungs quit working…wouldn't inflate as her gaze landed on his lips with a longing she didn't understand. No, she understood the longing all right. She just didn't understand why she'd never felt this way with Charles. She was tired of fighting this growing attraction as she'd done during the entire return trip back to the car.

"I wanted to thank you for one of the nicest nights I've had in a long time."

"It was nice," she said, praying he couldn't read her mind. Yet, when she glanced into those smiling eyes, the control she'd held on to for the last hour slipped a little lower. Of their own accord, her lips parted and her head lifted, sending a silent invitation. James didn't hesitate to respond. The next instant, his mouth covered hers. Disappointment hit when the warm kiss ended long before she was satisfied and he hurriedly ushered her into his SUV.

So this was lust, she thought, touching her lips as he drove south. She stared out the dark window, not seeing the passing streetlights and other cars on the road due to all the emotions swirling inside her just then. This was how she should feel with Charles. But she knew it would never be like that with him.

She should be disappointed, but she couldn't muster it over something she would never feel. She was a realist who planned strategy. She understood the rules. James wasn't long term. She also finally understood his allure, and she felt lucky to have shared this evening's experience, along with that last kiss with him. Hopefully she could use both to improve her current relationship.

Those thoughts and more like them played out in Sam's mind as James led her into her building. Like their earlier kiss, the wonderful night was ending much too quickly.

"Don't smile at me like that." His words interrupted her errant thoughts. He handed her the key after opening her door. "I read your signals loud and clear, and it's not a good idea to invite me in tonight."

Her grin spread. "Why?"

"I won't be able to leave," he murmured, bending and taking her lips with his. Though she'd kissed him before, too many times for comfort, nothing prepared her for the feelings that swamped her when his tongue invaded her mouth. Explosions of pleasure burst from within. She wanted to savor the sensation. Now knowing exactly what to do, she wasted no time in giving in to impulse and opened her mouth wider to meet the thrust of his tongue with hers. She moaned and wrapped her arms around him in an effort to get closer.

Abruptly, he pulled away. His breathing was labored, as if he'd run a mile. With a firm hand, he guided her inside her apartment. "Good night, Sam."

Stunned, she watched him turn and walk away with brisk steps. She closed the door and leaned against it, hugging herself. Now that he wasn't next to her, her rational, practical side slowly returned. Imagine that! The mighty James Morrison, hot and bothered from kissing her. She dismissed the thought that she'd been as hot and bothered, focusing on his abrupt exit instead, which meant she could handle him and she could handle lust.

"Charles Winthrope, you are mine," she stated triumphantly, heading toward her phone to give him a spontaneous call. James was a damned good teacher, she'd give him that.

"Charles?"

"Samantha?" he answered, his voice groggy. He broke off a moment. "Do you know what time it is?"

"Yeah. It's ten after twelve. I was lying here thinking of you."

"Have you been drinking?"

"No." How could he think such a thing? "I just had the most incredible evening and wanted to share."

"You couldn't call me in the morning to tell me this?"

"You're the one who wanted more spontaneity. And you were absolutely right."

"I was?" He sounded surprised and she grinned.

"Yes. We *should* do more to experience life."

"Okay, but I've had a horrendous day, so can we do this during daylight? Say, around eight a.m.?"

"Why not now?" she said, ignoring his teasing voice. "That's our problem. We let moments like this pass." If he wanted changes, he should be willing to listen to her no matter what time she called.

"And now I know you've had one too many. It's late. I'll call you in the morning."

She grinned at his now stuffy tone and tsk-tsked as James had done to her. "Have you ever ridden on a cable car? Eaten pizza at Mario's? Walked down the most crooked street?"

"Samantha." Her name came out in a long, exasperated sigh. "I'm really beat. Now is not a good time to discuss this."

"Don't you care about what I do? My feelings?"

"When did you ride on a cable car?" he said on another sigh, this time more resigned. "I thought you hated San Francisco."

He was the one who hated the city, but she didn't voice the thought. Instead, she said, "Not when you experience it as a tourist. Morrison's a great guide. I saw the world in a whole new way. Charles, we need to play more."

"Morrison?" She now had his complete attention, judging by the abrupt tone. "You were with Morrison tonight?"

"Yeah. So? We went out."

"Why would you go out with him?"

"Why not?" She caught jealousy in his voice and a jubilant thrill ran through her. "We're just friends. I mean, it's no big deal. After all, you took Lucinda to lunch."

"I didn't take her to lunch. We went to lunch together. Why wouldn't I? We're co-workers."

"I'm not stupid. I saw you with her this afternoon," she blurted out, as her own jealousy roared over his innocent tone. "Is that why you wanted a break? Have you slept with her yet?" Damn, now she sounded like a lunatic, and in Sam's mind, there was nothing worse than a jealous lunatic. Yet she couldn't get the picture of him laughing with Lucinda out of her head. Why didn't Charles laugh with her like that? Like James had done tonight? It should have been Charles. Not James.

"Samantha, it's late. Can we talk about this tomorrow when you're more coherent?" A stab of dissatisfaction hit her consciousness because he always brushed her feelings away. Unfortunately, she was just now noticing the fact. "Lucy is a friend. I know I screwed up the other night, but you don't need to use Morrison to make me jealous."

Her back stiffened at his mild rebuke and anger rose up. "But it's okay for me to see you two laughing together at lunch?" She knew she was being irrational, but his statement just irritated the hell out of her. Might be because it was twined with a bit of guilt for laughing so much with James earlier, the voice in the back of her mind shouted.

"I'm in the middle of the biggest deal of my career, and you interrupt my sleep to say something so absurd? Go to bed. I'll call you tomorrow. I'll be working most of the day, but we can go out tomorrow night. I've missed you."

Go to bed? He's telling me to go to bed like I'm a naughty child and he wants to see me tomorrow? Fat chance.

If he had no time for an impromptu call after all he'd said last week, then he could just take his night and...well...she had no intention of backing down now. Their relationship did suffer from tedium and, right or wrong, she planned to change that. "No. I'm busy."

"Busy?"

"Yeah, busy. Our three-week reprieve isn't over."

"I don't understand," he said, sounding totally confused. "Why did you call if you didn't want to see me?"

"Am I so predictable?" She pulled the receiver from her ear and stared at it in disgust. *We'll see about predictable, Mr. Winthrope.* "I'm busy tomorrow. I have another date with James. He's been keeping me company while you're being an ass."

"Okay, I'm an ass. Are you happy? You've made your point. Now, can we go to dinner?"

"No. This was your idea, and I'm beginning to think it's exactly what we needed. I'll call you on Sunday, since I'm not sure when I'll be home tomorrow. Wouldn't want to interrupt your sleep again."

She slammed the phone into the cradle, wondering why his offer annoyed her. A week ago, she'd have jumped at it. Why was the thought of spending the rest of her life with him suddenly so very unattractive? This was Charles, the love of her life. He made a mistake and, in his own weird way, she knew he was trying to rectify it. He might be stiff and stuffy, but he was also strong, stable, and secure—a good provider. Everything she always wanted...and more.

"It's his fault," she hissed, storming into her bedroom and yanking out of her sweater and jeans. This entire debacle would never have happened if not for James Morrison. He was fun. And he was a good kisser. That's why she was dying for more. No wonder women fell at his feet. He was hot. She snorted. *But it's not love…only lust.*

She'd never felt lust before. Had never given herself permission. Lust had been her mother's downfall. Her mom's quest for passion had kept them living in poverty and, as a teenager, Sam swore never to make the same mistakes. Passion always faded. Surrendering to lust wouldn't help her achieve her lifelong dreams of marriage and permanence. A sense of belonging that she knew marriage would give her. But now, understanding set in. How could she judge others so harshly for giving in to such a powerful, wonderful feeling?

Maybe her lack of experience was a bigger part of the problem with Charles than she realized. Her position on lust definitely needed more study.

As she brushed her teeth, she mentally debated her options. This situation was completely different from her mother's situation. Her mother always picked emotionally unavailable men to count on. Sam knew better than to expect anything more than a great time from Morrison. His lack of emotional stability might not provide what she needed in the relationship department, but that didn't mean she couldn't twist his actions tonight for her own means. She grinned, then spit out the last of the toothpaste and rinsed her mouth. That was exactly what she could do. It was a perfect plan.

And after that last kiss, the guy wasn't immune to her any more than she was to him.

James' shot about sex with him adding a spark to her relationship flashed and suddenly the idea held a lot more merit. A win-win situation. Why not experience sex at least once in her life for the simple sake of lust? Once she made love with James, lust would be out of her system and she could then use the encounter to spice things up with Charles. *If* she and Charles could work things out, which might be a toss-up considering that phone call. That thought stopped her. Damn. Awareness was a bitch. She wished she hadn't gone past the point of no return to ever be happy with the way her relationship was last week.

She had no clue as to what the future held. All she knew was that she couldn't let go of the idea of sleeping with James. But, if she did, she'd have to do so with her eyes wide open.

Chapter 5

James yanked the door open to stop the impatient pounding.

"Charles?" he asked, staring dumbfounded at the man's disheveled appearance. Winthrope was the last person he expected, much less wanted to see after dropping Sam off at her place. He was in no mood to deal with the guy, especially given the way her scent still clung to him after their parting kiss. Jealousy ate at him. And because it was an emotion he shouldn't feel, his voice was caustic when he added, "Isn't it a little late for a social call?"

"What have you been doing with my fiancée?"

"What do you mean, your fiancée?" He groaned inwardly at how his words sounded like a fierce growl. This was too much. He didn't want to hear about how Sam was his anything. He needed a drink. His thoughts definitely shouldn't be going in that direction. "Wasn't the break your idea?"

"To think and determine if spending my life with her is something I want. That doesn't excuse you taking her out to seduce her."

"She's a big girl, free to date who she wants."

"You know damn well we're almost engaged."

"Almost? Isn't that like saying a woman's a little pregnant?" *Almost engaged. What a crock.* Sam was right. The guy should know his own mind after three years. He'd used the same excuse with Kate, so he understood indecision. However, Charles should be honest about it.

"Don't play semantics with me."

"Well, you're either engaged or not. Last I heard, you hadn't popped the question and wanted time to think about it. What's she supposed to do in the meantime, wait on the shore while you test different waters?" Which is exactly what Kate had done for years. For some reason, the thought of Sam doing the same with Charles stunk.

"She has no business going out with you." Charles ignored his raised eyebrows and ranted on. "Now she's got a harebrained idea about taking time to play. Can you imagine? Samantha saying such a thing?"

"I thought that was also your idea." He snorted. "Maybe her priorities have changed and she wants more out of life than to have every element controlled. Maybe your priorities should change, too."

"That whole dinner was a disaster. I don't want change any longer. I know her…know what to expect from her. She's driven, yet reasonable. Sedate and settled. Exactly what I need in a mate. I see that now."

"Have you told Sam this?" In his opinion, the new Samantha Collins wouldn't be too happy with his adjectives. The woman in his arms tonight had proven beyond a doubt she was also sexy, vibrant, and unpredictable. On top of that, she kissed like an angel. Charles Winthrope had no idea what he pushed aside with his stupidity the week before, because, if their shared kiss was any indication, he could have been in her bed within minutes. Only friendship held him back—his friendship with her and also with the man in front of him, a man who was confirming with his absurdity he didn't deserve her. Given this new perspective, he wished he'd never introduced them.

"No. I intend to remedy the problem. She'll be only too happy to know I'm ready to commit. It's what she's been waiting for."

"What's the matter? Your new co-worker too hot to handle?" James said, irritated at Charles' smug attitude, also remembering Sam's concerns. She was a person who deserved respect, not to be treated as a commodity to be bought with a proposal.

"That nasty shot was uncalled for," Charles sputtered as a flush of embarrassment hit his features. "Especially coming from you."

"Uncalled for? Maybe." James shook his head in disgust. "And I'm sure it's not true." He turned to close his door. "Still, if I were you, I'd grovel. I suggest roses. She has a soft spot for roses."

Charles' hand on the door stopped its progress. "You've done this. You've put ideas into her mind."

"All I did was be her friend." James sighed, rolling his eyes, begging the heavens for patience. "I might have commitment issues, but I'm honest about it. I don't lead women on. Besides, I'm not the one you should be talking to. Good night, Charles." He slammed the door on Winthrope's stunned face and headed for his kitchen, praying he had a full bottle of wine. One glass would never be enough. Why had he ever gotten involved with Samantha Collins?

~

"Charles?" Sam blinked after opening her door and seeing him in front of her, holding a bouquet of flowers. His distraught appearance shocked her so much she forgot her earlier annoyance with him. Nothing about his humble demeanor resembled *her* Charles. "What are you doing here?"

"I came to speak to you." He offered the flowers. "I tried to find roses, but it's next to impossible at two in the morning."

She took the bouquet and stood to the side, her nod indicating her sofa. "Have a seat. Would you like a drink? I have wine." For the second time that night, she headed for the kitchen to fill a vase with water. The similarities ended there, however. Though James' gesture was premeditated, she'd been flattered at the time. Why didn't she feel the same with Charles' gift? She should have, especially since Charles never brought her flowers and she always wished he would.

Silly thoughts, but still troubling.

"Wine's fine."

He made himself comfortable, while she worked. Neither spoke. After filling both the vase and glass, she picked them up, placing the flowers on the coffee table before handing the wine to him.

"Thanks."

She sat, leaving the space of a cushion between them. She wrapped her robe around her tighter and redid the sash, then glanced at him with the question in her eyes. "Well?"

He took a sip and then studied his glass. For long minutes, she waited in deafening silence while he gathered his thoughts. Finally, he placed his wine on the table. He inhaled deeply and cleared his throat.

"I've come to a decision." He pushed his glasses to the bridge of his nose, and instantly the old Charles was back. "It's time we committed to each other."

"Oh?" He's come to a decision? What about her? Didn't she get a say? A week ago, she'd have been happy to let Charles make the full decision. Regrettably, that was a week ago when ignorance had been bliss. Now she deserved a hell of a lot more. Words of love would have been a good start. "When did *you* come to this decision?" She worked to keep her renewed annoyance bottled. It was late, and all she wanted to do was go back to bed…without Charles.

"Why are you getting upset? I thought marriage and a family were what we were working toward?"

Good question. Why am I so upset? She sighed, not understanding her disappointment. He was just being Charles and was offering her exactly what she always wanted. "It's late. Too late to talk about this tonight."

"Okay. We can talk in the morning. I like what you've done to your hair. Did you do that for me?" He narrowed the distance between them and put his arm around her. "I heartily approve."

"No. I did it for me." More aggravation washed over her. He pulled her closer and her spine straightened, one vertebra at a time.

"I still approve. I missed you."

He leaned in and kissed her, expecting her full compliance. His actions and comments only annoyed her further. He seemed so oblivious to the fact that she was still angry and didn't want to return his kiss. Had he always been so clueless about her feelings? Probably. What was sadder? She allowed it.

She shook her head to break their connection. "What about Lucinda? I saw you with her."

His head went back and he scrutinized her face. He clearly hadn't expected her to spout off about the woman. Did he really think it couldn't matter?

"There's nothing between us. I'm sorry you got the wrong impression and I'm sorry I went to lunch with Lucy. That was a mistake."

"A mistake? And by saying that, it absolves you from being a jerk?"

"I said I was sorry."

"Well, maybe sorry's not good enough."

"I see." He lowered his eyes and studied his hand for a long moment before his attention swept the room, stalling on the roses sitting on her dining room table. His back stiffened. Anger flashed in his eyes, as his gaze sought hers. "Are those from him?"

"Him?"

"Don't pretend you don't know who I'm talking about. You know damn well I mean Morrison."

"Morrison? The fact that he brought me flowers has nothing to do with this."

"You're using him to punish me, aren't you?"

"I think you'd better leave." She stood and crossed her arms. "Before we both say something we'll regret."

"I can see you're upset," he said, backing down completely. "Can't we talk about this? I never meant to hurt you. I love you."

Tears sprung into her eyes. "You weren't willing to tell me those things until you saw the flowers from James. If you had said something earlier, maybe I'd feel differently." Right now she simply wanted him to go. "I can't talk right now." She was more confused than ever. "I think we should stick with the original plan of taking a break. I need a few weeks to think. You owe me that."

"Okay." The word came out in a resigned sigh. "You're right. Tonight isn't the best time for this conversation." He stood and turned to leave. He stopped in mid-stride and pivoted, catching her gaze with his. "But while you're thinking," he said quietly, his expression somber, "remember, I do love you and I *am* offering marriage. Don't throw away three years over roses. Morrison won't give you what you want."

"This isn't about him. I wish it could be so simple." She brushed away a tear she felt break loose, then blinked, willing the others behind it to cease their trek. "I love you too, Charles, but something inside me has changed. Your actions hurt me. I can't turn back the clock and pretend nothing's happened."

"Then please give me a chance to make it right." His expressive eyes, amplified behind the lenses, begged, and worry etched his brow. "If you do, I'm confident we can work it out."

She nodded, watching him leave, then headed for her bedroom, letting the tears fall, not bothering to wipe them off, as she climbed into bed.

What was wrong with her? Why wasn't she ecstatic over Charles' spontaneous, late night visit? Why was the memory of James' kiss still replaying over and over in her mind, like an endless video, overshadowing Charles' vow of love and commitment? Was she the biggest fool on the planet or what?

She was a fool, because, while lying in the dark staring at the ceiling, she volleyed the pros and cons of making love with James for the hundredth time, with the pros winning hands down over the cons every time.

Mistake or not, she was dying to experience what he had to offer.

Chapter 6

Sam woke early the next morning in a totally confused state.

A shower and coffee did nothing to ease her uncertainty.

She changed into running gear and headed out the door. She needed to clear her mind, use the next five miles to think—to figure out her life.

Somehow her subconscious had another agenda. Within minutes, she found herself on James' front stoop, ringing the doorbell, without any clear idea of why. Well, she *knew* why. But James Morrison could only add to her troubles.

"Collins," James said, with surprise lighting his face. "I didn't expect to see you today. Thought you and Charles might be snuggling this morning." He left the door open and turned, aiming for his kitchen.

"How'd you know he dropped by last night?" She followed after closing his front door.

"Intuition. The guy's got to wise up sometime."

At the kitchen's entrance, she leaned against the doorjamb, crossing both arms and legs and watched as he poured a cup of coffee. He lifted the pot, and offered, "Want some?"

"Sure," she said. "He didn't spend the night."

"Why not? How could he not like the new you?" He reached up, opened the cupboard, and grabbed another mug. "What the hell is wrong with him?"

She shrugged.

"Is he still being an ass? Want me to beat him up for you?" His teasing grin twisted her insides. "I will, you know."

She laughed, unable to stop the burst of pleasure from bubbling out. How had she ever thought she was immune to that smile…to those laughing eyes? She was as susceptible as any woman, she realized. The idea reinforced the solution she'd finally decided on last night, providing her with more of her earlier determination. Maybe it was time to discover the benefits of lust.

"No need. I think I got through to him loud and clear." She smiled and unbent to take the cup he offered. "Thanks," she said, distractedly, then added, "He liked the new me all right…was all for spending the night, but I told him no. He needs a brain transplant if he thinks a bouquet of grocery store flowers will make up for his conduct." She quit talking long enough to take a sip of the hot brew. She swallowed and just like that, clarity set in. She sent Charles away because she needed time to be sure if *he* was what she *wanted*. "This was his idea. I have two weeks left and I don't plan to waste a moment."

"I thought you wanted to bring him to heel. Flowers and a late night visit say you achieved your goal. You should go home and savor your victory."

"Maybe I've changed my mind. Maybe I've decided I need more. Maybe I want to experience life before I settle down with one man."

"Experience life?"

"Maybe." She shrugged, then smiled. He didn't need to know that her definition of *experience life* really meant experience sex for its own sake. "As I recall, someone promised to play tour guide. Does the offer still stand?"

He snorted and shook his head. "I don't think it'd be such a great idea."

"Why? What happened to your two-week test?"

"Forget it." He glanced at her and she caught the sincerity in his gaze. "It was a stupid move on my part. I don't know what I was thinking to suggest it."

"But I want the McAlpin project."

"It's always been yours." He sighed and looked away. "I was being an ass, not a friend."

Disappointment engulfed her when she realized how right he was, but the knowledge didn't make it any easier to accept. "What about the kiss last night? What was that?"

"The point I was making, which translates into me being a bigger ass." He held up his cup and took a sip of coffee. "Let's forget I ever tried to bribe you. Spending more time together will only complicate matters."

More common sense. Still, she couldn't let her one chance of experiencing sex for the sake of sex go without some effort. She might never get another chance. Who better to use than her old buddy, James? "So, you only kissed me to make your point? No other reason?"

He shrugged. "Doesn't matter. The end result is the same." When she was about to argue, he put up a hand to halt her words. "We're friends. And we're going to stay friends."

"Oh no. You can't renege now. I won't let you."

"Go home and call Charles. If anyone can pull him out of that stuffed shirt he wears, it'll be the new you."

"I'm not a little kid who doesn't know what she wants." Well, she was, but he didn't need to know that about her either. She leaned against the counter, holding her cup to her mouth and said, before taking a sip, "And I'm not going home."

"Yeah? Well, I'm not about to play whatever game you've got in mind. The price is too high."

"What happened to friends and lovers?" She took another sip of coffee, then walked over to him, boldly holding his gaze. "You can't tell me you're not attracted to me. I've been present all those times you've kissed me. Remember?"

"I may find you attractive, but there's no way I'm acting on it."

"I only want what your kiss offered and you refused to give last night."

"You're practically engaged, for Christ's sake."

"Not yet, and I'm not going to pretend that Charles' comments didn't hurt me." She placed her mug on the counter and moved closer. "I am rigid and predictable. But no more."

"Revenge isn't the answer."

"This isn't about revenge," she whispered. His eyes narrowed as she clasped his cup, gently pulled it out of his grasp, and set it aside.

"What the hell are you doing?" He leaned away from her when she reached up to wrap her arms around his neck.

"You have to ask?" A chuckle burst free. His stunned expression spoke more words than the dictionary held. "I'm throwing myself at you. If you were a true friend, you'd catch me and give me the experience of a lifetime."

"Oh no! No way I'm ruining a friendship over sex." He tried to extricate himself from her. Holding her wrists, his gaze sought hers, imploring along with his voice. "I like you too much. Go home. Please?"

"That's so sweet," she cooed. She pulled one hand out of his grasp and patted his cheek. "You're worried about me and my feelings." Her arms went around his neck again and she tightened her hold, grinning all the way to her toes.

"Call Charles. He made a mistake. If he's offering commitment, take it."

His concern gave her the courage to continue, despite the impatient expression taking over his face and his chiding tone.

"Charles started this and he'll just have to understand my reasons." If he didn't? Well then, they weren't meant to be and she could live with that. What she couldn't live without at this moment was finding out about lust and what it entailed. She'd determined many things late last night. She wanted to know what caused her mother's downfall, why Sam's needs as a daughter fell far below the need for sexual fulfillment from some guy.

"Come on, James. I want the next two weeks with you." She exerted force, tugging on his neck, and brought his head closer, inches from hers. "I understand the rules of the game. I have no expectations, other than a wonderful experience. To be seduced by a true pro." This was her chance and she wasn't about to give it up without a fight. She tried to enjoy sex with Charles. After all, she loved him, but the act was usually perfunctory and uncomfortable, yet something expected in a committed relationship. Before kissing James, she hadn't realized how it could be.

She brushed her lips over his, back and forth, before her tongue followed, tracing his mouth. Then, she gave in to the need for more than a taste and locked lips with his.

His hands left her wrists, sliding down her arms and then back up again. Finally, he pulled away. "It's not a good idea," he whispered breathlessly, meeting her gaze with an intensity that curled her toes. "A recipe for disaster. We work together."

"You don't think you can separate business and pleasure?"

"I can. Question is…" He smiled, as his finger trailed the length of her arm, spreading pleasure in the form of goose bumps along its wake. "Can you?"

Her chin rose a defiant inch. "Of course. Charles may be the one or may not. Doesn't matter, because before I commit to anyone, I want more. I just want other experiences. Is that so wrong?"

"You're not cut out for one-night stands, Collins."

She grinned and pulled him closer. Slowly, her head moved from side to side, brushing her lips over his again, and she said softly, "Unh unh. Not a one-night stand." She took her time, fully using her tongue and mouth to make her point. She felt the rapid beating of his heart, before she broke the connection. She leaned back and caught his gaze. His breathing was more labored. She smiled inwardly.

Oh yeah, she'd given him a taste of his own medicine and it felt pretty powerful. No way she'd back off now. She had too much to gain from a night of sex with him. Sex for the sake of sex, where emotions would not intrude. She wanted him, and she'd have him. She released her hold, then stepped away to pick up her mug of coffee while he regarded her warily.

"We both know your affairs are never for only one night. I also know you like the women you sleep with. You're just not into commitment." She lifted her shoulders nonchalantly, taking a drink of coffee. "Since I'm not looking for a commitment from you, you should jump at the chance."

He spent countless minutes scrutinizing her face, his internal debate written all over his own. Finally, he sighed and shook his head, muttering, "I must be nuts," before adding in a louder voice, "If we do this, we do it my way."

"Of course," she said, hiding her satisfied grin behind the act of sipping.

"No. Don't give me your *of course* like you have no intention of complying. I know that tone." His sexy gaze caught and held hers.

He had her there. *He's good. Darn good.* It should irritate her that he knew her so well, but it only amused her. And, when he looked at her with such an earnest expression, she couldn't help but promise him darn near anything.

"Let's talk first," he said. "And I expect complete honesty or we can forget the whole idea."

"I'm always honest."

"Okay. Why?"

"Why? I already told you why."

"Tell me again so I'm sure I understand."

The soft command caught her off-balance and she had to think a minute for the right way to answer. "Why is very simple. I like kissing you, and kissing you makes me wonder how it would be to make love with you."

"What do you hope to achieve?"

Sam laughed. "You can't be that dense, Morrison."

"Okay." His eyes narrowed. "I'm going to make a few assumptions here, so don't take offense if I get personal."

"I think the fact that we'll soon be lovers gets pretty personal, so be my guest."

The edges of his eyes crinkled when he smiled, and his entire face lit up. The effect was as startling as the sun peeking out from clouds on an overcast day—warm brightness permeating the cool shadows, sending light and heat everywhere it landed. "I take it making love with Charles doesn't ring your chimes."

And he had to go and ruin her sunshine with such a statement.

"He does." She cringed, hating the defensive tone in her voice. When his eyebrow shot up and the look he flashed said no way he believed her, her chin inched higher. "We're in love, not lust."

"Ah! I see."

"What do you see?"

"Maybe I should be giving lessons to Charles rather than you."

"Charles is fine." Her focus moved to her hands. Fingering the designs on the side of the mug she held, she studied them intently. She sighed. *Might as well be honest, since he wants honesty.* "If you must know, the problem lies with me. I don't like sex all that much." She inhaled deeply and exhaled slowly. "Okay…there…I've said it and now you know. Whew. It's a relief to get it out. See? My seduction may not be such a great experience for you. I'm a flop in the bedroom."

"You're not serious?"

His tone held such an incredulous quality. The guy couldn't be so clueless. He'd find out the truth soon enough, since he'd agreed to her plans. Still, she hated having to explain, but he asked for complete honesty. Far be it from her to withhold information now.

"Is an IRS agent serious during a tax audit? Of course, I'm serious. You think I'd pour my heart out if I wasn't? I don't have much experience outside of Charles."

"How much is *much*?"

Looking down at the floor, she cleared her throat. "None," she said softly, feeling heat rush up her face and wishing more than ever she could add a couple of numbers.

"So, Charles was your first? Your one and only?"

Sam nodded, but still couldn't meet his eyes. She felt gauche and inept, a mere novice in the presence of a master.

"Hmmm. Interesting." James turned to open the refrigerator, asking over his shoulder, "Have you had breakfast?"

"No. What's interesting?" She finally found enough courage to look at him. "You're not reneging, are you?"

"And risk being assaulted again?" He grinned when she glared at him. "I want to think. And cooking helps me think." He pulled out eggs, cheese, and milk, along with green onions and ham. He put them on the counter, then reached into a breadbox and grabbed a loaf of bread. "Here, do something useful." He handed her the bread and opened a drawer. "Silverware's in here, and there's the toaster," he said, nodding at the appliance hidden in the corner of the granite countertop. "You're in charge of setting the table and making toast."

"Okay. I can handle toast and silverware."

~

James grabbed the sturdy frying pan and placed it on the burner to slowly heat up while he cracked eggs into a bowl. He whisked.

"You like ham and cheese, right?"

"Sure."

"I make a mean omelet," he teased.

Smiling, she filled the toaster with bread, pushed the lever, and started taking out silverware. Her genuine smile tied his insides into one big knot, which meant he should be kicking her butt out the door, not contemplating having sex with her. Only one other female had ever tied him in knots and he'd been crazy then too. Yep. Crazy. That's what he was to even be considering something so ludicrous.

He shook his head, and muttered, "I am crazy," then picked up a knife and chopped.

You're not crazy, Morrison. You know you're dying to have her and she's throwing herself at you. Don't think about what could go wrong. Just enjoy. That was the selfish bastard talking.

While they worked, James tried to focus on what Sam would gain, that this was her idea, anything to rationalize that going along with her plan wouldn't make him a bigger self-absorbed jerk. Even still, he wanted her, selfish bastard or not, and she'd made it perfectly clear she wouldn't take no for an answer.

Once he had everything chopped, he added a few spices to the bowl of eggs, whipping everything together before he went back to the stove. Now, heated to the right temperature, he added a dab of butter, letting it coat before he poured the whipped eggs into the hot pan.

"Smells heavenly. I didn't know you were a gourmet cook."

"Kate's the gourmet. In eight years, a few things rubbed off. Now, I like tinkering with food." Her smile yanked on his gut again, twisting the knot tighter. And a little niggling idea of self-preservation reared its ugly head, doing what his conscience couldn't, adding doubt into the mix. He had no sense. He should know better. Only an idiot would proceed with her crazy proposal. True, he'd instigated it with his outrageous test, but he hadn't been serious about following through on his threats. Shit, he couldn't believe he was even arguing with himself over this. "This shouldn't take too long."

"Table's set and toast is almost ready."

"Good," he murmured, watching as Sam buttered the browned bread, and noting her intense concentration. James grinned.

Hell, why shouldn't he take what she offered? This new Samantha Collins was hot. After their kiss last night, he'd had a hard time walking away. He didn't have qualms about stepping on Charles' toes. He gave a mental snort. The guy had to be a lousy lover. Given their few shared kisses, Sam was a responsive, warm woman who knew what she wanted and Charles obviously wasn't giving it to her. It would serve the arrogant bastard right for his complacency in not satisfying his partner, and judging from her admission, a good sexual experience for her could only help their relationship. Once she knew what she was missing, she'd demand it of him.

Remember, Morrison…she loves the guy. In a flash, he realized why he was balking. Experience—his history with Judith Reid, now Judith McAllister, who loved his best friend, Dev. On the other hand, this was different. Judith was different and someone he could see himself with long term. Sam wasn't. She was too serious…too intense…definitely too rigid. Not at all like the women who usually attracted him. He would have to make sure everything remained light. It wouldn't do for Sam to get too involved. They worked together. He damn sure didn't need the complications.

None of his reservations mattered because he couldn't stop his mind from working up a scenario that would give her exactly what she wanted. The experience of a lifetime.

"Just keep things simple and fun," James muttered, as he dished up their breakfast.

"What?" Sam asked, looking at him expectantly.

"Nothing." He picked up the heaping plates of food and nodded at the plate of toast and the jam he'd put out earlier. "Grab those, would you? And I'll fill you in on our plans for the rest of the weekend."

"So, what do you have in mind for today?" she asked, after he'd placed the food on the table and helped her into the chair. "Are we going to play tourist again? I'd love to go to Pier 39 or Fisherman's Wharf."

"We can do that next weekend." He grinned, ate a few bites, and nodded at her plate, watching her as she brought the fork to her mouth. "What do you think of my omelet?"

"I've died and gone to heaven. I never thought ordinary eggs could taste so delicious. Who knew you could cook?"

"I get tired of eating out." Her warm smile and heartfelt praise stroked something inside him, making him want to do more to keep both coming, like purring. Now he knew how a cat felt.

"I wish I had such skill. I can barely boil eggs, much less get them to taste like this."

They ate in silence a few more minutes before Sam caught his attention, and lifted an eyebrow. "Okay, you've kept me in suspense long enough. If we're not going to Pier 39, what did you have in mind for today?"

"What do you think of hitting the wine country?"

"The wine country?" Sam shrugged. "I've never been. Sounds fun."

"After we eat, I'll make a few calls. We'll spend the night in Sonoma and head to Napa in the morning." He glanced at her. His brow shot up. "If you approve?"

"We're spending the night?"

"Yeah. I'll reserve two rooms."

"That sounds counterproductive. I thought the purpose for doing this was to have sex."

"No. The purpose is to give you the experience of a lifetime. One you can savor, not rush. We're not taking shortcuts or forcing the issue."

"Hmmm. I don't mind shortcuts."

James shook his head. "Making love is an art form. You deserve the full effect. Sex will happen." Judging from both their responses last night, not to mention her little display this morning, he knew he needed to slow things down, not speed them up, if she was going to enjoy the full effect, which was the point of all this. Hell, based on her earlier revelation, he doubted Samantha had ever had an orgasm. If anything, she deserved to know what she was missing. Then, she'd demand more from Charles. He sighed. *The things we do for friends.* "But we're going to have fun, so that it evolves naturally." He snared her gaze so she could see the seriousness in his. "I'm in charge. Got it? We do this my way or not at all."

She nodded and they both went back to eating.

"Need help with the dishes?" Sam jumped up and reached for her plate once the meal was over.

"Sure." He grinned. Might as well use the time to begin her first lesson in Romance 101. He followed her into the kitchen and set his plate on the counter next to hers. When she turned to go back to the table, his hand on her arm halted her in mid-step.

She glanced at him, her brown eyes full of curiosity. His fingers made a light trail up the length of her arm, pausing at her shoulder, before brushing strands of lustrous brown hair out of the way, exposing a lovely, Audrey Hepburn-esque, swan neck. *Yeah. A young Audrey Hepburn. That's who she reminds me of, staring at me with those luminous brown eyes.*

James felt a tremor beneath the pads of his fingers and gently pulled her closer.

"Time for the first lesson. We begin with touch," he whispered, while his fingers lightly massaged her nape, ignoring both her shivers of delight and the goose bumps making an appearance. When Sam nervously chewed on her bottom lip and her expression turned solemn, he sucked in a deep breath and concentrated on what he was about to say, totally unprepared for the surge of lust infiltrating his mind as blood rushed south. "Touch is an important element. Used correctly, it can stimulate and sensitize. Create anticipation." His steady voice amazed him, given that his heart rate was nearing two hundred.

"Touch?" The one word came out in a breathless sigh.

He nodded. "Mmm hmmm." *Damn. She's the one who's supposed to be getting all hot and bothered, not me.* He took several deep breaths before he felt able to continue without letting her know that both her look and her breathless reply had his guy at full attention, more than ready. What the hell was wrong with Winthrope?

"To stimulate and sensitize?"

James nodded again and the smile she bestowed on him did nothing to still his overwhelming urge to lower his head and kiss her senseless. Then, Sam did something he never expected, but should have. Her movements mimicked his. Her hand slowly slid up the length of his arm, pumping a blast of pure heat directly to his groin. When she went up on tiptoes, reaching around his neck, her fingers, feather light, played with the hair on his nape. He never meant for his lesson in touching to end in a kiss, but he couldn't stop himself from giving in to the urge to taste her. His head lowered and he captured those full lips with his. He spent long minutes doing nothing but letting his mouth slowly savor hers.

Blood rushed past his ears, like a freight train hurtling inside his brain. At the same moment, her lemony scent rose up, filling his nostrils, sending more sensation to his mid-section. His hands ached to reach underneath her t-shirt. To touch those luscious breasts. He stilled the longing, but it took tremendous effort.

Damn. The woman knows how to kiss. She was like an exotic drug, intoxicating him. He didn't want to end the kiss, but he knew he was at the point of no return. The desire to lift her in his arms and take her to bed, right then, was all encompassing. God help him, but he was going to enjoy making love to her. Too much. Friendship no longer mattered because all of his common sense flew out the door.

He pulled back and rested his chin on her head, gaining a moment of sanity while his breathing slowed to normal, wishing it hadn't been so long since he'd last had sex. His self-imposed exile from dating after Veronica wasn't helping matters any.

Get a grip, Morrison. You're not a horny teenager, for hell's sake. Don't rush things.

"You sure we can't take shortcuts?" Her question pulled him out of his thoughts and he glanced down at her.

Taking into account her swollen, pouty lips and noting the same sensual longing he felt reflected in her eyes, he reached deep inside for strength and gave his brain a mental shake.

He grinned. He was back in control. He'd have to be more careful about kissing her is all. Though the task seemed impossible, he'd made love with too many women to believe he couldn't slow things.

"No shortcuts. I've got reservations to make, so go home and change." He let go of her, turned her toward the front door, then swatted her butt. "I'll pick you up in an hour. Pack a bag with something elegant for dinner."

Chapter 7

"You're from the Bay Area? Went to grad school at Berkeley, right?"

James' questions brought Sam out of her daydreams, as she watched a container ship head under the Golden Gate Bridge, probably heading for Oakland. They drove north on US 101, the start of what James referred to as her introductory lesson on wine tasting in Sonoma, where they'd be spending the night. He had a favorite resort in mind along with his favorite wineries. They'd finish up in Napa the next day to round out the tour.

She glanced over at him, answering his question with a nod. Her eyes narrowed. "Why?" She hated talking about her past, so much so that she pretended she had a different one...pretended she was just like everyone else. Even though James seemed more understanding than Charles, she had a hard time confiding such ugliness to anyone.

"No reason." His shoulders lifted nonchalantly. Then he grinned. "Okay, maybe there *is* a reason. I was just curious as to how long you've lived here."

"All my life." Mary Ann was the only person who knew the entire truth about her sordid past, because she'd watched her climb out of it.

"Then how is it you've never played tourist in San Francisco or visited the wine country?"

"I've never been interested in either, I guess," she said evasively, thankful his question was going in a different direction than the one her mind had taken. "I've been too busy focusing on work or school, but not anymore."

"What interests you?"

"Art. I love visiting the museums." She shrugged. Heavens, listen to her. *Why not shout, "Boring!"* Oh, how she wished she had taken more time in the last ten years to play, so she wouldn't come across as such an uninteresting person. Viewing herself through James' eyes, she felt lacking. For some reason, she didn't want him to think she was so bland.

"What do you and Charles do for fun?"

"Opera, symphony. We eat out a lot." Charles loved fancy restaurants. She sighed. How could she tell him "fun" didn't quite depict their time together? They enjoyed each other and she felt comfortable in Charles' company, but fun? Not really. "And we did go to Hawaii last year." Sam smiled wistfully, remembering their four-day island getaway. At least it was something.

"I like Hawaii. The islands can be very romantic."

"I guess." She stared out the window, focusing on the passing scenery. Romantic wasn't exactly the word she'd use to describe the trip. She'd tagged along with Charles, who had a business conference to attend. They'd spent less than ten hours together as a couple, and she'd been on her own for the rest of the time. Since she hadn't been much of a shopper back then, she'd hung out at the beach behind her hotel, slathered in sunscreen and hating every moment.

"What?" James' gaze moved to her for a brief moment, capturing her attention, before he refocused on the road. "Why do I get this feeling you don't find Hawaii as romantic a place as I do?"

"I do." Even she could hear the defensive tone of her voice. Why was she trying to sound so convincing? She breathed deeply, ignoring the twinge of irritation rising because he seemed to hone in on a problem area she was just now noticing in her relationship with Charles. Why had she been content with mediocre for so long? Why had she never demanded more?

Good questions.

But she didn't want to think about Charles.

No. I'll deal with him, once I experience these two weeks with James. After he taught her the basics, she'd implement them in her relationship. If she still had one. *So far, so good.*

In Petaluma, James veered off on another highway, heading east. Looking out the window, Sam loved everything she saw.

"Though we've been driving over an hour, I never realized all this was so close to San Francisco." The northern California road wasn't desolate, but it was obvious they'd left the congestion of the city, along with its bedroom communities, far behind and were in the country.

"You need to get out more. See your state. The rural areas here aren't much different from rural areas anywhere."

"Learn something every day," she murmured, her attention remaining fixed on the scenery outside her window.

The conversation died, until he slowed the car and pulled into a parking lot.

"Since our time is limited, we're only stopping at a couple of the wineries I like." He shut off the motor and turned to face her.

"Wine's wine."

"Don't let anyone in there hear you say that." He nodded toward the stucco mission-style building that looked like someone's home, rather than a place of business.

"I thought all wines from northern California were good. So why should it matter?"

"For the most part, they are, but they're also competitive. I have my favorites. From here, we'll work our way south, to the inn where we'll spend the night."

"I'm yours to command." She was having another grand adventure, which only added to her confidence. She'd made the right decision. She couldn't hold on to her smile as it made a full appearance. "I've put myself totally in your hands, so be gentle. Don't forget I'm a virgin at this touristy stuff."

"I'll keep that in mind." He grinned. His hand went to hers, resting on the center console. He gave a gentle squeeze before lifting her hand to his lips. James turned it over, kissed her palm, ran his wet mouth several inches to her wrist, and seized her gaze. "Why do I get this feeling you'll be a natural. At everything?"

Warmth streaked up her arm and spread sensation everywhere. Sam's grin stretched from ear to ear. She couldn't help it. Everything inside her wanted to smile when he looked at her with those intense baby blues.

Down, girl. He's done this before, and he's doing this on purpose. Remember his words about anticipation. At that moment, she prayed for shortcuts, was dying to see what happened when they actually did more than kiss. For the entire drive, she'd felt electricity crackle inside the car, as if a current ran nearby. Every once in a while, when he glanced at her, she felt the hairs at her nape stand on end, felt a slight jolt of expectation. Right now, she tried to keep the heat his sizzling stare generated from burning her insides even more.

He placed her hand back on the console, then reached out and smoothed her cheek with his fingers. They lingered for a second too long, before he brushed strands behind her ear.

"Ready?" he whispered. The pads of his fingers made a slow journey down the side of her face. Chills raced along her spine. Her breath caught at the back of her throat.

Oh yeah. She was more than ready if her heart rate, galloping out of control, was any indication. She forced herself to breathe. First one breath, then another. It took several more before she could nod.

The spell was broken when he let go of her face and turned to open his door. Sam used the distraction to gather her wits. Wouldn't do to melt in a puddle in front of him. James was probably used to that.

In the few seconds it took to jump out of the car, she gained control of her senses. She pivoted and inhaled deeply, buying more time to secure the rest. "I like this place. Looks nice."

The quick flash of his smile, along with the amusement she caught in his eyes, told her he knew of his effect on her. She should be irritated, but why waste time trying for something she couldn't feel? What she really wanted was to give him a little of the same, to drive him as crazy as he was driving her. She didn't recognize herself, didn't recognize this she-devil who'd taken over her body. *Look out, world—Samantha Collins is on the make.*

"This winery delivers a good chardonnay, which is why I put it on the list for today."

"I like chardonnay. I'm not particular about brand, though. Don't know enough about them to be picky."

"Stick with me. You'll learn all kinds of things. Come on."

She smiled warmly when he grabbed her hand and led her in the direction of the entrance.

Inside, she looked around. This first winery had a charming tasting room, reminding her of an inviting country inn. Plush sofas and chairs, done in earth tones, were situated around a roaring fire, despite the warmth of the September Indian-summer day outside.

They walked up to a long bar with eight stools in front and a wine steward behind. Two other couples sat at the counter. James pulled out an empty stool for her, before perching on the one next to it.

"Welcome. I'm Mike, and I'll be your host today." Mike nodded as they introduced themselves, then asked, "Are you familiar with our wines?"

"I am, but she'd like the full lesson," James said.

"Okay." He picked up a bottle. "Today we're tasting two whites, a Riesling, and a young chardonnay, and two reds, our house varietal and a cabernet sauvignon." He spent a minute talking about the grapes and fermentation process, then ended his spiel with, "California wines compete with their French counterparts so well because we're on the same latitude. Our fertile valleys are blessed with perfect weather nine months of the year, and plenty of moisture in the late fall to late spring. After a long, hot, dry summer, all grapes are harvested, usually in September."

He then poured. "We'll start with the chardonnay. This wine has been aged in oak barrels for a year."

Sam glanced at James to watch what he did. He swirled the contents in the glass and breathed in the scent. His eyes sought hers and he lifted one brow.

She followed his movements and laughed. "Why am I doing this?"

"Tell me what you smell."

"What do you mean, tell you what I smell?" She sniffed again and shrugged. "Smells like wine."

He chuckled. "You swirl gently to release the aroma. Open your nostrils and slowly inhale. Let the signals reach your brain so you can appreciate the flavors. Do it again." She copied his movements and brought the glass to her nose, taking in a slow, deep breath, really trying to discover the smell. She looked at him and smiled. He nodded approvingly.

The warmth in both his smile and his animated eyes heated her insides, and worked in conjunction with her nostrils. Her system seemed on overload as little sparks of pleasure shot from her core, traveling out through her hands and toes. She closed her eyes to break the connection, and in doing so she could then let the full sensation of the scent fill her. Who knew sniffing wine could be such a sensual experience? That's exactly what it was with James. Sensual.

"What do you smell?" His whispered voice slid over her, adding to the phenomenon. Her heartbeat quickened, though she was sitting. "Tell me!"

Sam tried to think…to satisfy his soft command. What did she smell? She inhaled deeply again, let the scents surround her, and it hit her. "Almonds and crisp apples and a hint of sweetness," she said, pleased to have come up with an answer.

His response was a deep grin followed with, "Now see if you can taste them."

She took a sip. Spent seconds letting the liquid flow inside her mouth, working to taste the flavors she smelled. Sam sipped again. This time she was more successful. She couldn't hold back her triumphant grin as she caught his gaze.

"See? A natural," he said.

As she finished the last few drops, James poured the remaining contents from his glass into a container on the bar. Mike picked up the next bottle and added more liquid, talking about the specifics of this wine.

By the time she'd finished tasting the other three samples, her confidence about the day increased. She ignored the fact that she'd consumed more than a full glass of wine, which probably amplified the feelings. It didn't escape her notice that James had only taken a sip or two, but she understood his reasons. He was driving and this experience was hers to savor, not his.

"Ready to move on?" James asked, as Mike placed a case of chardonnay on the counter. He pulled his wallet from his pocket and handed the wine steward his charge card.

"I liked their cabernet," she said, watching the guy ring up the sale on the cash register.

James nodded at the box. "Can you add a case of the cab to the total and have someone carry them out to the silver Sequoia?"

In minutes, James slammed the hatch after depositing the wine in the back, while she snapped her seat belt into place and waited as he climbed in beside her.

The next winery produced a parallel experience. Even the wines were similar varieties, and they were treated much the same as the one they'd just left. Sam enjoyed learning more about something she always took for granted, loved the lessons about the little nuances of the different grapes. She drank chardonnay, but only because Charles did. Before she dated him, she didn't drink at all.

Once they were seated back inside his SUV after the tasting, James turned to her. "Are you hungry?"

"I could eat."

"Good. I'm starved. We can eat, then finish with a couple more wineries. There's a little place right down the road."

They drove for ten miles before the place came into view. They were out in the middle of nowhere, but the parking lot was packed, indicating someone knew about it.

Wonderful scents hit her nostrils when they entered the restaurant. The food had to be delicious; her nose told her as much. Sam didn't question James' choice for their late lunch. As usual, she was overwhelmed with all she was seeing and experiencing. The guy really was a lot of fun and seemed to know where the action was: right where they stood. The décor—walls filled with memorabilia and funky, stained glass windows—could only be called interesting. One thing she was learning about James, he was flexible in his choice of restaurants. He could easily enjoy the nitty-gritty, like good food and atmosphere, unlike Charles, who preferred more pretentious, snooty places. He'd never step into a joint like this.

"This is a marvelous choice," she said, after being seated and taking the menu the waitress handed her. "How did you find out about this place?"

"Dumb luck. I just pulled in one day and decided to try it. I've been coming back ever since."

"Others must've done the same," she said, her nod indicating the crowded, noisy room.

She ordered a glass of wine she recognized on the menu as well as a cheeseburger and fries. She didn't give a thought to how much she'd already consumed or how her choice might not be the most nutritious item on the menu. The idea of the greasy, mouth-watering meal sounded delicious. She was tired of not doing things just because they might not be good for her. She was tired of not experiencing life. Most of all…she was so tired of being boring.

"I'll be right back with your order," the waitress said as she finished writing in her notepad, then pocketed it and grabbed their menus.

Sam watched her weave through the crowded tables and let out a long sigh. It hit her right then. If she lived the next half of her life like she'd lived the last, she'd have nothing but boring memories to look back on. Success and achievement were all well and good, but she wanted the decadent feelings she got when she experienced things with James. They made her feel alive.

For the rest of the afternoon, Sam dropped the usual restraints she placed upon herself, determined to make the most of this trip.

After eating, they visited the third winery. By then, she'd gotten the hang of tasting different wines, and was surprised to discover that she could now tell the subtle distinctions in the flavors of each.

By the time they pulled into the parking lot of their hotel, she was having the time of her life. A bellman opened her door and she clambered out feeling slightly tipsy.

Despite the humble three letters over the marquee that spelled out "inn," there was nothing humble in the fancy resort Sam spied when she looked around. *At least a five-star rating...figures James would know of this place too.*

James came up beside her, handed the valet his keys and a tip. "Will you take care of the wine?"

The guy nodded, and after giving him more instructions, James turned to Sam.

"Ready?"

She nodded, grinning. She felt his hand on the small of her back. Warmth, starting from the spot where his fingers touched her waist, spread through her system, as he guided her toward the entrance. She had to concentrate on walking so she wouldn't trip and make a fool out of herself. Not in front of James.

In minutes, they'd checked in and were headed for the bank of elevators. The whole time, including the short elevator ride, anticipation of what would happen once they were totally alone wouldn't let her relax. Her body tingled every time James brushed against her as they walked down the long hallway. She was so ready to climb to the next level, after kissing.

She tried to tamp down her mounting frustration when, after opening her hotel room door and giving her a light kiss on her forehead, he gently pushed her inside.

"Dress for dinner. I'll pick you up in an hour." His grin spread. "Don't look so disappointed. I promise the wait will be worth it."

"I happen to like shortcuts," Sam snapped, irritated because James seemed so amused.

His answer was another burst of laughter as he walked away, shaking his head.

She groaned and slammed the door. She stalked inside the room, deciding right then she wasn't the only one who was going to be hot and bothered.

Screw anticipation.

Enough of his subtlety. It was time to increase the pressure and give him a taste of what waiting meant. No way she'd let him play the game of seduction single-handedly. She'd use what he'd already taught her to aid in her strategy.

Laughter filled the room as she hugged herself and fell on the bed, giggling. Just the thought of her plans had the blood pumping through her system as her heartbeat quickened.

What a heady feeling.

She rose to begin unpacking, humming while thoughts of how she'd go about seducing him roamed through her brain. Tonight, James Morrison would be hers for the taking, or her name wasn't Samantha Collins.

~

An hour later, James knocked, fully unprepared for the vision of Sam in a flimsy red concoction once she opened the door. It flowed about her and clung to her curves, showing off her figure to perfection.

"Like it?" she gushed, doing a complete three-sixty. The delicate fabric followed the turn and wrapped around her, drawing his eyes to sexy legs that went on forever.

He cleared his throat, using the moment to gain the wind that had been knocked out of him.

"Yeah, I do. Very much," he managed to get out without disgracing himself or giving himself away. The effort cost him.

"You don't look so bad yourself," Sam said, grinning.

When his gaze moved up the length of her body and ended at her lovely face, his spine stiffened. He mentally groaned. He knew that determined look. He'd seen it before, watched her in action too many times with her clients. He should have known better. He should have expected the unexpected. But he hadn't.

She wrapped her arms around his neck, stepped closer, and pulled his head to within an inch of hers. Her lips grazed his before she locked on firmly with her mouth, using her tongue, giving him one of the hottest kisses he'd ever had, shocking the hell out of him. Everything went haywire as need and want exploded inside him. A desire swamped over him to get her out of the insubstantial bit of fabric she wore to see what else she was hiding. He had to force himself to pull away…force himself to breathe, once he did. And, the hardest part of all? He had to force himself to ignore the way she clung to him.

"Shit, Collins. We're supposed to be taking this slow and easy." James stepped back. His hands fell to his side, but he had to clench both fists to squelch the desire to pull her back into his arms.

"I've changed the rules." She let go and caught his gaze. Amusement spilled from her eyes, making him even more wary. "You have until after dinner to finish what you started, otherwise you'll leave me no choice but to take action."

He ignored the pure shot of lust her words sent surging through his system and grabbed her wrist in one hand, yanking her none too gently out into the hall while closing the door behind him. At the moment, retreat appeared to be the best option.

The thirty-second wait for the elevator seemed to last hours. He stood immobile, reaching for normalcy. The doors opened and they stepped inside. The space instantly shrank after the doors slid shut. He stared straight ahead, pretending the subtle, lemony scent wafting under his nose every few seconds didn't bother him. Nor would he let the fact that he felt her presence next to him, could feel the outline of her body so close to his, affect him.

He was a horny bastard. His mind waged one enormous mental struggle. He so wanted to skip the rest of his plans and jump right into bed. No sweet words…no dinner and dancing to add to the experience…no finesse…just raw sex to dampen the need strumming through his bloodstream. With her doing her best to incite his senses, the task was even more arduous.

Why not step up the timing? Sam's obviously ready and willing. You've achieved your goal. Given her a romantic day she'll never forget. Why wait?

James risked a glance at her and sucked in a breath. *Shit!* He knew why. He'd never forget today either. Their relationship was changing, right in front of his eyes. He couldn't slow the progression as it shifted into something more than friendship. He wasn't quite ready for those changes. Though this new Samantha was someone he wanted with a passion, she wasn't someone he recognized. He was stepping into an unknown—some kind of *Outer Limits*—and once he strode over a certain point, he had this feeling he'd never be able to retrace his steps.

Shit, shit, shit. What if making love changed their working relationship?

No. She was well aware of his issues and wasn't expecting happily-ever-after. All she wanted was an experience to remember.

He still meant to give her one, but he realized he would also receive a hell of an experience to remember.

The thought petrified him as well as exhilarated him.

Thankfully, the short ride came to an end. The doors opened and she walked forward, momentarily interrupting his mental battle. He followed, rolling his eyes to the heavens, asking for divine intervention to hold on to his resolve to keep things slow and easy.

"How do you know of all these great places?" she asked with a hint of awe in her voice as they entered the darkened room. Even her expression told him she was impressed with the elegant restaurant. "It's very romantic."

James shrugged. As always, her approval touched something deep inside him. "I can't remember how I found this place. I've been coming here for years."

He placed his hand on the small of her back and gently guided her toward the table the maitre d' indicated. A full band played in the background and a handful of couples were making use of the dance floor centered in the midst of cloth-covered, candlelit tables.

"Sterling place settings and crystal," she said, fingering a wineglass. "Fancy. Yet not overstated." She waited until he pulled out her chair, then gracefully slid into her seat. "Since you wouldn't let me pay for my hotel room, why don't I buy dinner?"

"No."

"No?"

"Exactly what I said. No."

"What? I'll have you—"

"You got a problem with understanding the word no?" he asked, cutting her off.

She grabbed the menu and opened it with an impatient flip. "This is the twenty-first century, you know. Women don't need to be wined and dined for sex."

"Fine. You can pay for the next date, but tonight is on me." He held her gaze with his, so she could see he meant business. "Call me old-fashioned. It's my gift to you as a friend."

"Friend?" She quirked an eyebrow and waited a split second before adding, "That's it? Friend?"

"Maybe lover," he conceded. "The evening's outcome is still too early to call."

She laughed. Her obvious amusement sent a shiver of unease

down his spine and told him he'd truly underestimated Collins' determination, mainly because he'd never been subject to its full effect before. He sighed and went back to his menu.

"Would you like to dance?" he asked, watching their tuxedo-clad waiter stride away after taking their orders.

When he took her grin as an answer, she pushed her chair back, and he stood and helped her out of her seat.

The minute she was in his arms, connecting so closely, there was no way on earth he could hide his response. He was hard…to the point of pain. Every once in a while, she'd brush against him, and for an endless second, white-hot lust would shoot straight to his groin, eclipsing every thought but one. He knew she was doing it on purpose when it happened several more times. Being so close to her didn't help matters any. In fact, it made him more uncomfortable when his nostrils picked up the lemony scent of her and slammed into his senses from another avenue. After that, James lost the struggle for control and let Samantha Collins take the lead for the rest of the meal.

He might as well quit struggling, especially since his body wouldn't shut off to her signals.

"So, whose room are we going to end up in?" she asked, once the waiter departed after taking away their dessert dishes and leaving the check discreetly next to him.

"You know, Collins, you should wait until you're invited."

Sam laughed coyly and shook her head. Under the table, she'd kicked out of her slingback and her bare foot was suddenly caressing his crotch. "I feel your invitation, Morrison. You know damn well, you're not sleeping alone tonight."

She did have a point, or rather he did. He grabbed her foot and, while massaging it, his eyebrows rose. "You're playing with fire, you know."

She gave a throaty laugh. "Then we'll burn together."

James looked to the heavens. Please Lord, just let him make it through the next few minutes without disgracing himself. Though waiting another day would intensify the anticipation of their lovemaking, no way in hell he could stick to his original plans of not having sex tonight. Not when she clearly had her own strategy going. She'd pulled out all the feminine artillery from her arsenal, and he was battle weary from dodging her intentional flirtatious blows.

Especially after sitting across from her for over an hour and being held hostage with that enticing smile. And those radiant, coffee-colored eyes. Whatever she'd done to them tonight made them appear bigger, more soulful. The desire spilling from them was transparent. She meant to take no prisoners. Primed and waiting, he intercepted every silent signal she sent his way.

"You wasted your money, paying for two rooms. You know that, don't you?"

"Maybe." He grinned. He had to admit, he was enjoying her seduction. Seems Sam had a few moves he could learn from her. "But the price was worth every penny."

He groaned inwardly when the band struck up another slow, romantic number and he noticed a touch of wistfulness form in the depths of her eyes, replacing part of the earlier desire.

He wished he could ignore her unspoken request and just take her upstairs.

He snorted. *Yeah, right.*

He could no more ignore her silent pleadings than he could ignore the need raging through his body.

After signing for their dinner, he stood and held out his hand. "Come on. One more dance won't kill me. Go easy on me and remember, I'm only flesh and blood." Besides, he wanted to hold her in his arms. He'd just be happier if they weren't on a crowded dance floor.

"You're too far away," James said minutes later, drawing her closer. He glanced down, gazed into her brilliant brown eyes, and couldn't resist their pull. Her soft mouth, melding with his, wielded all she'd promised for the past few hours. He tasted her tongue, met it thrust for thrust, while inhaling her scent and stilling the urge to touch her breasts. Need burst inside him. With a firm grip, he leashed in his desires and lifted his head. The sensual promise in her eyes was his final undoing as his last bit of resistance unraveled.

"We're done here," he said, releasing his hold. He stepped away, grabbed her hand, and hurriedly headed for the elevators, pulling her behind him.

"That was the most romantic three hours of my life." Sam leaned against the wall outside her room, laughing, as she dug into her bag, and finally waved a keycard.

"Come here," James said, ignoring the key and pulling her

toward him. "You've been inciting my senses from the moment I picked you up for dinner and I need a bit of retaliation. More than that, I need another kiss."

His lips met hers. As on the dance floor, need and want exploded inside him. In a flash, all fun and games ended. Blood rushed to his head and groin simultaneously while her scent filled his brain. His hands found her breasts and weren't gentle. There was no way he was dragging this out one more second. His patience for finesse was shot. Lust roared through his veins and he had only one thought. How to get her out of that flimsy, red bit of gauze as quickly as possible so as to finally make her his.

Geez, Morrison. Get a grip. Wouldn't do to go at it in the hallway.

Somehow, he was able to pull back. Still, the move took supreme effort. He released her, yanked the key out of her hand, and hurriedly inserted it in the slot. Then he strode into the room, pulling her with him and slamming the door behind him.

Chapter 8

Uh-oh. I've pushed him too far.

The door closed with a final click. A streak of concern slid down Sam's spine as James pulled her further into the room. Suddenly, he stopped abruptly, jerked her none too gently into his arms, and his lips and hands were everywhere.

She felt quite like a person who'd prodded a wild animal with a stick…one who understood she had nowhere to run…had nowhere to hide from the unleashed beast. Though the thought excited her, she had no clue how to deal with this side of James Morrison.

Charles never lost restraint. For that matter, neither did she. In fact, everything about today was new to her and added to a niggling guilt for feeling so alive, for wanting to go further, for reveling at seeing James in such a frenzied state.

The thoughts were short-lived, however. Due to his untamed advance, sensation swamped her, giving her no more time to think. All she could do was feel. Her arms wound around him and her fingers plowed into his hair, pulling him closer. Utter yearning exploded inside of Sam when James' aggressive mouth met hers, inhaling her tongue, offering her a loud moan.

Seconds later, cool air brushed against her body where her dress, now slithering to her feet, once covered. She hadn't even realized he'd undone it. The next instant, he had her moving backward until she felt the mattress behind her legs. He didn't slow his forward momentum, had them both falling onto the bed while his hands molded to her body. He grazed her mouth with almost kisses, before taking her bottom lip between his teeth and sucking. A hot streak of heat raced straight to her core, surrounding her with intense pleasure. His lips continued sucking emotion from her.

Sam closed her eyes. Sensations rushed too fast to hold on to. She moaned, opening her mouth wider, meeting his tongue's thrust, and parrying with it. Wave after wave of molten, white-hot heat coursed through her as his lips moved lower, trailing wet kisses in their wake, following his magical fingers. He was so good at using his mouth and hands to bring her body alive with need.

Leave it to Morrison to know exactly how to touch a woman. Exactly how to kiss her.

She fought desire, tried to reciprocate, and though he was still fully clothed, she did her best to meet him head to head, matching his enticing movements. If his hands slid up and down her legs, she let her hands wander the same way over his legs.

His caress moved lower, touching her in that private spot. She couldn't hold back a low moan. The sensual quality of the sound shocked her—excited her further. That couldn't be her making such a feral noise? Could it?

His exquisite fingers didn't give her a chance to contemplate for long. Pure joy burst forth in a flash of intense heat when fingers slid inside her and kept moving in and out. Flames of ecstasy built, until seconds later, she exploded in his hand.

In swift motions, he yanked out of his clothes, and after he took a quick moment to sheath himself in a condom, she found herself back in his arms, with his lips working their magic once again, generating more warmth.

And finally, he pushed inside her, extinguishing all thought but the heat of pleasure rushing from her core. Nothing prepared her for this mating. His passion swept her away with him, to a place where she was too caught up in the wonderful torture. All she could do was hang on for the ride of her life as he pumped vigorously. The inferno built so quickly, Sam was blindsided with an intense, searing blaze of pleasure that burst from her center, streaking throughout her entire body. At the same time, James' body flexed, then he shuddered uncontrollably and his loud groan sounded around them before he collapsed in a dead weight on top of her.

"I'm sorry." Sam was still having trouble catching her breath when James' apology cut through the silent room long minutes later. He rolled over, pulled her into the curve of his arm with one hand, while rubbing his eyes with the other. He sighed. "That wasn't supposed to happen."

"You're sorry we made love?" A pang of apprehension hit her, eclipsing her joy. She could never be sorry for the most incredible experience of her life. For someone like Sam, who'd never had an orgasm, to have two within minutes was a miracle and something she'd remember forever.

"Of course not." He chuckled and kissed her forehead. "Making love was inevitable. I just shouldn't have lost it like that."

She closed her eyes and heaved a sigh of relief, enjoying his soft touch, as his hand idly skimmed up and down her arm while his breathing slowed, along with the rapid beating of his heart. "That was too fast…too hot. I meant for it to be perfect."

She giggled and let her fingers run through the bit of soft blond hair on his chest. "Any more perfect and I don't think I could survive."

"Yeah? It was damn near perfect, wasn't it?" His head moved lower and he captured her lips with his, leisurely sucking and biting. He broke apart and paused with his mouth an inch from hers. "It gets better. You'll see."

"Then what're we waiting for?" She wouldn't take James' word for it. Already she was dying to see. "I want to experience what comes after perfection." She wrapped her arm around his neck and closed the narrow gap between their mouths. The next thing Sam knew, he filled her, showing her with his body what was better than perfection. Everything, but the sensation of him languidly moving inside of her, slid from her mind.

~

Sam woke before James. She stretched, then glanced over and a smile touched her face as she took in his sleeping, naked form. Waking up next to him was almost as nice as making love with him…almost. Nothing was nicer than making love with James.

The guy was gorgeous. Had the perfect body. Her gaze fell on his long, artistic fingers, where it lingered for a brief moment, before roaming higher, along strong, muscular arms to his broad chest and ending at his face, where a lock of blond hair covered his forehead. She itched to brush it out of the way…itched to run her hands through its softness once again. When her focus rested on his mouth now relaxed in slumber, the memory of how those lips kissed every inch of her only hours before flashed inside her brain. A flush of pleasure washed over her, leaving goose bumps in its wake.

Who knew a night of lovemaking could be so wonderful.

Everything about his actions, his heated glances, his trembling touch, his slow sensual kisses, made her feel beautiful. She'd never felt so desirable. She finally understood what all those love songs meant. Such a heady, exhilarating feeling. The only thing that would make the weekend better would be for him to say he loved her. She couldn't quite subdue the idea of James replacing Charles in her life.

No…Sam…Don't go there. James isn't long term. You knew that going into this. This is a learning experience. Nothing more. Despite her mental rationalizing, she didn't see how she'd ever share the same passion with Charles.

The disturbing thoughts disintegrated in the next instant when his eyelids fluttered open and his amused stare caught and held hers.

Busted!

She could feel the heat rising up her face because she'd been eyeing him and he knew it, given the sensual, knowing smile making an appearance.

"Good morning, beautiful." He stretched. Then in an unexpected move, he grabbed her naked waist and pulled her underneath him. His erection poked her. It was one thing to act brazen after a few glasses of wine in a darkened hotel room, but in broad daylight, the thought mortified her. His face had the feel of sandpaper as he nuzzled her neck, kissing his way to her ear before he spent a moment biting and tugging on the lobe.

Sam giggled. "Don't," she gasped, shrinking from him, feeling totally embarrassed, as shivers of excitement burst inside her. "I have morning breath."

He climbed out of bed as his teasing laugh rang out. "You have exactly two minutes to fix it," he said, swatting her butt. When he turned and strutted to the bathroom, totally unconcerned about his unclothed state, she had to look away, hiding her inhibitions in the pillow. James Morrison, in his naked splendor, took her breath away and she wasn't quite comfortable with her reaction.

At the bathroom door, he glanced back at her with a quirked eyebrow. "Well? You're wasting precious time. You now have one minute and forty-five seconds."

She put the pillow over her head to stifle a nervous laugh. James couldn't expect her to brush her teeth with him watching. Seemed too intimate. She jumped out of bed and reached into her bag for a t-shirt.

James grinned. "Leave it off."

"I can't." She straightened and began donning the shirt. Now that she had something covering her nakedness, she felt a little braver.

"Don't tell me you're shy." He shook his head and grabbed his toothbrush out of his travel bag he'd retrieved the night before. He started brushing, eyeing her as she walked past him. She waited till he spit into the sink before she shooed him out of the way and shut the door for privacy.

When she turned on the water to wash her hands and face, as well as brush her own teeth, he knocked and she heard the laughter in his voice, as he mumbled, "Hey, hurry up in there. I have to spit."

She opened the door. He finished with his teeth and took a drink of water.

"I find your modesty sexy as hell." James kissed her shoulder and grinned, capturing her glance in the mirror. "But a little ridiculous, don't you think? After last night?"

Her face flamed so much she had to look away. "Some things are too private," she murmured, moving past him.

James laughed. In an unforeseen move, he caught her around the waist and lifted her off her feet as if she weighed no more than a feather. He strode purposefully to the bed and dropped her. Her laughter erupted as she bounced when he plopped down next to her. In one fell swoop of his arm, he had the t-shirt pulled up and over her head.

"Don't need this," he said, tossing it over his shoulder.

He moved closer. Sam forgot her embarrassment the moment their lips met. After sheathing himself in hurried movements, he filled her. She couldn't believe how quickly her desire built. Charles never made her feel so sexy, so hot, so wanting more, and she wondered why it wasn't like that with him when she loved him. Then she wondered if she didn't love the security and stability he offered more. The thoughts got lost in a wave of emotion as a moan she couldn't contain rose up. She barely recognized herself—this new Sam—the one who was eagerly moving with James. She never thought she'd be someone who could make love so readily. Not this morning; not after the multitude of times they'd gone at it last night. Then, even those thoughts were brushed to the back of her mind, replaced with the sensation of his touch, sweeping her away to oblivion.

~

"I had a terrific time, James," Sam said, grabbing the door handle once he shut off the car after pulling into a parking spot in front of her apartment building later that afternoon.

Another perfect adventure and she needed space. She had to get away, take some time to distance herself from him, so that she wouldn't end up making a total fool of herself. The past two days had been extraordinary.

"So, that's it. A terrific time?"

Something in his voice kept her from climbing out of the car. She turned back to him and eyed him warily. "What are you saying?"

"I had more than a terrific time and I'd like to see more of you."

"Oh?"

He smiled. "I'm not promising anything. You already know my track record. I can deliver roses, but delivering the garden isn't exactly my specialty. If I were you, I'd be running for the hills."

Yeah, she was well aware of his record. James couldn't promise love and commitment. He wasn't long term. Most of all, she knew seeing more of him wouldn't be such a good thing. Not when she was already half in love with him. She should be sensible. Take what he taught her and be happy with the experience. But damn it all, she wanted so much to do something reckless…just because it felt wonderful…not because it was good for her. She wanted James for as long as she could have him.

He reached over and, with a forefinger and thumb, caught her chin. He angled her head so she had no choice but to stare directly into intense eyes that had become deep blue pools of liquid heat.

"Maybe I'm the one who should be running for the hills. This is a disaster waiting to happen. I know better." He leaned over to give her a gentle kiss. He pulled away, then offered a self-deprecating smile before he let go of her face. His attention moved to a point out his window. "I know you've got unfinished business with Charles. You love him. Hell, I know I should back off, let the two of you work on things." He sighed. "I can't. Not now. Not after last night."

She closed her eyes and let his admission roll over her. He didn't want to back off any more than she did. Still, she couldn't ignore her rising trickle of dread at the mention of Charles.

Geez, Sam. What are you doing? You should grab on to Charles, take what he's offering, and show him how things could be. Get out while you can…while your heart is still intact. All these thoughts whizzed around in her mind but none of the thoughts stuck except one—James still wanted to see her. She didn't have the will to refrain from diving deeper into temptation, from yielding to the need to have him for as long as she could.

"Well? How about it? Shall we give dating a try?" He turned back to her and she was positive her eyes showed what she couldn't hide. She could no more deny him than she could deny herself.

She nodded. "I'd like to see more of you too." She'd deal with the consequences later.

"You don't have to bother. I'm fine," she said, when he reached for his door handle.

"Humor me. I *do* have to bother," was all he said, as they climbed out of the car together.

After handing over her overnight bag, James retrieved her case of wine, and they walked inside the apartment building. When they got to her unit, he set down the box and held his hand out. She sighed and tendered the key and waited as he opened the door. He stuck the wine inside before turning back to her.

"I'll pick you up at seven for dinner." He bent to give her a kiss on the cheek while placing her keys in her hand.

When she nodded, he spun around and walked away without another word. She kept her gaze on him until he was out of sight. Then, she shut the door and leaned against it with her eyes closed. She was in deep trouble. Deep, deep, deep trouble. No. Cavernous trouble.

~

As James drove the few blocks to his house, conflicting thoughts of Samantha Collins invaded his brain.

What in the hell are you doing, Morrison? She's a good friend. You shouldn't have let things go so far. Though he mentally chastised himself for probably acting like the jerk Kate accused him of being, he didn't regret their weekend together. How could he regret the best night of lovemaking he'd ever experienced? Which spoke volumes, given his background.

He shouldn't be pushing to see her again. Especially so soon. Yet, somehow he couldn't make himself do what he should do…leave well enough alone…walk away with a wonderful memory.

She's not asking for a commitment. She has that with Charles. She wants an affair. All you're doing is giving her one. You even tried to talk her out of her crazy idea.

Of course, he'd been crazy to go along with it, but he wasn't a monk. She understood the rules of the game. He hadn't lied to her. She was well aware of his commitment phobia.

Face facts, Morrison. You're rationalizing. He knew damned well he wanted her for as long as she would be there. Her motivations didn't really matter. Which only proved Kate right, once and for all.

He pulled into his garage, shut off the motor and sighed. He looked to the heavens, wishing he wasn't such a selfish bastard. Selfish or not, he couldn't get the genie back into the bottle.

He hopped out of the car as one thing registered. Nothing on God's green earth would prevent him from taking his affair with Sam to the end. He only hoped their business relationship could survive the turmoil. He headed inside, thinking of ways to maximize her experience. If he was going to continue, he might as well do it right.

Chapter 9

Sam's cell phone rang. She glanced at it. Charles' name appeared on the caller ID. Going back to her blueprints, she sighed and decided to let voice mail pick up. Almost two weeks had gone by since she last saw him and she wasn't exactly sure how to deal with him. Heck, at this point she wasn't even sure what she wanted. All she knew was that she didn't want her old relationship. What's more, she didn't want to think about Charles right now. She'd call him later, once she figured it all out.

After another hour of working, she set her pencil down and stretched. Her back ached from being hunched over the drafting table for too many hours. Still, a little pain was worth the effort, she thought, pushing on the kinks. Her initial ideas for McAlpin's office building were finally coming together into a solid plan. She couldn't wait to show her design to James and ask his opinion.

Thoughts of James led to other more memorable thoughts, like what they'd done last night. She smiled. She'd worked until nine, then he'd cooked dinner for her at her place, and afterward they'd stayed up past midnight just talking. After making wonderful love, of course.

An affair with him wasn't anything like her relationship with Charles. She and Charles never spent hours just talking about nothing and everything. Charles hated to talk, called it a waste of time and never talked about his dreams or hers, little alone about mundane daily stuff. Not James. He was interested in her life and her thoughts. And shared his. Too many times during the evening, she'd caught herself in the nick of time before mentioning something about her past. Revealing too much would only create questions she wasn't comfortable answering.

He didn't need to know the worst about her. After all, she had to remember this was only an affair. One that would eventually end. So far, things were going as smoothly as possible. Except he'd disappeared earlier that afternoon without a clue as to his whereabouts, exactly as he had last week. Just like then, Sam had wondered where he spent his Wednesday afternoons. She still wondered.

A noise from behind drew her attention and as if her thoughts had conjured him up, she turned around to see James standing at the door.

"Hey." His smile twisted her insides. "You've been burning the midnight oil every night this week."

"Hey, yourself. I'm working on my new project."

"It's not due for weeks." He stepped inside and sauntered up to her.

"Yeah, but I wanted to get my ideas organized and on paper."

He glanced at his watch and grunted. "It's after eight and I say it's time for a break."

"I guess it is." She pushed on her aching back and rolled her shoulders again. "I'm beat."

"Have you eaten?"

She shook her head. She'd worked nonstop since early morning.

"Then I know just what you need." His eyebrows rose up and down suggestively. He leaned closer and kissed her neck, working toward her ear. He spent a moment nibbling, then whispered, "Let's go to your apartment and I'll cook you a quick dinner. I've already stopped at the store for pasta and sauce." James' wonderful hands then gripped her shoulders and he started massaging. "Then afterward, I have just the thing in mind to make you feel a whole lot better."

Instantly aware of his ultimate goal of spending another night together at her apartment, she tried not to respond to the way those fingers dug into the kinks. This was getting to be a habit. James liked to cook, said it relaxed him, and he'd already demonstrated his cooking skills, among others, twice this week. She should slow things, not let them burn out of control, as their affair seemed to be doing in only a matter of weeks.

Yet, when he took another nip on her neck, her insides melted. Why bother pretending he didn't speak the truth. She *would* feel better, despite niggling concerns over getting in deeper. "Ah. That's the spot. You've got great hands, Morrison."

He chuckled and his soft breath teased the wetness his kisses had left behind, sending more sensation directly to her heart. "So you've said before."

Was this how her mother had felt? Knowing in advance the relationship would probably go nowhere, but unable to resist the temptation of being with someone who wasn't offering anything more than great sex? Oh, God. Sam didn't want to think about that now. This was different. She didn't have a child to consider. Besides, she went into this affair with her eyes wide open. Neither had expectations of the other.

James straightened. When he remained silent for too many seconds, she glanced up and caught him studying her face, wearing a concerned frown. "Is something wrong?" he asked.

"No." Offering a smile, she shoved the troubling thoughts away and lifted her shoulders in an unconcerned shrug. "What could be wrong?" Sam wasn't about to push for more than he was willing to give. To do so might spoil their time together.

"I don't know. You seemed sad all of a sudden." He threw her a careless smile that eased a little of the tightness in her chest. "Must've been my imagination."

Slow down. Don't get your hopes up. James is good at making a woman think she's the one. Nothing has really changed since this began.

"I'm just tired," she murmured. That smile could melt an iceberg. It certainly warmed her heart and made her feel as if she were the only woman on the planet. If only she could believe it would last.

He held her gaze and more sparks shot off inside her tummy. It was hard to keep from falling further under his spell.

He reached for her jacket, holding it out. "Come on. Let's go."

"No, wait. I've changed my mind. I can't," she said, clutching on to a dose of self-preservation. She picked up her pencil again and went back to her plans. They'd already spent too much time together—four out of the last six nights. A break seemed a safe move right now. "I have too much to do. I'll grab a quick bite on my way home. I can't seem to get the atrium in my mind to work the way I want it." They were meeting McAlpin in less than a month to present the initial plans and she meant to be prepared well before then.

More than that. Her plans had to be perfect. A successful project like this one would validate Sam's professional dreams—dreams with a hefty price tag. In order to follow them, she'd turned her back on her mother's way of life. On welfare, no ambition to be better, the wrong men parading in and out of their lives…men with no means of support who only sucked her mother dry…all of these things had been Sam's early memories. In her mind, her mother's actions only resulted in more poverty. Poverty was something Sam hated, the main reason she spent so much energy on her career, so as not to repeat one of her mother's many mistakes.

"Let's talk about it after dinner." He laid the jacket aside, began gathering her plans and rolling them, then reached for a circular container. He stuffed them inside and said, "Maybe I can help."

Still gripping the canister, he handed her the jacket before taking her arm to help her off her perch.

Now standing, she opened her mouth to disagree, but he bent and locked lips with hers, cutting off her protest.

"Let me cook you dinner, Sam." Grazing her mouth lightly, he spoke in between his light kisses, each back and forth sweep breaking down her resistance a pass at a time. "I just want to be with you…make love to you. I can't seem to get enough," he whispered, before lowering his mouth for a longer, more heated kiss.

She closed her eyes, inhaling his essence, as need clenched her soul. Neither could she, it seemed. Why fight the desire to be with him, she thought, melding her mouth to his and letting him take her away to that place where she felt like she belonged. The end would come soon enough. When it did, she would have all the time in the world to work.

"So, you're cooking me pasta?" she asked with a quick laugh once the kiss ended, dismissing the depressing thoughts while letting him lead her out of her office. "I'll follow a guy who'll cook for me anywhere."

~

While waiting for the pasta water to boil, James kept surreptitiously eyeing Sam, who looked mighty alluring leaning against the jamb. She was wearing some kind of t-shirt that showed off her breasts to perfection and her jeans fit snugly to her hips, showing her definite curves. The sight was all too reminiscent of that first night they got drunk together. It seemed like a lifetime ago, he thought, observing her watch him cook while she contentedly sipped a glass of cabernet. Yep, Samantha Collins had a body meant to entice a man's hunger. And not for food.

His attention returned to the pan in front of him, and as he stirred the red sauce, the sadness he spied in her eyes earlier entered his consciousness.

His stomach constricted tightly, the memory's full impact returning and suddenly reminding him all too much of his relationship with Kate in the beginning. She, too, had a hot body and he enjoyed their sexual relationship without a thought to the future. For years, Kate was more than patient in dealing with his commitment issues. Yet, in the end, and though things turned out for the best, he disappointed her.

Not his finest hour, that was for damned sure. He would always regret his lack of courage for not ending things much earlier, because she wasted so much time on him. He'd been careful about not making a repeat performance with other women, which is why he tended to end things once he realized they'd never go anywhere. With Sam, he just didn't know how he felt. Hell, right now it felt perfect…like it was meant to be. She made him laugh. He could be himself and relax around her. That alone was appealing. He prayed this contented feeling would last.

Face it, Morrison. Commitment scares you. He added spaghetti to the boiling water and stirred, then lowered the heat on the steaming broccoli. Sooner or later, Sam would push for more. In his experience, women usually expected more sooner, rather than later. As much as this relationship was different from all of his others, or from the one he shared with Kate, he couldn't help thinking the outcome would be similar. He would disappoint Sam too, so much so that he could almost feel the end rushing toward him at the speed of light, crushing his chest with an overwhelming need to escape.

Get a grip. You can handle this. You've only been seeing her for a short time. Besides, it was past time to overcome his fear. How hard could it be? He took deep breaths. Slowly the hemmed-in feeling subsided and his chest felt lighter. He turned down the heat on the red sauce, grabbed the vegetables, and moved to drain the water. As he added a dab of butter, he glanced over once more. Sam was now looking at her wineglass and appeared lost in thought.

Could he ever love her? Enough to commit? Damn. His heart started pumping faster and he had to wipe his sweaty palms on his jeans.

He honest to God didn't know how he would feel about her in a month…two months. With Kate, they just sort of fell into a pattern that seemed to continue for much too long.

Just then her cell phone blared on the counter. Before she reached for it, he glanced down and noticed Charles' ID on the front.

Shit. That's all he needed now. Reminders that Charles had been on the brink of proposing before all this started. He might only be twelve days into this, but they were twelve intense days, and while with her, he tended to ignore his main concern. That by not ending things now, before emotions got out of hand, he was being more of a selfish bastard. He already felt guilty about his inability to commit; he didn't need added guilt for destroying her relationship with Charles. He didn't know which was worse.

No way in hell he could just stop seeing her. Not yet. Maybe she was going to dump Charles anyway, without his interference. He once read that sex was usually ten percent of a relationship, unless there were problems. Then it became ninety percent. They clearly had a few problems. The guy had to be a lousy lover to leave her thinking she was no good in the bedroom.

As if she sensed him staring at her after silencing her phone, Sam looked up and smiled. The effect further disturbed his equilibrium.

"Is everything okay?" she asked.

"Couldn't be better," he lied, forcing a smile. James sighed and went back to watching the spaghetti boil, along with his rationalizations. Charles had to be crazy and worth leaving. She was one of the sexiest women he'd ever known. Definitely different from any woman he ever dated. At this point, his feelings seemed to go deeper than what he originally felt for Kate, and he wanted to believe that it was enough to incite change in his usual MO. One could only hope.

Minutes later, he stuck his hands in oven mitts before gripping the stockpot of pasta. He emptied the boiling water into the colander in the sink and hoped he wouldn't disappoint her in the end.

~

Sam picked up the plates James had dished out and headed in the direction of the table. He followed with the garlic bread. They sat.

"When we're done eating, I'll take a look at those plans." James placed his napkin on his lap. Just before he took a bite, he added, "In the meantime, tell me about your afternoon."

She smiled. "I skipped lunch to work." Discussing the day's highlights was becoming a comfortable habit—one she loved. He seemed so much more interested in the mundane events of her workday than Charles ever had. "I like what I've done so far and can't wait to show you." She spent a moment updating him. "So, how was your afternoon?"

"Fine. Nothing unusual. I went to lunch with Dev, then had a meeting with a potential client." He gave her a rundown on the retail space the client wanted designed, ending with, "It's not a big project like McAlpin's office building, but it's still business."

Meetings like the one he described normally lasted an hour or so. What had he done for the rest of the afternoon? She was dying to ask him about being MIA, just like last Wednesday, but didn't dare because she'd be getting too personal and then he might expect her to reciprocate. Instead, she said, "This is really good. I haven't had spaghetti since my college days." She didn't add the reason: because it was cheap and filling. "I have to admit I got kind of sick of it."

"Really?" He laughed. "I could never get sick of it. When I was a kid, spaghetti was my favorite meal and my mom complained about making it so often. According to her, when I was eight, I had to have spaghetti at least once a week. That was before I switched to PB&Js."

"I've eaten my fair share of those too," Sam interjected, laughing. Peanut butter was one of the cheapest proteins out there, which made it another staple in her cupboard during those lean years. She kept that little tidbit to herself too. James was inquisitive. If she opened up too much, he'd start asking questions. Her biggest fear was that sooner or later he'd ask something about her past, and she didn't want to talk about her dismal beginnings.

"I see Charles called."

Stunned to hear the comment, she glanced up with the question in her eyes.

He shrugged. "I peeked. Don't mean to be nosy." He cleared his throat. "Well, yes I do. Does he know you and I are dating?"

"I'm not sure." Sam took another bite and considered her answer while chewing. She swallowed. "I told him about our first date and he's a smart man, so I think he's put two and two together."

"Do you still love him?"

Irritation rose up and she blurted out, "Of course I do," a little testier than she'd meant to. She sighed heavily and softened her voice. "He's a great guy and I can't pretend we didn't share three years together." They just weren't great years, she added silently.

Talking about Charles depressed the heck out of her and made her feel guilty for enjoying James so much and for not missing him. "Can we talk about something else?" Unfortunately, the more time she spent with James, the more she realized how very little she had shared with Charles. Sam truly didn't know what she was going to do once her time with James ended. If she and Charles ever did get back together, things would have to change. A hell of a lot.

Thankfully, he did as she asked and steered the conversation back to work.

With dinner out of the way and the last plate placed in the dishwasher, she led him to her drafting table in her bedroom.

She reached for her plans as he said, "Tell me what you've done so far."

For twenty minutes Sam did just that.

"I like the atrium adjacent to the lobby looking out over the bay. It's insightful," he said, after she explained how most of the first floor would be exploited for the view. They then spent another half hour discussing ideas on how to angle the atrium to capture the best view.

She made a few notes. "So, what do you think about utilizing the space for more than just the view? Do you think McAlpin will like it? I mean, it *is* different." She was worried that it might be too different.

"I know Fred and he's a free-thinker. He'll love it. Hell, what's not to love? The café-like seating area for lunches or office breaks is a brilliant utilization of the space. At the same time, it allows all employees—as well as any person entering the building—access to the awe-inspiring scenery."

"I'm designing the atrium to easily handle most of McAlpin's receptions, too," she added, feeling more confident about her idea.

"Nice and well thought out." He glanced her way, grinning.

She shouldn't care about his opinion. Yet, she had to admit she craved the approving nod. The warm admiration spilling from his voice, his eyes, even his smile, made her feel like a glow stick. She wanted to beam. She couldn't stop the flush of pleasure his praise drew from seeping out. He liked what she'd done.

"Fred will be pleased. I knew your artistic talent was perfect for this project from the minute he told me about the property."

She started to roll up the plans. While sliding them inside the canister, she felt his hands grip her shoulders.

"Now it's time for the massage I promised." He kissed her nape. Goose bumps sped along her skin. His fingers started their slide up and down her arm then moved to her spine, digging in and making her forget all about office buildings and Charles and what she would do once this was over. She'd worry over everything later. Much later.

Chapter 10

Thursday morning, a week later, James rushed from Sam's apartment to his house to shower and change before going into the office. This was the third time this week and the ritual was getting old, he decided, pausing outside Sam's open office door after stepping off the elevator.

He'd never spent as much time with one woman since Kate, so he hadn't encountered this situation before now. He felt like a displaced person, plus he was too damned old to be sleeping on a double bed with a woman. He'd have to remedy the problem and soon.

He shoved the thoughts aside and stood, unnoticed, silently observing for moments, taking pleasure in the view. Sam sat at her drafting table, lost in drawing, oblivious to the outside world. The sight made him realize they shared a huge connection. They shared the same passion. They shared the same ability to immerse oneself in creating.

He must have moved because she looked up. The inviting smile she bestowed him stole his breath. His lungs malfunctioned…he couldn't breathe. All he could do was stare.

"Good morning. Is there something I can do for you?"

"As a matter of fact..." He grinned and grabbed the doorknob, shutting the door behind him as he sauntered into the room. "…there is."

Once he stood behind her, he placed his hands on her shoulders and slowly swiveled the stool fully around.

Sam's eyes grew wide and her mouth opened slightly, drawing his focus. Then his head followed his gaze and lowered.

With lips locked, he pulled her off her perch and angled toward the sofa catty-corner from her drafting table. Together, the two tumbled on top, but he didn't break their bond.

He spent long minutes just kissing. That's all he wanted. A kiss.

After sharing several weeks with her, he felt he could spend a lifetime kissing Sam and still he didn't think he'd get enough.

He broke away, grazed her lips, and whispered, "See. Told you we'd be necking on your sofa after a few dates."

She shook her head and grinned. She placed a hand on either side of his face and bit his bottom lip, gently sucking, then said in between nips, "Wasn't my idea."

"Are you saying you don't want to kiss me back?" He pulled away and snared her luminous brown gaze.

"And if I said no?"

"I'd have to call you a liar," he stated softly, leaning in to take her mouth again as her light laughter floated past his ears. He added his tongue, let his hands roam, and continued kissing her.

Finally, he sat up and righted the clothing he'd mussed with his amorous behavior. Wouldn't do to get too carried away. Not at the office.

He cleared his throat and ran a hand through his hair. "There's a reason I dropped by."

"You mean, besides taking advantage of me?"

He grunted. "I got a little sidetracked."

"A little?" She stood and smoothed her skirt before walking back over to her drafting table. She leaned against it and turned to face him, smiling brightly. "Ya think?"

"Quit giving me that look," he said, watching her from the sofa, wanting more than anything to drag her back and continue kissing her. "Otherwise I'll be forced to respond."

"I wasn't the one who came strutting in here with his macho moves."

"Macho moves? Oh no!" He shook his head and waved her statement away. "You invited my kiss. Just like that day in my office. Just like you do every time I see you."

"Humph," was all she said, eyeing him through a narrowed gaze. "You go on thinking that, Morrison. I understand the male ego."

He laughed. He shouldn't be amused. "You're distracting me with your very presence and you damn well know it." He stilled the urge to take her into his arms to show her exactly what her heated glance did to his insides, and said instead, "I left too early this morning to ask about tonight. And it slipped my mind last night during dinner."

"Oh?"

"Yeah." He sighed and stood, stepping over to her window. He spent a moment staring out at nothing. "I don't expect you to spend every minute with me, but I was hoping you'd go with me tonight."

"Go where?"

"Kate and Paul are having a small get-together at their house." He pivoted to face her. "They have one every so often and Dev and Judith are usually there. It's family. Most women get the wrong idea if I take them anywhere near my family, so I usually go alone." He cleared his throat. "I thought since you know everyone, you might enjoy it."

"Oh?"

"Never mind. It was a stupid idea." He shrugged and headed toward the door. "Forget I asked."

"Wait!"

He slowed his retreat, then turned back to her, hoping his thoughts weren't reflected in his eyes. For reasons he didn't understand, he wanted her to go with him, but he didn't want her to know how much it meant to him.

"I'd love to go. Can I bring anything?"

He grinned, relieved with her positive response. "I thought you said you can't boil eggs."

"I can't, but DeLuca's puts out a mean potato salad."

"Sounds good. We can grab it on the way if you don't have a chance to stop after work. I'll pick you up at seven."

~

Sam paced the length of her living room, waiting for James' arrival.

The past three weeks had gone by in a sensual blur. Each night she spent with him built on the last, leaving her feeling as if she'd been hit with a tidal wave of emotions. She understood before going into this what the outcome would be if her heart became entangled. What she felt for Charles was minor compared to what she now felt for James.

You have no sense of self-preservation, Sam.

How had she ever thought she would be safe from his charm? She snorted. Safe? No female was safe from Morrison if he put his mind to charming her.

Sam desperately fought to resist falling more in love with him, but like all those others before her, she had no control over falling hard and heavy, at the same speed a boulder hurls from a mountaintop toward the bottom.

What was she going to do? She wrung her hands and paced some more.

Despite having no one but herself to blame, she wouldn't trade any moment spent with him. The thought of being included tonight sent a surge of hope through her, especially after the last week. Plus, his actions in her office this morning added to her optimism. Maybe…just maybe...he was falling a little in love with her too.

"One can only hope," she muttered, as she strode to the door to answer his knock.

"Hi." She grinned at the sight of the gorgeous hunk in his usual body-hugging, faded and worn denim, silently appraising her with an intense gaze.

Instantly, all doubts dropped away. No matter what happened, she would never regret spending whatever time she had left with this engaging and sexy male specimen who was eyeing her as if she were a delicious dessert. An adventure like this was sure to come around only once in a lifetime.

He stepped into the room and closed the door behind him. "I've been dying to do this since I left your office this morning." He pulled her into his arms and in seconds he was kissing her.

Sam wondered, as his lips progressed to her neck before ending up nibbling on her ear, if she'd always feel this zing of anticipation whenever he was near.

Oh God. How was she going to endure working with him day after day when their interlude ended? For that matter, how could she ever go back to Charles after experiencing James?

No, Sam. Don't think of any of that now. Just enjoy.

He lifted his head and the smile taking over his face caused her breathing to become labored. She forced herself to concentrate and breathe. Simply taking in air seemed an immense chore.

She cleared her throat and smoothed her blouse, using the distraction to gain control. *Remember, Sam. You're not an ice cube in the sun, so don't melt in front of him.*

"You ready?" He offered the same smile that always made her heart beat faster.

"Yes, I'm ready." Damn. Would she ever be immune to him again? Probably not. Her back stiffened and she took in another deep breath, knowing without a doubt she'd totally underestimated that Morrison charm for all those years. "Just let me grab the potato salad I bought on the way home."

In minutes they were seated in his SUV, heading south toward Redwood City, where Kate and Paul lived.

James turned into a bedroom community and drove a few more blocks before pulling into the driveway of an attractive two-story house that had a charm of its own, despite being a cookie-cutter copy of the other homes in the neighborhood.

Kate opened the door just as they reached the front porch, which meant she must have been watching for his car. When she spied Sam, she stopped short. Then, she nodded. "Hi, Sam. I wasn't expecting you." She put her hand to James' forehead. "Are you feeling okay?"

"Very funny. Sam brought the potato salad, so I had to invite her," he said, lifting the covered container.

"What happened to Charles? I thought you were working to impress him?"

"I decided he was right. He wanted a break and he wants me to be more spontaneous," Sam said flippantly, coming to James' rescue and not having a better excuse. "So, I'm obliging by going out with your brother-in-law."

"Oh?" Kate's raised eyebrows spoke loudly and James sighed.

"Yeah. We're spending time together. You got a problem with that?"

"No." She stepped back and held the door open. "Come on in. I'm sure everyone's dying to see this."

"Don't mind her," James said after Kate yelled over her shoulder, "He brought a date!"

"She thinks eight years gives her license to be a nosy, annoying pest." He snorted and rolled his eyes, but his smile as he bent to kiss her cheek deflected his words.

"I like to see him squirm," Kate said, winking at Sam and grabbing her hands after she closed the door. "It's the only payback I get for all those wasted years."

Sam grinned and put her face up for Kate's kiss, only the petite woman had her in a bear hug before she could step out of her reach.

Kate turned and pulled her along with her into the room. "Look, you guys. Samantha Collins is here with James. Can you believe it?"

Kate's husband, Paul, was a slightly taller and slimmer carbon copy of his brother James, with the same coloring, the same blue eyes and streaked blond hair. He came out of the kitchen, grinning broadly, holding a bottle of wine in the air. "I'd say this calls for a toast."

"You're real funny too," James said, chuckling, clearly taking their teasing in stride. "See, this is why I never bring anyone around my friends and family. They can be brutal."

"Payback's a bitch, isn't it, bro," Paul retorted.

"Hush, Paul. Don't scare her away before he has a chance to win her favor," Kate chided.

"What makes you so sure I haven't already won her favor?" James asked.

"A little overconfident, aren't we?" She offered a ready smile and pointed in the direction of the patio. "Judith's outside, taking advantage of this magnificent weather. We're eating out there."

Sam had to bite the inside of her cheek to keep from laughing as her focus followed Kate's hand. The sun hadn't completely disappeared from the evening sky. Warm air wafted through the screened windows and doors. A picnic with friends seemed a perfect idea.

"Sounds nice." Sam waved to Judith McAllister, who waved back from her perch, visible through open doors off the living room. Her husband, Dev, stood and headed toward them with his hand out and a smile on his face.

"Mac," James said, pumping Dev's hand. "Don't you start, too. Sam's a friend."

Dev's amused gaze gave Sam a lengthy perusal before he quirked a brow and stated with the same amusement in his voice, "Friend?" He nodded. "Got it." He held his hand out to her and asked, "You've done something different to your hair, haven't you?"

"Like it?" Patting her head, Sam blushed.

"Yeah. I do." She grinned when James' charismatic best friend brought her hand to his lips, and added before kissing it, "Looks great," totally charming her.

Remember, Sam, these men are in their element. He probably does this with all the ladies. Still, she couldn't help being flattered. With that jet-black hair, accentuating a pair of startling blue eyes, and his killer smile, he could have any woman he wanted eating out of his hand. A thought struck just then. Three very fascinating, very attractive males filled the room with their presence, and two of them appeared to be very happily married.

Dev nodded, let go of her hand, and turned back to James. "Your *friend* is too nice for the likes of you. What's she doing with you?"

Sam laughed good-naturedly as James grumbled, "Yeah, yeah, yeah…just had to chime in, didn't you?"

Dev chuckled. "There's wine on the counter, and beer and soft drinks are in the fridge. Kate and Paul don't stand on ceremony. Help yourselves."

"I'll get us a drink. What would you like?" James asked, catching Sam's eye.

"Surprise me." Sam's gaze moved to James' back while he started for the kitchen. She wondered if he'd ever fit the mold of the contented, married male, complete with baby, house, and white picket fence. The idea kept the smile on her face. Good grief, he'd probably have a heart attack if he knew which direction her thoughts traveled. A woman could dream, couldn't she?

"Come on," Kate said, grinning. Sam had no more time for thoughts or dreams, as Kate tugged her exuberantly toward the sliding screen door. "Let Judith see the full effect of how good you look. I love that outfit. I don't remember you buying it on our shopping spree, so our lessons must've taken hold."

"I had excellent teachers," she murmured. Shopping was something she'd taken a liking to, especially since she could buy outfits that she thought James might like.

"Doesn't she look great?" Kate asked as the two stepped out onto the patio.

"You do. I love that color on you," Judith said, indicating the green silk blouse Sam wore with stylish jeans she'd found on sale at Macy's. "Brings out your eyes." She scooted over.

"Exactly. She's hot, which is why James brought her." Kate's voice held much conviction. "But I don't understand? What happened with Charles? I thought you were trying to impress him, not James."

"I was and I did. Now, I've changed my mind. I guess you could say I'm the one questioning our relationship at this point," she said honestly. Heck, she had no reason to hide the truth. Not from these two. "James and I kind of connected, so we're spending time together, like he said."

Kate clapped her hands, almost jumped up and down her delight was so evident. "I knew it. I knew there was more to that night than they let on."

Feeling slightly put on the spot, Sam cleared her throat. She tried to keep her face from flushing but Kate didn't seem to notice and changed the subject in midstream instead.

"Nicky's teething. Got another one coming in, so he's cranky." She turned to Judith and added, "See what you have in store in less than seven months. I love my son to death, but quite frankly, I was looking forward to James being here tonight to distract him."

Sam couldn't hide her stunned expression at the news.

Kate laughed. "Don't look so shocked. It was only a matter of time before Judith got pregnant, seeing as how she's been trying. And James never misses a chance to play with his nephew. That man loves kids. Which is why I always thought he'd make the perfect husband. He should have a few of his own."

Judith's amusement shone in her eyes as she grinned. "She's obviously not used to your candidness, Kate." She turned to Sam and shook her head. "Don't mind her. I'm immune to her blurting out exactly what's on her mind. Been friends for too long to be upset she told you about my pregnancy. Something that was supposed to be a secret," she scolded, giving Kate a teasing glare. She patted the seat next to her. "Sit and I'll tell you all about my news."

Sam sat and Judith started talking until James appeared at the door with a glass of cabernet in his hand. He moved to set it on the table in front of her.

"It's similar to the wine we tried, so I figured you'd like it." He unbent and looked around. When no one spoke for a long moment, he grinned. "Oh, I get it. You're discussing girl talk. Guess I'll let you gab and see what Nick's up to."

"That's why we love you. You're so perceptive," Kate said sweetly, batting her eyelashes. "And Nicky's been dying to see his uncle."

He snorted. "I hope you're not talking about me." He leaned over and paused to smile. "And if you are, don't believe a word of it," he said, before kissing Sam's cheek. He straightened then spun around to leave.

Sam's attention moved from James' departing form to the two women and she caught them exchanging knowing glances. "It's not what you think."

"We don't think anything," Kate said, her expression all innocence. She then turned to Judith and winked. "We were discussing Judith's pregnancy, weren't we?"

Sam gave up trying to convince them, and in a short space of time, her usual mental guard went down as the three talked about babies before moving on to work. She glanced up after Judith asked her a question about her latest project and smiled from the inside out. Seemed these women were just like her…well, almost. Both had committed husbands and she didn't. Still, she felt a strong connection with them. "My latest is the McAlpin project, an office building in Half Moon Bay that I'm designing," she answered. She then spent a little time explaining what the client wanted, feeling completely comfortable—like she belonged here with these people who seemed to accept her for who she was, quirks and all.

For as long as Sam could remember, she'd felt out of place, like the odd person standing outside looking in, wanting so much to fit in with groups like this. Oh, she had Mary Ann. Her family had become a surrogate family of sorts, but she'd always felt lacking, which had kept her from totally connecting with them. Not like this, as she sat chatting with Kate and Judith about babies, work, and career goals.

"I've still got a couple of weeks to work on my plans before James and I meet with the head of the company to finalize the contract. This is a big deal, what I've been working my entire career for, so I don't want to blow it." She couldn't. Having a successful career meant every bit as much as having a successful husband.

"I know how that goes," Judith said, in response to her comment. She was a commercial designer who specialized in refurbishing old buildings. "Dev understands my need to work. I think I'd go crazy without it. Success is important to me."

"Paul says that investing in my shop was the best money he ever spent," Kate said of the antiques store she owned and operated not too far away. "He laughed when I told him I would pay him back, with interest. He's not laughing any longer…not after seeing my balance sheet. Now he just says what's mine is his and vice versa. You know, cuz we're married. Secretly, I think he loves having a successful wife."

Sam nodded. Like them, success meant everything. She wasn't content to live without it. Though their reasons differed, the results were the same. She'd vowed early on never to be like her mother, and she'd achieved her goal. Her life now held no similarities with Vickie Collins' life. Because the world she was trying to fit herself into was so alien compared to the one she was from, she never felt totally comfortable in it. It was as if she fit in nowhere…until now. Had her efforts to control everything stemmed from wanting to belong somewhere she hadn't really believed she deserved to belong? The thought brought her up short.

Was that why she'd picked Charles for a husband? Would marriage to him validate her place in this world? "Definitely something to think about," she murmured, as Dev opened the sliding screen door.

"You three are being antisocial."

James followed carrying a squirming Nicky.

"We're man-bashing. Were your ears burning?" Judith teased. Dev's response was an elevated eyebrow. Judith laughed and jumped up to give him a kiss. "But I only had good things to say about you," she purred.

They all laughed.

"Paul says it's Nicky's bedtime." James glanced at Kate. "I was hoping he could stay up a little later because Uncle James is here." He jostled the boy in his arms, his attention remaining on Nick's mom, his gaze pleading. "You're the boss, what do you say?"

"I'd say Paul was dead on." Kate crossed her arms. "He's cranky enough after you babysit. All you'll do is corrupt him."

"But that's what uncles are for." He looked at the child busy flapping his arms, and cooed, "Tell her we men have to stick together."

"The answer is still no, but I'll let you put him to bed. He's ready for his bath."

"Hear that, tiger?" James said, his smile taking over the bottom half of his face. "She says I can put you to bed."

Kate was right, Sam thought, observing James' easy way with his nephew. He would make a perfect father. Out of nowhere, the thought of what he did Wednesday afternoons filled her mind, when he'd always disappear for a couple of hours without any explanation. She wondered about it before, but now she was more concerned. Of course, she was too chicken to mention the subject. She wasn't his keeper and asking him outright might also be a tad presumptuous when she already felt as if she were treading water in this relationship. How wonderful it would be if their relationship grew into one where he would want what Paul and Kate had. A loving marriage and kids.

Paul sauntered out carrying a platter of steaks. "You have barely enough time before these are grilled, Uncle James." He caught his brother's eye. "You know, instead of corrupting mine, you could have one of your own. It's not hard. Just find a woman who'll put up with you and settle down." He then glanced at Sam and winked before starting toward the barbecue.

She felt her face flame. *Real smooth, Sam.* Paul's speculative grin told her he'd guessed exactly what she'd been thinking about James being father material…for her children. She sighed and looked down at her wineglass, studying the liquid intently as Kate said, "Oh hush, Paul," coming to her rescue and interrupting the moment. "You shouldn't gloat over the fact that you realized perfection sooner than he did."

"You're right, sweetheart. I can't forget that James did help me with my perspective."

"Whoa there, tiger." James leaned his head away from his nephew. "That hurts." Thankfully, he appeared too focused on Nicky's attempts to grab at his hair to pay attention to his brother and sister-in-law's conversation. He looked over at Sam. "You don't mind if I spend a few minutes putting him to bed, do you?"

Mind? How could she mind? Most men avoided such mundane tasks. Somehow the fact that he didn't made him even more attractive in her mind. *Slow down, Sam. Quit thinking of happily-ever-after with him.* Still, she couldn't quite squash the little burst of pleasure his actions brought forth.

When James came back to the patio after putting Nick to bed, Paul handed him a fork. "Here." He nodded toward the barbecue. "Watch the steaks while I go and get a drink. And don't screw them up," he warned over his shoulder. "They're almost done."

"Sure." James poked at the steaks and Sam took in the cozy scene around her. A little ray of hope that had begun the moment she'd stepped inside this house started to shine through, lighting and warming her insides. Maybe things could work out.

"I got it now," Paul said, returning and relieving James of the large fork. He then turned the steaks and tested them. "I think we're ready."

"Plates, silverware and napkins are over here, along with the side dishes, Kate said, as she set down Sam's potato salad with others on the long table. "It's buffet style, as usual."

Paul added the steaks and they all rushed to grab dishes, forks and knives, and soon everyone surrounded the table and began filling plates with food. The scents of baked beans, steak and buttered corn rose up. Sam's stomach made a gurgling sound as she sat with the others at the glass table Kate indicated. Within minutes someone mentioned a football game coming up and the men went back and forth over who was the better team.

Sam remained optimistic during the meal, until the three women cleared off the table while the guys were distracted with an impromptu poker game.

"Don't let him know you love him," Kate said in a warning tone, grabbing the plates out of her hand as she and Judith finished cleaning up. Sam's attention returned to Kate, who continued with, "The thought will send him running in the opposite direction faster than a greyhound after the bunny." She then turned and headed inside, her hands full of dishes.

Sam felt a flush of warmth slide up her face at being caught staring at James again—a recurring incident that had happened too many times throughout the evening. Nor was she prepared for Kate's concerned words. They hit her hard, shattering the bit of hope that had been building inside.

After picking up two more plates, she followed Kate and set the dishes on the counter.

"What do you mean?" Sam asked nonchalantly, schooling her face to show no emotion while meeting the petite woman's gaze. If Kate, who'd only been with her for a few hours, could read her so effortlessly, then surely James must see it too.

"Ah, ah, ah. Can't fool me. I've been there, done that." Kate began rinsing the dishes and placing them in the dishwasher. She smiled and added, "He's a complex man. I spent eight years chasing him, and I know firsthand that loving him isn't exactly easy." Then, she sobered. "Anyone can see he cares for you. But, hell, he cared for me too. I'd hate to see you make my mistakes."

Sam wasn't quite sure how to respond, so she stayed quiet, as she scraped the remaining dishes and handed them to her.

Kate laughed, put an arm around her shoulder, and squeezed. "Don't worry, your secret's safe with us."

"Us?"

"Yeah. Judith and I won't tell anyone. James seems clueless. Men usually are." She hesitated, then grinned. "Well, some men are. Paul knew right away we were meant to be together. But then, he's a special male. At least, I think he is. Judith and I are placing bets as to how long before James realizes what's right in front of his nose."

"Really?" They were taking bets? The thought should irritate her, but all she could think about was Kate's earlier revelation. "You think James cares for me?" She thought so, but that his friends and family made note of it, substantiated the idea. She'd take anything at this point.

Kate nodded. "Whatever you're doing seems to have made an impact. You're the first date he's brought here. I've never seen him so relaxed with a woman, excluding moi, of course." She snorted. "For all the good it did me."

Sam examined her hand, absorbing the news. A drawn-out moment later, she cleared her throat. "So, what do you suggest I do?" Maybe Kate's insight would help. Certainly couldn't hurt.

"He always told me I was too available. But I think it goes deeper. It's like he's denying himself happiness or something. He gets to a certain point and then does little things to sabotage his relationships. Granted, I'm no psychologist, but that's how I see it. I realized too late James wasn't ready for marriage when I was. Lord only knows if he's ready now. I don't know what to tell you, except follow your heart. If it's meant to be, it will be."

Follow my heart? Seemed such an easy answer, yet she knew it was anything but. What did her heart know? Less than a month ago, her heart belonged to Charles, and now James, a man who may never give her what she craved, held her heart.

Chapter 11

Friday night, a week after Kate and Paul's informal get-together, Sam prepared for another date with James. Negative thoughts kept bothering her despite spending five more glorious nights of that week with him. She couldn't help falling more in love with the man. The task of hiding her feelings was overshadowing everything else, making her a nervous wreck. It was compounded by another disappearance last Wednesday and she was still afraid to ask him about it.

She grabbed the tube of mascara and unscrewed the cap. While stroking her lashes, Kate's words played over and over in her brain. If she'd been so obvious to Kate, how could she keep her secret from James? She shouldn't be going out with him, prolonging her misery. A tear trickled down her cheek at the thought of working with him day after day while he ran from her. She blinked it away so she wouldn't to ruin the makeup's effect, and remembered back to when she first started with the company. Back to when she, like everyone else at the time, could never understand why James didn't grab Kate and head for the altar.

What makes you think you can get him there when someone as polished and vivacious as Kate couldn't?

And what the hell was she going to do about Charles? Their agreed-upon separation had ended. Over a week ago. He'd called and left several messages, begging her to see him. Like a coward, she'd texted back, saying she wasn't ready to see him just yet. What would she tell him? She did love him. Just not in the same way she loved James.

When her doorbell rang, Sam was prepared physically, but not mentally. She rushed to the door, working to stifle her unease and wondering how she'd survive the night without letting her feelings slip out. Whether in a long sigh or a furtive glance, he had to sense it. She felt it in every fiber of her being.

"Red roses?" she gushed, opening to James' smiling countenance as he held out a bouquet of the most beautiful roses she'd ever seen. "What happened to yellow?"

"We've long surpassed friendship and are now full on into an affair." He kissed her cheek and offered an amused chuckle. "One that's become hot and steamy, and yellow just didn't seem to fit any longer."

"Okay." She took the flowers. "They're absolutely breathtaking and they need water," she said, masking her disappointment in the act of racing toward the kitchen to put them into a vase.

Don't think about it. Just have fun until it's over. Memories. I'll have lots of memories and none of them are boring.

"Is there something wrong with hot and steamy?" James asked, after a long moment of silence. He'd followed her and now leaned against the doorjamb, eyeing her thoughtfully.

She shook her head and flashed a quick smile. "Not a thing." When finished with the flowers, she picked them up and brushed past him to set them in the same spot her yellow roses had gone.

He came up behind her and placed his hands on her shoulders, turning her to face him. "You're sure nothing's wrong?"

"Of course I'm sure. What could be wrong?" She met his concerned gaze, without letting him see any of her inner torment.

"I don't know, but you seemed sad all of a sudden." He bent to kiss her. "And the thought of you being unhappy bothers me."

"I'm fine." She nodded and let her smile spread, unwilling to remain gloomy. *Sadness would come later.* "What's on the agenda for tonight?"

"A culinary delight. But it's a surprise."

Her grin became genuine when she spied his pleased, smug expression. Her time wasn't over yet and she meant to fully savor…*everything.*

"Then what are we waiting for." She grabbed his hand and pulled him toward the front door, determined not to waste precious moments.

She'd have plenty of time to reflect—like the rest of her life—once her time with James was over. Besides, she still had Charles. *Damn. Charles.* All of sudden, he felt like a consolation prize, and the thought left her bereft, but she wouldn't think about that, either. Not now. Not when the night was young and James promised a culinary surprise.

"So, where're we going?" she asked, as he waited while she locked her front door.

"You'll see. I told you it was a surprise."

Sam slid inside his SUV and he slammed the door shut. After watching him run around, hop in next to her and start the engine, her attention moved to his competent hands. He shifted into gear. She couldn't curb the slow smile taking over her face at the thought of those same fingers roaming over her in much the same manner.

She could come up with a surprise of her own for such a sexy man. James was the sexiest man she'd ever known. She'd just remember all the little things he'd taught her, use her lessons well, and leave him with a night full of memories.

Oh, yeah. She definitely had a few surprises.

When he parked outside his San Mateo home, her eyebrows shot up. "We're having dinner here?"

"Yeah. I'm cooking for you. That's the surprise."

"At your house?" The news stunned her. Kate's comment, spoken so candidly the morning after the tequila incident regarding James' space, was still embedded in her brain. Neither had broached the subject but, sure enough, during those nights together, they'd spent them at her small apartment, not his house.

Uncertain of the exact extent, she realized his pleasant bombshell held significance.

~

James opened the door and let Sam go in front of him.

"Hmmm. Smells heavenly." She stopped and sniffed. "Those scents have my mouth watering. What's for dinner?"

"Wait and see." He took her jacket and hung it up alongside his.

James was more uncertain than ever of how he felt about Samantha Collins after sharing so much time with her. One thing he did know. He wanted to wake up with her so they could enjoy a leisurely morning in his big bed, not her uncomfortable double bed, which is why he planned this dinner.

"Would you like a drink?" He walked further into the living room. "I have the wine you like."

Her ringing cell phone interrupted her reply. She picked it up and looked at it.

He waited while she shut it off.

"Not anything important, I hope?"

"No." She shrugged. "Just Charles. I know I should talk to him, but I'm not sure what I'll say." She offered a wan smile. "Which means I'm procrastinating." She sat on the same sofa they drank shots in front of only weeks ago and added, replying to his earlier question, "Wine would be nice."

A lifetime had passed since then and in that amount of time, his need to be with her grew substantially. This need worried him. He cherished his privacy. Didn't like anyone invading his inner sanctum, including the woman he was currently dating. Having Samantha here felt different. Made him realize he'd successfully altered his usual pattern for her.

Don't think about what will happen if I revert to my old pattern. Plus, he didn't like the jealousy that had streaked through his system the instant she'd mentioned Charles' call.

James moved to the bar, uncorked a bottle, and poured two glasses of wine. He picked one up, walked over, and handed it to her.

She nodded. "Thanks."

He snatched his glass and brought it to his lips. With his gaze remaining on her, he took a sip, wondering how long before that hemmed-in feeling got too hard to ignore. The thought triggered his memory of the earlier sadness he spotted in Sam's expression and a trickle of apprehension rose up his spine.

He should quit dragging this out and end things before she got hurt. *What about Charles? Does she still love him? Will she be able to go back to him after what we've shared?* Somehow the last thought unsettled him. He shouldn't care. He still couldn't offer commitment. Not yet, so he had no business expecting more from her.

He gulped a bit more, hoping to loosen the dread gripping his insides over the thought of Sam being intimate with Winthrope.

"Is something wrong?" Sam asked, watching him intently.

He shook his head and swigged another mouthful, ignoring the fact that he'd asked her that exact question earlier. "Nothing's wrong."

"Then why are you eyeing me as if I'm the enemy and I've invaded your territory?"

"Is that what I'm doing?" He smiled at her acuity.

She met his smile with raised eyebrows. "I don't know. You tell me."

He sighed and set his glass on the bar. "I've got to check on dinner." He strode with purpose to the kitchen, pushing out his morose thoughts. She didn't need to know how conflicted he was. It might lead to other questions. He couldn't risk her demanding more. If she did, he honest to God didn't know what he'd do or say. As much as he wanted her and as good as things were between them, he just couldn't commit to her. Not right now. Most likely not ever. Once that conversation took place, the fun and games would be over. She'd be gone, probably back to Charles who, judging from that phone call, was obviously waiting for the inevitable to happen. The guy was no dummy.

James grabbed the needed items from the fridge to whip up a hollandaise. He felt her presence as he placed a saucepan with butter on the burner to heat, then separated egg yolks into a bowl.

"Almost ready." He turned to face her.

She handed him the glass of wine he'd left on the bar. "I think you need this." She leaned against the counter, keeping her attention on him.

"Okay, I'll concede." He grinned, brought the wine to his lips for a healthy drink, then went back to his task. "I hope you like shrimp and crab, the main ingredients in tonight's meal."

He combined everything into the blender and was ready for the crepes warming in the oven.

"I love seafood."

He filled the crepes on each plate with the seafood mixture he'd spent part of his afternoon making, before adding the sauce, then lemons and parsley for color.

"How about spicy? This is a Cajun recipe and it's pretty hot." He grabbed the plates, intending to head for the dining room, but Sam blocked his path.

"I love spicy," she murmured, gently pulling the plates he'd prepared out of his hand and setting them on the counter. "Especially if it's cooked by a blond god."

"God?" He peered down and watched a Mona Lisa smile slide over her face. He couldn't take his eyes off that supple mouth.

"Mmm hmmm. God," she whispered, wrapping her arms around him and tugging him closer before grazing his mouth with hers.

The move was erotic as hell. He closed his eyes and breathed in the scent of her. An instantaneous erection resulted. His senses came alive as her lips softened and he received a mouthful of her tongue. He gripped her shoulders, stilling an overwhelming urge to be inside her. He ached to feel her breasts, to roam lower, touch her in places he knew would draw out her pleasure.

How could he want her so soon after that morning when they'd made love after waking? Lord help him, but he wished he could push her away and let her go back to Charles. Getting more involved would only complicate an already complicated situation, but he simply didn't have the strength.

She's here tonight, so enjoy her. Don't think about complications. The inevitable end will come soon enough.

He pulled back and rested his chin on her head, holding her close. He took numerous deep breaths to contain the lust raging through his body. Eventually, his pulse rate dropped and he managed to regain a modicum of control.

"Come on." He kissed the top of her head and broke contact. "I'll be hot and bothered for hours, so we can make love later. My dinner will only stay hot for minutes. It's not as good cold."

He grabbed the plates and started for the dining room.

"Wow." She halted in mid-stride, obviously having just noticed his efforts. Wanting the evening to be special, he'd pulled out all the props. Using china, crystal, sterling, and his artistic eye, he'd created a startling, elegant effect. "It's beautiful. You went to all this trouble for me?"

"You're worth spoiling," he murmured, bending to kiss her cheek after placing the meals on the table. He pulled out her chair and helped her sit. Lifting her napkin, he shook it out before positioning the square cloth on her lap.

Next, he lit the candles and turned the chandelier down to the lowest setting. The result was a romantic glow that highlighted her smiling face. He flipped the switch to the CD player. A soft love ballad crooned from the speakers, filling the room with more romantic ambiance.

"I don't know what to say, except thank you. No one's ever gone to so much trouble to make an evening special before."

He sat next to her and smiled. Samantha deserved romance and he meant to give it to her tonight. He didn't quite understand why, but this dinner held importance for him too. Yet, he didn't want to think about that. He didn't want to think about anything other than enjoying Sam. Later. He'd think about his motivations later.

"This is delicious," she said after taking a few bites. "A five-star meal. I'm so impressed."

He couldn't pretend her praise didn't affect him. He loved hearing the admiration in her voice. He leaned toward her. "Glad you can appreciate my culinary talent."

His hand snaked around her neck and he gently tugged her closer. His lips hovered inches above hers and an irresistible urge to kiss her streaked through him. When he noticed a flush of red stealing its way from her neck to her hair, warmth pooled in his groin.

"Quit distracting me!" She giggled, pulled back, and waved a hand, clearly working to compose herself.

His eyebrows shot up and she giggled again.

"This is too good to leave on my plate—even for your lovemaking," she said, once her giggles died down. "That look in your eyes says it all, tells me exactly what you're thinking."

Her soft voice full of amusement sent another surge of white-hot desire through him. "What am I thinking?"

"That I'm the main course. You'll just have to wait until dessert."

His rich laughter rang out and she grinned.

"That's why I keep you around. You seem to know me so well." He kissed her cheek. "So, eat. I should warn you though, the minute we finish, we're having dessert."

Sam sighed and dug into her meal with gusto.

The two ate in a companionable silence.

"Since you cooked, I'll clean up." Sam scooted back from the table.

The music changed to a slow, sensual number by the Eagles.

"Dishes can wait." James stood and grasped Sam's hand, pulling her with him. "Dance with me. I love this song. 'I Can't Tell You Why'—it seems an appropriate theme for tonight."

"How romantic," Sam murmured, as she stepped closer.

He wrapped his arms around her. It felt wonderful to be dancing in candlelight with the lights from the view outside the big window presenting a darkened San Francisco Bay as a backdrop. The entire time he danced, all he could think about was making love to her.

"I can't tell you why," he whispered, accompanying the music filling the air. "I find I love having you in my arms."

His lips roamed from her ears to her neck, nipping as they went. Every move he made leading her around the room was calculated to arouse. He wanted her with a passion.

"Was this supposed to be part of the meal?" she asked in a breathless voice. She closed her eyes, and laid her head against his shoulder.

"And if I said yes?" he asked with a chuckle. The slow beat of the music thudded in cadence with his heart as he swayed in unison with the woman he was doing his best to seduce. She fit so perfectly in his arms.

Her soft laughter permeated the air. "I'd say you've succeeded."

The words sent his need for her off the charts. Like the song said; he couldn't say why. By this point in his past relationships, he'd be long gone. Maybe, just maybe, he could make this work. At that moment, he wanted nothing more than to hold Sam in his grasp forever.

Barely rocking in time as the music slowly faded, they swayed in silence for prolonged seconds. When James finally realized it was over, he straightened and peered down. Her eyes were closed and the serene expression he noted took his breath away. Then she opened her eyes and a knot of tension tightened in his stomach. James had to force himself to breathe as he stared into lovely, enormous brown eyes that promised everything he craved, beckoning him to yield everything he had to give. Unable to resist, his head lowered.

The second their lips met, a spark of hunger ignited desire and consumed him.

Kissing Sam was similar to drinking a kind of elixir of life he couldn't live without, drugging his senses, creating a need that stemmed from his very soul. Together they sank to the floor. Their dance progressed to one of completing the slow, sensual seduction—one where both participated. In front of the huge window, with the romantic night landscape as a stage, he spent long moments taking one piece of clothing off at a time. Kissing, nipping, licking, and touching every square inch he uncovered.

Once naked, she reciprocated, leisurely undressing him, mimicking his movements. He grinned into her neck as he felt her fingers slide over his erection. Sam was definitely an adept student. No one made his blood boil as quickly as she did. The thought was snuffed out when those same fingers cupped him and stroked while her lips found his. There was nothing gentle in their kiss as mouths and tongues melded together. From that moment on, he could only react to the desire pulsing throughout his body.

~

Sam woke and stretched, feeling absolutely marvelous. She couldn't stop grinning as she admired James' sleeping form. Her gaze wandered the length of well-defined arms and legs, connected to a muscular torso. He appeared so peaceful in sleep, so contented and relaxed.

Her sigh came out in one long, wistful breath. She squelched an urge to touch him…to run her fingers over his gorgeous nakedness. A rush of pleasure saturated her inner core. If she hadn't loved him before last night, the dinner and dancing by candlelight, along with their unhurried lovemaking that followed, would have stolen her heart.

What about James? How could he not love her after last night? Actions spoke louder than words. His actions had definitely been those of a lover.

He stirred. She bent to kiss him awake. Having spent too many mornings waking next to this sexy male, she no longer had any shy qualms. She now had a purpose. To use everything he'd taught her. Make love with wild abandon. In seconds, her goal became reality as James expertly complied, filling her with his essence.

Sam didn't recognize herself. Would she ever get enough, she wondered, as he moved inside her? James gave her no further time to think, pulled her with him in his lovemaking. All thought fled from her mind and she met him wild thrust for wild thrust.

When it was over, and he held her in the crook of one arm, slowly sliding his hand up and down her arm, she wanted to shout her love to the world. More than anything, she wanted to hear those three short words. She wanted to be able return them without feeling as if he'd turn and flee in the opposite direction. Kate's warning kept her silent. Her heart would break if James ran from her. She loved him…maybe too much after such a short time. She should be worried, but she shoved all negative thoughts aside, unwilling to allow anything to mar the deep satisfaction overwhelming her this morning.

"I love to wake up making love with you. It's a perfect way to start the day," he said moments later.

"It is nice." She weaved her fingers through his wispy blond chest hairs. She smiled into his neck when his muscles flinched, knowing full well her touch was the reason. *Such a heady feeling.* She sighed longingly. "If only it could last forever."

James stiffened, the move so distinguishable from his flinch a moment before. His body radiated a rigid tension under her hand.

Way to go, Sam. Just blurt it out. Please, Lord. Give me more time. Don't let him push me away. Not now. Not after last night.

He placed his hand over hers, stilling her movements, before picking it up and intertwining fingers. He eyed their raised hands thoughtfully.

"I want you," he whispered, taking her hand to his lips and kissing it. "I can't say where we're going, or how I feel because it's happened so fast, but I can say with all honesty I've never felt this way about anyone."

"Even Judith?" The question just popped out. Geez. She needed a muzzle. Why not advertise the fact that she'd been wondering?

He grinned and his gaze snared hers. "I see you ladies have been talking."

"Maybe." She bit her lip to keep from laughing at his raised eyebrows. His expression said *no maybe about it.* She finally gave in to the urge and laughed. "Okay, so we talked."

"I'll bet. You probably know all about me and my sins." She shrugged in response when his gaze seemed to require one. He chuckled. "And I know next to nothing about you before you started with the firm, except what's on your resume and in your personnel file. Getting information out of you is like pulling out fingernails. Why are you so secretive?"

"I'm not," she replied, as beads of unease slid over her and her heartbeat quickened. "I told you, it's all very mundane and not worth mentioning." She didn't want to think of her past right then, and she certainly didn't want to tell him about it. She'd been evasive to his many questions over these last weeks on purpose. Charles hadn't dealt well with the few hints she'd given him, worrying more about what his parents would think, rather than her feelings. Only Mary Ann and her family knew of the true ugliness she'd grown up with. She hid her past from the world, buried it deep inside and pretended she came from somewhere else. No one, especially someone like James who'd grown up with all the advantages of love and security, could understand what she'd endured. She didn't know how to make him understand, so it was better off left unsaid. "I was boring until I went out with you."

"I must be a good influence because you're anything but boring now." He sat up and met her gaze again. His expression was earnest. He inhaled deeply and let the air out slowly. "I'm torn. I want to keep seeing you, but I don't want to hurt you."

She put her hand to his mouth to prevent more torment from spilling out. She'd already jumped in and she was well past the point of no return, so she certainly didn't want his regrets or for him to think about backing off. "Shush. I'm here for now."

"But that's just it. I can't promise anything right now."

"I don't recall asking for any promises."

"You were expecting them from Charles. You can't tell me you don't expect them from me. All women do at some point."

Not quite sure how to respond, she remained silent and glanced at her hand on his chest to break the visual connection. She swallowed the lump of need lodged in the back of her throat and studied her fingers intently.

James wouldn't let it go. He lifted her chin with a thumb and forefinger, forcing her to meet his gaze again. His intense focus held her spellbound.

"Let's be honest, at least," he said softly. "Anything less will diminish what we're doing. Our relationship has taken a completely different path than either of us anticipated."

Nodding, she closed her eyes and took a deep breath. Though she agreed, she also understood there was no way she could be honest with what was in her heart without risking the consequences, no matter how it diminished what she felt. She wasn't willing to take the chance of him hustling out of her life just yet. "I'll let you know when I can't handle things. How's that for honesty."

Chapter 12

James' cell phone rang and he glanced at the screen to see his mom's name pop up. "Hold on. I'll be right out," he said to Brad Stone, one of the other senior partners. "Let me answer this call first." He sat back down, pressing the On button and leaning back, then swiveled to look out at the glorious sunny day. "Hey, Mom. What's up?"

"I just heard you took a date to Paul and Kate's last get-together."

"Yeah." He stiffened. While not exactly at the speed of light, news did tend to travel quickly within the Morrison family pipeline. At times, like now, it could be annoying. "So, what?" Obviously, someone had spoken up and now Alicia Morrison was out for more information to fill in whatever gaps Paul or Kate left out.

"What do you mean, so what?" She paused a heartbeat, then asked, "So, what's going on with Samantha Collins?"

He laughed. "She's a friend. And a colleague. You know that." He shook his amusement and swiveled back around, sitting up straight. "Why the sudden interrogation? I've had lots of friends over the years."

"Well, A. You've never taken anyone to their house before this, and, B. Kate says you really like her."

"Ah, the truth finally comes out. Kate put you up to this, didn't she?"

"Silly boy."

Her devious chuckle drew a trickle of unease from his consciousness. He recognized her tactics. Had seen his mom in action too many times over the course of his thirty-five years on this planet not to be a little wary.

"Kate doesn't care, except to cling on to any information that might cause you embarrassment. Since she couldn't yank your chain that night, she gave up. Too easily, I might add," Alicia went on. "But I'm not Kate and I have more of a vested interest in my children, so

I'll remain as nosy as I can be until my curiosity is satisfied or until you're married, whichever comes first."

"Mom." He couldn't contain the laugh that broke free. He knew better than to admit anything to Alicia Morrison. Still, she was like a dog with a bone. She wouldn't let go until she gnawed through every crevice, taking any amount of meat off before she'd let it go. "Even if there was something there, I'd be nuts to tell you. So, don't ask." His gaze focused on his hand as he added, "That way you won't be disappointed."

"Come on. Give an old woman a break."

"Mom," he warned, biting the inside of his mouth to keep from laughing again. "You're being invasive and I don't appreciate it."

"Okay." She remained silent for too long, obviously thinking of what to say next, if James knew his mother. She sighed. "Look, I know this may be interfering, but if you're really interested in Sam, you should listen to my theory of why you're having such a hard time with commitment."

This time he let out another laugh. "Alicia," he said more firmly. "Give it up."

"No," she shot back just as firmly. "Not until you hear me out."

She broke off and by not speaking again, set his nerves on edge. Finally, he sighed, knowing he had no choice but to listen. Otherwise, she'd figure another way of getting through to him. "Make it fast. I have a date with the kids at the community center," he said, glancing at his watch. "You have one minute, so start talking."

Her laughter filled his ears. "You're so smart to give in, sweetie."

He rolled his eyes. "Clock's ticking."

Another laugh sounded. "Okay, okay." She exhaled a long sigh, then hesitated. He was just about to prod her again when she asked, "Do you remember when Uncle Ed died?"

He glanced at the phone and frowned. That wasn't a question he expected. He remembered, but the memory was vague. "What's a dead uncle have to do with me and Sam?"

"You were what, twelve or thirteen?"

"Eleven. I was going to be twelve in three months." He remembered that now as the memory formed firmer in his mind. The funeral was held during the winter because he also remembered how dead everything looked back then. He made mental note of the time, thinking the season fit with the first death in his family he'd ever experienced. In fact, the idea had spooked him at first, but then he'd been able to shove the memory aside, once all the hoopla was over. After all, death wasn't something a kid dwells on. Not something a thirty-five-year-old man dwells on either, he thought as his mom's voice pulled him back to the conversation.

"Do you remember what you said to me at the funeral home, when Aunt Chloe burst into tears?"

"No." He wiped his face, reaching for patience, not really wanting to get into this. "I've said a lot of things over the years I have no memories of. Why would I remember something I said to Aunt Chloe over twenty years ago?"

"Well, of course you wouldn't remember. On the other hand, I've been thinking and remembering. Enough so that I've come up with a hypothesis."

"A hypothesis?" If only he had a dollar for every time she offered one of her hypotheses, he would be a rich man.

"Yes, and considering how torn up my sister was, I now believe seeing her like that was more of a pivotal moment for you than I first thought. What's more, you should've remembered or be forced to remember back so you can understand the ramifications," she interjected.

"You're not making sense." Though she thought her conclusions logical, they seldom followed logic. He checked his watch again. "I'm really running late."

"Okay, cool your jets, I'm getting there. You asked, why Aunt Chloe was so sad and when I told you, you answered, and I quote, 'I'm never going to let anyone matter to me so much that I'll cry like that.' You were quite emphatic at the time, as I recall." Alicia sighed into the phone. "I shrugged it off as a child's reaction, but now I'm starting to wonder if that experience didn't skew your thinking about love and life and marriage."

"Mom. I highly doubt seeing Aunt Chloe in tears is the reason I can't commit." He laughed outright. "I was eleven, for Christ's sake. I don't even remember saying that."

"Then you'll bring Sam home for dinner one Sunday?"

"No," he blurted out. Hell, no. Not when he could tell by this phone conversation that she was on her one-woman crusade to see him happily married. To Sam, it seemed. Alicia had never held back her opinions concerning his single status, always spouting off that as the oldest he should be years ahead of Paul. This was his life she was meddling in and until he knew he could handle where his relationship with Sam was headed, he'd be better off avoiding Woodside and parental influence for the time being. Otherwise, she'd never allow him to deal with his commitment issues in his own way.

In the past, he'd always ignored her. Yeah, but that hadn't stopped her attempts then, any more than ignoring her would stop Alicia now. He snorted, imagining his mother figuring out another means of attack. He had to offer something. "Look, Mom. My relationship with Sam is new. I like her, as more than a friend, okay? We're happy for now," he said, remembering their hot weekend together and smiling. "When I get to the point I need help, you'll be the first to know. How's that?"

"Not good enough." He was afraid she'd say that. "You know, I've held my tongue all these years, but now I'm worried." No, she hadn't, he thought, as she droned on. "More than worried. I expected you to be happily married by now. My goodness." Yep, here it comes. He glanced at the ceiling and recited her favorite warning inside his head, his inner voice matching hers word for word. "You're past a third of a century, heading into middle age. If you want a family, you'd better get cracking."

"Your point?"

"Kate obviously wasn't for you, but I never said anything. Just let you both prolong your miseries until you figured it out, which you never would've without Paul's interference."

"Mom—" he tried to interject, but she cut him off. "But now, with Sam, I pray you don't back off. If you're afraid of pain, I'm here to tell you having a person love you for any amount of time is worth any pain. Don't hide yourself. Give of yourself. Give Sam a chance. You won't be sorry."

"Thank you, Mom. I appreciate the advice."

"But you won't heed any of it. Will you?"

"Good-bye, Mom. Like I said. Thanks for the help." He clicked off and stood, pushing everything she said aside. Rubbish. Pure rubbish. Hell, he was making progress with Sam all on his own, and he damned well didn't need his mom psychoanalyzing his motivations and actions.

He left his office and hurried down the hall.

~

"Come on, Collins. I could use your help."

Sam looked up to see James at her door.

"Morrison," she said, smiling at how mighty fine he looked standing in her doorway. "Is there something I can do for you?"

"As a matter of fact, there is. How are your plans coming? Can you take the afternoon off?"

"Sure." She nodded. A break would do her good. "What do you need?"

"Basketball." He pushed his way into her office, ending in front of her desk. "Ever play? If not, it's time to learn."

"Basketball?"

"Yeah. You know, the game where you bounce a ball down a court and shoot at baskets to score."

She laughed. "I'm familiar with the game." Of course she was familiar, though she hadn't played or thought about it in years. At one time, she'd lived and breathed the game. Her biggest scholarship had been a basketball athletic scholarship. She'd spent four years as a center on her team in college.

"Good enough for me." He nodded behind her desk. "Grab your running gear. You're partner of the week."

"What?" She could only stare at him, totally confused.

"Community service. Consider it part of your new duties."

"You didn't think you made partner just because of your talent, did you?" Brad said, after poking his head in. "You're part of the team now and as such you're subject to the same arm-twisting. Being female is not an excuse."

"What are you guys talking about?"

"Morrison has this thing where we all have to participate as Big Brothers…and now Sisters…with a bunch of disadvantaged kids."

"I didn't know you were a Big Brother." She looked to James for verification. This was the first she'd heard of this and a side of him she'd never seen.

James shrugged. "No big secret, but I don't advertise it. I've been playing B-ball with the same group of kids for a couple of years now. When a new community center opened a few months ago, they asked for my help. The partners agreed to a couple of hours a week. I pay for the time. It's my way of giving back."

"Yeah. Doctors play golf on Wednesday afternoons and the partners of this architectural firm play basketball. We've all taken turns accompanying Morrison. He goes every week. I hate basketball. Since you've made senior, it gives him another body to recruit. Ain't life grand?" Brad turned and left. His echoing laugh bounced off the walls of the hallway before slowly fading.

Sam eyed James thoughtfully. So that's where he'd spent all those Wednesday afternoons. "Wow!" she said, grasping the relevance. Every time she turned around, she found something more attractive about him. He'd come from money. His dad was a CEO of a major corporation based in Mountain View, and she never thought he'd care about disadvantaged kids who were so far beneath him socially.

A warm fuzzy feeling infiltrated her tummy. James was so much more than a charming man.

"Well?" he asked, interrupting her thoughts. "What are you waiting for? Grab your gear. I'm already running late, thanks to my mom."

Her eyes narrowed. "You really expect me to drop everything?"

"Yes." He nodded and held out a hand. "I do."

"I guess I could give it a try." Grinning, she grabbed on to his hand and let him pull her out of her desk chair. Once standing, she reached for the gym bag she kept in the corner of her office. "Give me a minute to change, and then I'll be ready to show you how basketball is played."

"No time. There's a ladies' locker room at the center. You can change there." He flashed a ready smile before adding, "Come on. I'm sure the kids will love you."

When they arrived at a community center twenty-five minutes south of San Mateo, she and James walked inside. Sam spied a group of kids huddled around one who seemed to be dominant.

"Go and change." His head indicated a door marked WOMEN. "Then I'll introduce you to the guys."

She nodded and he sauntered toward them, bouncing a basketball. She spent a moment observing him laugh and joke as if he was one of them. Their acceptance of him seemed so natural. Seeing him in such a light gave her a glimpse of another side he rarely showed the world…had certainly never showed her. Yep, James Morrison was much more than a pretty face. Like her, he had hidden facets, yet his seemed so much more altruistic.

She hurriedly changed, then rushed out and looked around. She halted, uneasy all of a sudden. James wasn't there yet.

It's okay, Sam. They're only kids. Except, nothing in their expressions reminded her of children. As she started toward the group of guys, her mental encouragement did nothing to curtail the tension tightening in the pit of her stomach. They weren't the mean girls of her youth, but they still made her feel self-conscious and their presence conjured up too many memories of kids she'd known in her early teens. Her uneasiness grew the closer she got. The feral gleam coming from the one she deemed their leader was hard to ignore. Their obvious interest in her had her slowing her steps until the locker room door opened.

She turned and relief washed over her to see James saunter in her direction. She wasn't completely comfortable, but she no longer felt threatened like she had only seconds before.

"Hey, guys, this is Sam." James came to a stop next to her. He rattled off their names and she made note. "Tamal, Jeron, Michael, Tyrol, LaQuon, and Duantez. She's here to play basketball."

"Umm hmmm, hear that, gentlemen?" Tamal said, after James' introduction. "Look what the big M brought along for our amusement. She's here to play. I could jus' eat you alive."

"Tamal," James said, his tone firm. He shook his head as annoyance flashed in his eyes.

Paying no heed to his implied warning, Tamal puckered his lips and made smacking noises.

Sam ignored him, but he did it again, only louder. His sneer, as his gaze took an explicit trip over her body, had her reflexes going into overdrive. This scene was all too familiar and after years of blocking them, those ugly days of high school snuck right back into her mind. Sam clenched her fists, wishing she could wipe that leering grin off his face. Despite not being that same kid any longer, the hairs stood on end at the back of her neck, reminding her of a few similar encounters in her mother's world. The way people acted in that world had kept her from ever going back. She only had to remember she wasn't her mother. She'd worked too damned hard to become someone who deserved respect and she refused to let the morons get to her.

"Someone needs to teach you manners," she said coolly, showing nothing of her inner struggle to maintain her calm. Seemed no matter how far she tried to run from the human animals in the world, it wasn't far enough. She couldn't quite catch her breath, had to force herself to take in air. *You're in control, Sam. This is different. He's just a kid. So what if he doesn't respect you? It doesn't change anything.*

Thankfully they couldn't hear her heartbeat galloping out of control as she worked to quell the apprehension strumming through her system.

"So, you're a teacher?"

"That's enough, Tamal."

His grin spread and he licked his lips suggestively, ignoring James' second and very clear verbal warning. "You c'n teach me anythin', anytime, white bread. I'm not picky."

Her spine stiffened, one vertebra at a time, until her back felt as rigid as a board. She regarded the kid in front of her, as total disdain for his punkish behavior seeped out of every pore of her body. She'd vowed long ago that no one would treat her in such a disrespectful way ever again.

"I didn't drive all the way down here this afternoon to be insulted." She grabbed the ball out of James' hand, interrupting what he was about to say. "I came to play basketball." She dribbled the ball, maintaining complete control. She'd show him. No one, especially a street kid who needed to learn a lesson about respect, pushed Samantha Collins around. Not now, not ever again.

"What do you say, tough guy?" she asked, bouncing the basketball with a few intricate moves, before tossing it to him with force. "You're tough enough to throw out insults, but are you tough enough to take on a woman?"

"She's mine," Tamal told the guy who'd come up behind her. James and several other players followed.

The game began in earnest, as they split into teams with James and her on the same side.

Tamal started toward the basket, dribbling. She stayed on him. His height gave him a definite advantage. His long legs, despite being hampered with baggy shorts hanging off his butt, carried him swiftly down the court. Sam was quicker. In seconds, she'd stolen the ball and now headed for the other end of the court.

Her move took him by surprise, but not for long. Given the predatory gleam in his eyes and the speed at which he recovered, she knew he was out for blood. Hers. She got one good shot and took it before he almost knocked her down as he shoved into her. She smiled inwardly.

He wants to play dirty. Fine, I'll show him dirty.

She then proceeded to get down and dirty, playing the game with the finesse she'd spent years learning, while also adding a few tricks her coaches wouldn't tolerate if they'd caught her at it. Samantha Collins knew how to play at their level…it was the level she'd launched herself from thirteen years ago.

Like riding a bicycle, she thought, shooting for a basket. Once learned, the skill came back rather quickly, especially given the added threat to her body after she jabbed Tamal in the chest with enough force to send him back a few feet. Her college teammates hadn't called her dexterous for no reason.

"For a white bitch, you're cool," a sweating Tamal said, sixty minutes later.

"More than cool. I whipped your black ass." Sam grinned and nodded at his mouth. "Still got all your teeth?" she asked sweetly.

"Never saw it comin'. You got some moves." He rubbed his jaw where her elbow happened to connect during the rough game.

After that action, she'd had to stay on the move and out of the kid's reach. But she knew how to avoid getting caught with a trip or an elbow. An hour on the court with only a few bruises proved she hadn't lost the footwork. Still, she was thankful James had been behind her, protecting her, because she was sure his threatening presence kept Tamal from taking out a switchblade and slicing her throat for a couple of the stunts she pulled.

The two ended up shaking hands before Tamal and his friends headed for the locker room, laughing, joking, and slapping each other on the back. Noting James' puzzled look, Sam hurried in the opposite direction, hoping to avoid questions.

"What was that all about?" James asked twenty minutes later when she came out of the locker room after she'd showered and changed.

"What do you mean?" She knew full well what he alluded to, but did not want to discuss it.

"You've obviously played basketball before, and you're quite good at it. Hell, you won Tamal's admiration. I could tell by the others' reactions, you earned their respect too. They're a tough bunch. Took me months to break in and you did it in less than an hour."

Her shoulders rose in a nonchalant shrug as they started for his car. She remained silent, praying she could skirt the issue. The few people in her adult world she had confided in about her childhood didn't respond positively, so she was better off not discussing those years.

"I'm impressed. I saw two Samantha Collins out there today." He smiled. "So, which one is the real you?"

"I'm both, I guess." She didn't offer any other explanation and he didn't push for more.

They walked the rest of the distance to his SUV in silence. Neither spoke during the drive to the office parking lot.

"Are you going to give me any clue as to what was going on inside your head back there?" James asked, after he'd turned off the engine and both had stared out at the scenery for countless minutes, neither moving to get out of the car.

She shrugged. "It's in the past."

"In the past?"

Sam nodded, wishing he'd just drop the subject. She didn't want the feelings such memories dredged forth to infiltrate her life now.

"I see." The irritated edge in his tone got her attention. She risked a glance in his direction and was stunned to see anger flash in his eyes, as he said, "So, what am I supposed to do when you won't open up? Guess and form my own conclusions?" He sighed and raked an impatient hand through his hair. "It's such bullshit. I think I deserve a more honest response, don't you?"

He wants me to open up. And if I do, he'll run like a rabbit in the opposite direction.

Suddenly, emotion she'd been so careful to keep under wraps broke free and everything hit her at once. Her tears slipped out. She couldn't stop them from streaking down the sides of her face as the full truth dawned on her. James wasn't the only one running. She was too, and she couldn't run far enough, it seemed.

Those kids reminded her of exactly what she was running from. Herself and her past. James wanted her to talk about it. Why wouldn't he? He had no idea it wasn't wonderful. He had no idea her greatest fear was sliding backward to becoming someone like Tamal once again. Or worse. Someone like her mother.

"I am such a fraud," she finally got out, once she could speak.

"Fraud?" His probing gaze sought hers and the concern she spied spilling from his eyes brought on a fresh round of tears.

What the hell was she doing? Months ago she had a clear idea. Yet, right now her focus was as blurred as James' sympathetic expression in front of her.

"What's going on, Sam?" His gentle tone did nothing to stem the flow of teardrops from her eyes. His hand cupped her face, bringing her attention back to him. "Why the tears?"

"I'm so tired of running. Tired of pretending."

"You're not making sense. What have running and pretending got to do with basketball or with me expecting you to open up about your past?"

"Everything." She shook her head to break free from his hold and stared out her window.

"I still don't understand."

Through tear-filled eyes, she watched several people leave the building and head to their cars. At that moment, she wished she could trade her childhood with any one of theirs.

"Sam?"

She sighed and worked up the courage to reveal information she'd spent most of her adult life burying. Only right now, her memories had congealed after rising to the surface of her thoughts, as ugly and thick as the lard that settles at the top of a fat-laden soup when cooled.

"In the past few weeks, you've asked about my background. Are you sure you want to know?" She turned and met his gaze. If he wanted to know the sordid truth, she might as well enlighten him. "Even if it isn't pretty?"

"Yes." James nodded. "Of course I want to know. I want to know everything about you." When she didn't speak for a while, he prodded softly, "I'm listening."

She took a deep breath. "A big part of my past is locked inside, has been for years. Memories I wish I could forget. You want to know the worst part? Seeing Tamal made me feel as if I was looking into a mirror, only to see the worst of myself." Her tears began anew, increasing when James wrapped his hand around her neck, and pulled her to him. She resisted the urge to bury herself in his warmth. He might not be so caring once he knew all of the grisly details of her ugly past.

"Shush. It's okay."

"It's not okay." She leaned out of his consoling embrace, unable to endure the thought of losing his sympathy after she told him the rest. "It'll never be okay. Don't you see? I was Tamal. A dirt-poor kid from the projects. I used to play basketball with kids like him on a daily basis. Not to give back, but because it passed time. Until one day, a punk like him thought he could play more than basketball with me. He attacked me. Only my speed and wits saved me from being raped that day."

"Shit, Sam. I'm so sorry. I never knew."

"Not too many do." She snorted, thinking back to a time so long ago. She sucked in a huge breath without looking at him. If she spotted any kind of repugnance or loathing in his expression, she wasn't sure she would be able to continue. "After that happened, I knew I had to get out, or I'd end up defeated…end up just like my mother. The animals that poverty creates can do more to conquer the human soul, keeping it in bondage, than anything society does. I know from experience." She sniffed, wiped her eyes and dropped her hands to her lap. "My own mother laughed when I told her to call the cops and have him arrested. She said I should shut up about it. They wouldn't care and worse, they'd think I'd done something to provoke it." Sam never liked thinking of that incident. "Can you imagine a mother saying such a thing to her daughter? She's not what I consider a candidate for mother of the year, and by then I didn't want to be like her. Yet I remember a time when I thought she was the most beautiful woman in the world. What did having looks get her? Nothing but trouble, because she attracted the wrong kind of men who only used her and made our situation worse."

She glanced over. The compassionate look on his face brought on a fresh supply of tears. She couldn't seem to slow them…worked to wipe them away as fast as they fell. No longer concerned about shocking the hell out of him and needing to get the rest of the sordid details out, now that she'd begun, she said, "I don't even know who my father is. He left months before I was born, which wasn't any great loss from what I understand. Yet, the experience didn't teach my mother much. She ended up repeating the pattern. Too many times. I got so tired of watching her make more mistakes, especially when I knew if she'd simply quit making them, our life would've been drastically altered."

Her reality was so different from his.

"I didn't come from a warm, loving family as everyone, including you, assumes. I came froma chaotic hell and I'm never going back." Thank God she'd had Mary Ann and her nurturing family. "When I was sixteen, I ran away to live with my best friend. The Murphys lived in the same neighborhood and were struggling like everyone else but, unlike my mom, Mrs. Murphy was my guardian angel…she made room for me until I could finish high school. To show my gratitude for their taking in an extra mouth to feed, I graduated early. Worked my tail off and got a scholarship. Basketball was my salvation. I was fast and could shoot baskets. I used the game and education to better my life."

"That's a lot to hold inside. Why couldn't you tell me all of this before?"

"Why would I?" Charles hadn't been the least understanding when she'd broached the subject and she'd expected much the same from James. "I hate talking about something so hideous." She offered a self-deprecating smile. She stared at him through tear-glazed eyes as sadness filled her. Sadness for all the times she wished she could describe her life any other way, and couldn't. "I saw your reaction. I don't want anyone's pity, especially yours. I realize now, I was running from the ugliness. Thought if I pushed the memories away, took control of my life by surrounding myself with success and people I admired, I could pretend it never happened." She shook her head and sighed. "But I can't do that anymore." He'd just have to accept her as she was.

"I'm so sorry." His hand reached out. He tucked an errant strand behind her ear before wrapping his fingers around her neck and pulling her to him. He kissed the top of her head. "I guess anyone who survived a childhood like yours would become a little rigid."

"I had to be. I didn't have the luxury of being anything else, because my biggest fear was losing control and reverting back to my ugly roots and becoming someone like my mother."

Sam broke away and her blurry gaze moved out the car window. She observed a squirrel running haphazardly around the grass before he made his way up a tree. Was that what she was doing with James? Chasing after nothing? Had she become her mother? Chasing a feeling? Chasing at nothing like that squirrel? She certainly wasn't acting any better than her mother, chasing after something that might never happen.

"Are we moving in the right direction?" she asked, unable to hold the question inside.

"I think we are. I didn't lie when I said I've never felt about anyone else the way I feel about you. But it's all new and…" James broke off and cleared his throat and ran a hand through his hair. "Shit, Sam. I'm no good at this." He looked her square in the eyes. "But give me a chance. We're making progress." He hesitated, before asking, "Don't you think?"

She nodded. She even thought he might love her. Her biggest fear was that with his track record he'd run from love, just as she'd run from her memories.

"I care about you." His voice interrupted her musings. "You know I do."

She smiled. He'd cared about Kate too. Look what happened there. The memory of Kate's warnings rushed back and, unable to bear the thought of him running from her, she sighed and slowly shook her head, wondering at her own foolishness. It seemed she was her mother's daughter after all. Despite knowing what she wanted, and foolish or not, she wasn't willing to give up the passion she'd found with James. Not just yet. Not without giving him a chance. Still, she couldn't ignore the niggling thought that like her mother she was rationalizing her actions.

"Oh, God," she cried, as a fresh round of tears emerged. Why couldn't he see what she saw? They were perfect together. Why couldn't James just say he loved her and commit?

He pulled her into his arms and kissed the wetness streaming down the sides of her face. "It's okay. We'll deal with it."

She offered a sad smile. "Yeah. We will." Or she would, she thought as more doubts consumed her. Her stomach clenched when he looked away and turned to gaze outside the car.

He sighed heavily while his focus stayed on a distant point above the steering wheel. Her uncertainty grew.

"Maybe we can slow things a little. This whole thing is overwhelming."

"Sure. That'll work," she said, backing down completely from blurting out more of her true thoughts. Now was not the time. Maybe slowing things down was the answer. Let him catch up to her.

She reached for the door handle and was out of the vehicle before he had a chance to realize her intent. She leaned back inside. "I gotta go." If she didn't leave now, she'd end up saying something she'd regret and she just couldn't risk that just yet. "Playing basketball put me behind."

"You want to grab a bite to eat later?"

"Not tonight." She scrunched up her nose. "I'm fine-tuning the McAlpin project."

"You can do it at my place," he offered.

As tempting as the offer was, she knew it wasn't a great idea. "No." She shook her head and placed a hand over her hair to stop it from whipping around her face. "I need some space."

"Then when?"

She shrugged. "Saturday?" When his expression said *no way*, she smiled. "You're the one who suggested slowing things down."

"We'll go out tomorrow. For dinner. But we won't sleep together. How's that?"

"Okay," she agreed, knowing they'd probably end up in bed. "It's a date." At this point, denying she didn't want to be there seemed futile, which also meant she *was* following in her mother's footsteps.

~

James sat, immobile, and watched her departure, feeling more torn than ever. The entire time the selfish bastard lurked in the background, mocking him, telling him he could never be that person she needed, that someone to count on. The right thing to do would be to end things. Before he really hurt her. Hell, he could tell he'd already hurt her somehow.

His phone conversation with his mother came back to jeer at him and he realized her hypothesis held more truth than he cared to admit. He hated seeing people in emotional pain and what's more, he'd never wanted to be the cause of such pain.

Sam's obvious pain while revealing her past had almost paralyzed him. He could barely imagine how she survived such a screwed-up past to become so successful, without the nurturing and love his parents gave him. His track record stunk, which only made him feel lower than dirt. He was worried that if their relationship continued, he would only add to her pain.

Damn. He wiped his face as self-revulsion filled him. Maybe he'd already become what Kate had accused him of being because, despite loving her, he couldn't jump in…couldn't commit. Not yet. Hell, they'd only dated a short while. He knew perfectly well it was time to cool things a bit so they could both take a breather, but he couldn't stomach the thought of not being with her. Somehow he had to figure out how to proceed without hurting her further, while giving them both what they needed.

He emerged from his SUV and slammed the door with purpose. As he hurried toward the glass double doors, his mind spun. He would try his damnedest to give her what she wanted. At this point, he would continue ignoring that hemmed-in feeling crushing his chest and push past his fears. He wouldn't think about failure. He would only think about the present and how much he enjoyed being with her.

Chapter 13

The rest of the week flew by swiftly. As Sam predicted, their resolve to slow things lasted about a day. They were miserable apart and as much as Sam knew she shouldn't, she spent every available moment with James.

To add to her worries, Charles' frequent calls hadn't slowed. By Monday, she returned them at James' urging, unable to procrastinate any longer on making a final break with him. As James emphatically pointed out, he also deserved her honesty.

On Tuesday night, she paced, waiting for Charles' arrival. As she strode back and forth, her thoughts weren't pleasant. Moments such as these made her realize honesty sucked. She would much rather hide her head in the sand and let life go on around her than face Charles.

When had she become such a coward?

His knock sounded.

Sam sighed and wiped her hands on her slacks. It was time to face the piper. She opened the door. How had her life become such a mental mess?

Charles offered her a bouquet of red roses.

A flare of annoyance burst inside her. What was it with him and flowers all of a sudden? He'd never brought her flowers before.

Patience, Sam. Hold on to your patience.

"How thoughtful. Thank you," she murmured, pushing irritation aside. "You're so sweet." Thank goodness, James' red roses were now drying upside-down in her bathroom. She didn't think his seeing them would make this any easier.

"You look fabulous. Very feminine. I like that dress." He bent to kiss her. "I love the new you."

She pulled away when he tried to deepen the kiss and hurriedly said, masking her annoyance, "Let me get these in water."

"Okay." He stiffened as she turned and started for the kitchen.

Tension oozed from every cell in his body as he followed on her heels.

She kept a furtive eye on him as she placed roses in the vase she filled with water, observing the speculation roaming over his face. He wasn't fooled by her actions.

She took a deep breath and let it out slowly. "So, have you finalized your merger?" Hopefully small talk would get her out the door.

"Yes. Over two weeks ago." He cleared his throat and pushed the glasses higher on his nose in a typical Charles move, causing her to smile. He wasn't an enemy. Just someone she no longer loved as much as she loved James. The smile died when he added, "I called so we could celebrate, but obviously you had other more important things to do."

"I'm ready to go," she said, ignoring the little dig and holding on to her temper as she put the last rose into place.

Charles nodded. He walked toward the chair, picked up her coat, and waited while she slipped into it. He reached for her hand and led her out to his car.

Both remained silent on the ride to the restaurant.

"What happened to us?" Charles asked, once the waiter took their orders, along with their menus, and made a hasty retreat.

"Us?"

"Let's cease with the pretenses, shall we?" His tone drew her attention. At least he'd waited until she had a glass of wine to help give her liquid courage, she thought, noting his serious demeanor. "I think a proposal justifies more than a month of unanswered phone calls, don't you?"

"Of course." She nodded. "I'm so sorry."

There was no way she could postpone her news now. She sighed heavily, wishing more than anything she felt differently. "I…umm…can't marry you. We …umm…I don't think …we're…umm…meant to be together," she was finally able to get out.

His expression took on a lost little boy look, appearing so hurt. She clenched her fist under the table.

Damn it all. He started it, with his request for a break and his pointing out the exact status of our relationship.

"You were right to be concerned with our relationship. It was tedious."

Was she supposed to accept his words and actions? Pretend they hadn't hurt while she did all the changing and then wait patiently for him to come to his senses? She swallowed the bit of regret rising at the back of her throat. *Yeah. That's exactly what he expected, all right.* Why should he expect anything different when that's what she'd let him get away with for too long? Had she traded her soul for marriage and someone to count on?

"Is that what this is about?" he asked in a voice laced with torment.

"What you said woke me up to problems." She shook her head and softened her tone to ease his anguish. "I'm not doing this to hurt you."

"Have you slept with him?" She eyed him, too stunned to answer. But he must have read the truth in her guilty expression. He snorted, clearly not expecting a reply as he added in a derisive tone, "I ask you to be my wife and you sleep with him." He took a swallow of his wine and examined the glass carefully before meeting her gaze. His eyes appeared huge behind the lenses, the intensity amplified a hundred times. "Though you deny it, I know you did it for revenge. To get back at me."

"No, I didn't. It just happened," was all she offered. Somehow, she didn't think telling him the truth, that she was attracted to James and wanted to see what it was like to be with him, was what Charles wanted to hear. The truth would only hurt him more. She never wanted to hurt him. How could she have been so cruel?

"What about us? Were we a lie?"

"No." Her hand covered his and she squeezed. "Don't you see? We were both settling. For less than what we deserve."

"Yeah, right." He laughed. There was nothing pleasant in the brittle sound. "You're so naïve. What do you think we deserve?"

She cleared her throat and stated fervently, ignoring his mocking tone, "Passion."

"What about commitment?" he asked. When she stayed silent, not quite sure how to respond, he added, "I don't see a ring, which means Morrison's not giving you what you deserve." She knew this wouldn't be easy, but seeing his pain, as he spewed his sentiments in such a venomous manner, was much harder than she anticipated. "Or am I wrong?" he prodded, quirking an eyebrow. When she remained motionless, unable to refute him, he slowly shook his head and gave a grunt of disgust. "Passion's overrated. Fades over time. We shared so much more than passion. You were always satisfied with our relationship before this."

He did have a valid point. They were comfortable together, but now comfort seemed totally insufficient for building a life together. She shrugged. "We all change and evolve."

"You said you loved me. You expect me to believe there's nothing left after three years?"

"I do love you." A tear broke loose. She brushed it away. "But it's not enough any longer." She tried to make him understand. "I've changed. At one time, I was content to spend the rest of my life with you. I'm not that person any longer."

"I see." Seconds ticked by and his earnest gaze never left her face. Finally, he sighed. "You may have passion with James, but it'll be fleeting and he'll never give you what you truly want. I will. You have to know that."

Of course he'd go for the jugular—her biggest fear. She schooled her face to show no emotion, unwilling to give him the satisfaction of letting him know this. "I'm aware of James' track record."

"I love you, Sam. This *passion* will die. I can wait." His resolute expression told her he meant it. "I know exactly what commitment means to you. You'll come to your senses soon enough. Then we'll be even for my lustful thoughts concerning Lucy and can go from there." A streak of unease ran through her at his admission. Charles wasn't for her. But he obviously didn't share the same perception.

~

After Charles walked Sam back to her door and said goodnight, she was too upset to face an empty apartment. She didn't want to see James either. He'd guess her thoughts.

She hurried to her car and in minutes she let herself into her office building.

"Hey, Sammy," Alvin, the night watchman, said as she started for the elevator. "You're working late again."

She nodded. "I have a big presentation next Monday and I thought of several things that I can work on tonight." She smiled. "I hope it's not a problem."

"No, ma'am." He returned her smile and then went back to the book he'd been reading.

She pushed the button and waited for the elevator. The doors opened and she stepped inside. On the fourth floor, she unlocked her office with every intention of losing herself in work. At least one thing in her life was totally on track.

Recently, Sam had become a senior partner, a goal achieved and one she had since coming to work at Morrison, Morgan and Stone—now Morrison, Morgan, Stone and Collins. Her mixed emotions over her relationship with James now overshadowed her success.

She flipped on the light, grabbed her stool to sit, and began looking over plans that were almost perfect. If only her love life were as perfect, she thought, remembering the way James deftly skirted the issue of their future at every turn. Outside of encouraging her to talk to Charles, he hadn't offered her any more than what he'd already offered. He cared about her and what he felt for her he'd never felt for anyone else, including Kate. Yet, he hadn't mentioned anything about love. Sam was beginning to doubt he ever would. Kate's comment about being too available suddenly made her wonder if she, like Kate, was too available.

She pounded the table in frustration. Geez, she hated playing games. He either loved her or he didn't. Sadly, she had no way of determining whether he did or didn't. Heck, at the office, James acted as if nothing had changed when for her everything had changed. Only now, both of them danced around the issue of long term.

Charles' parting shot rushed back just then and kept replaying—an endless DVD that wouldn't shut off. His words had hit their mark and she couldn't dismiss them. Right now, one thought persisted. James might never give her what she truly needed. Maybe Charles was right about passion. Maybe it was a pipe dream to believe she could have both passion and a committed partner. Was this how her mother had felt? Torn and hopeful? It was a horrible feeling and no one should have to feel this way.

She laughed, but there was little humor in the sound. Yeah, loving James wasn't easy. Kate hit that nail dead center. It was damned hard.

In the quiet of the empty offices, she heard the elevator descend, stop, and then start an ascent, which meant she wasn't as engrossed in her plans as she should be. Worse, she had a good idea of who'd called the elevator when it finally stopped on the fourth floor and the doors opened. James. She squared her shoulders and prepared to face him. No other partner worked her late hours. She should have expected he would make an appearance. She rolled her eyes. Hell, he was probably looking for her, since she also ignored his phone calls and texts.

Seconds later, his sexy form filled her doorway. "Hey, gorgeous." He offered her his usual cocksure smile, the same one that could charm a tax auditor into allowing a questionable deduction. "So, how'd it go with Charles?"

"Fine." Still eyeing him, she threw out a half-hearted laugh, trying for a levity she didn't feel. Then abandoning the effort, she said with all honesty, "How would you expect it to go? He reminded me of the facts."

"Facts?"

"Yes, and I quote, 'James won't give you what you need. I will.' Seems he's waiting until we're done." She hadn't meant to reveal so much or sound so curt, but damn it all. He asked.

"I see." James nodded, considering what she'd said. "And?"

"And I don't know." She sighed, losing some of her bravado in the exhale. "I don't know how I feel about it." Liar. She knew exactly how she felt, but she just couldn't bring herself to end it tonight. Geez, she was a coward. How she craved to tell him exactly how she felt. Craved to hear him say those three little words in return. Craved some kind of commitment from him. And so much craving caused her heart to ache. Yeah. Loving James was damned hard. The hardest thing she'd ever done.

She cleared her throat and pushed the heartache away, striving for normalcy. "I don't want to talk about it right now. I really need to work on the finishing touches to my proposal."

"Okay. We'll talk later." He smiled and nodded at her plans. "Let's see what you've done since last week."

She forced out another laugh and put her hand over them, blocking them from his view. "They're not completely ready yet. Give me a few days."

"Sure." He glanced at his watch. "It's almost ten. Why don't you call it a night?"

"You go ahead." This time she wasn't about to cave on adding distance to their relationship and slowing it down. "I'm on a roll and I want to add a few things while they're fresh in my mind." She took a big breath and leveled her gaze at him, so he would get that she was serious. "I need to be alone tonight. I was hoping you'd understand."

They both would benefit from a night apart. Since she wasn't ready to throw in the towel just yet, only distance would allow her to shore up her defenses against loving him.

Chapter 14

On Monday morning, the day of her big presentation, James opened the passenger door and she climbed into his SUV. Spotting her usual *venti* cup of Starbucks coffee resting in the cup holder, she ignored a sliver of pleasure and glanced at him with raised eyebrows.

"I snuck out while you were getting dressed."

They'd spent the weekend together after a few days apart. Even though nothing had changed, the small break had given her a chance to reinforce her resolve to wait for him to catch up emotionally with her.

Her gaze then hit on the apple he'd obviously put on the console earlier. She snatched it up and grinned as he slid in beside her. "Thanks."

"Rituals are important, especially on big days like today."

"I could've done without an apple for one day and I could easily have waited till we got to the office for coffee."

"But it wouldn't be Starbucks, would it? Besides, you've got a big morning ahead of you. Can't have you cranky because you're not getting your daily apple."

"Now you're poking fun."

"Maybe. But, I happen to know you don't eat anything except the apple for breakfast. And I wouldn't think of depriving you of caffeine for the drive to work." He chuckled. "Besides, how can I poke fun when I'm wearing my lucky shirt?"

"You have a lucky shirt?" Her glance flew to the impeccable suit he wore with a stylish tie.

"Mmm hmmm. My mom says it's seen better days and I should buy a new one, but I can't quite bring myself to throw it away."

"Doesn't look old."

"It is." His grin was infectious. "You don't recognize it, do you?"

She shook her head. "Should I?"

His shoulders lifted in an unconcerned shrug as an answer. "I've worn this shirt to every important event I've had since grad school. Hasn't failed me yet. A new one wouldn't be the same…wouldn't be lucky."

Smiling, she nodded, wishing she didn't love him so much. It was just too hard to ignore his charm, especially when he seemed to know her so well.

Neither spoke for the rest of their ride, but the silence hummed with an underlying companionship.

After pulling into the parking lot, James parked. Too eager to get inside to set up for the meeting, she jumped out.

"Wait." James slammed his door after climbing out. "Before you go, I just wanted to wish you luck. I know you don't need it because you're going to knock 'em dead." He'd caught up with her by this point and leaned over to kiss her. "Break a leg, Collins."

She blinked to keep from tearing up. James truly believed in her. It was written all over his face.

"Thanks," she said, before rushing toward the building's entrance. Lord, she loved that man. Why couldn't he see what she saw? They were perfect together. Realizing her thoughts were nose-diving, she shoved them away. This morning was too important to worry over James' inability to commit.

~

James sighed, then looked at his watch. Leaning back, circling his foot that rested on his knee, he couldn't quit fidgeting. Would this meeting ever end? For over three hours, he'd sat across from Sam, the entire time subjected to the torture of every male at the table ogling her.

Like you're any better? You can't keep your eyes off her.

Did she have to dress so provocatively?

She smiled and nodded at the handouts she'd distributed. "If you'll turn to page six, you'll see a rendering of what eighty percent of the offices will look like." She waited until those present flipped pages.

As she droned on, her voice wrapped around his ears and caused more torture. James couldn't shut off his mind to her nearness.

The suit she wore bordered on sexy, especially when she took off her jacket, revealing a flimsy blouse that all but shouted *look at my curvaceous breasts.* No one could mistake her feminine lines, the curve of her hips, her rounded derriere, and those shapely legs, all highlighted with the short skirt slit to mid-thigh. What happened to those boxy clothes she used to wear? He definitely liked them better when other males were around.

Still, he was proud of her. She deserved this moment. Respect for her filled him, listening to her dignified voice, so full of enthusiasm as she explained her plans. She had every person leaning in, totally absorbed in her presentation.

Everyone but him. While maintaining his focus on her, he had a hard time concentrating on what she was saying, thinking more about making love to her. He shouldn't be harvesting daydreams of laying her on the conference table and kissing every inch of that luscious body.

He shook the vivid image and sat up straight, forcing his attention to the handout.

Ten more minutes—less than half an hour.

"Any questions?" she asked, once she'd completed detailing her ideas. No one spoke. She took a deep breath and smiled. "Well, if you think of any, you know where to reach me. Thanks for being such a great audience."

"And thank you for an excellent presentation," Fred McAlpin said, beaming, as he stood and turned to James. "Once we get the financials out of the way next week, I can work on starting the construction process."

James rose and grasped his offered handshake, only too thankful his agony had ended, as the others at the table began filing out. James stood patiently waiting while Fred shook Sam's hand, filling her ears with glowing accolades. Sam deserved all the praise. She'd done an outstanding job and made him and his firm proud.

Eventually, the three headed out the door. At the elevator, Fred said his good-byes, still gushing about how pleased he was over Sam's plans, and finally left them once the car arrived.

James then turned to her. "Exceptional presentation, Sam." He made eye contact and caught her blush. God, she was gorgeous when she smiled. Her eyes were lit with animation and she practically vibrated with happiness. He flashed a sincere smile and said, "You outdid yourself. The firm is lucky to have such a talented partner."

"Thanks."

"I'd say this calls for a celebration."

"Darn straight it does. My presentation was awesome, wasn't it?"

She tucked a strand of hair behind her ears and rocked back on the heels of her feet. "Still, there's this little part of me that thinks it's all a dream and soon I'll wake up and nothing will be real."

~

Sam sat in the darkened restaurant, sipping wine after finishing a steak and lobster dinner cooked to perfection. Even James couldn't outdo this meal.

"This was a great choice for our celebration." She peered across the candlelit table and smiled, trying hard to ignore the dissatisfaction niggling in her subconscious. She didn't want her perfect day marred with negative thoughts. Even though she'd enjoyed James' glowing attention all night, they lurked because he still hadn't mentioned anything about love. The longer she waited for something that might never happen, the more the dissatisfaction grew.

"Sam?" James' voice interrupted her musings, drawing her gaze. "Is something wrong?"

She offered another smile and shook her head, knowing damned well she should voice her concerns, but too afraid to spoil such a wonderful day. "I'm just a little tired," she said instead.

"Then, let's go home." He stood and was beside her in a flash.

"Sure." Sam let him help her out of the chair and assist with her jacket, thinking it was his home not hers. With as much time as she spent at his place, she basically still lived out of a suitcase. Oh, she had a few items in the bathroom and he allowed her some closet and drawer space, but she felt as if she were interloping to leave anything extra there. He seemed to be resisting the next step and she couldn't pretend it didn't hurt.

Thankfully, he accepted her excuse of being tired and the ride to his house was made in relative silence. For self-preservation alone, she probably should have gone back to her apartment, but she couldn't muster the strength. Not when his scent enveloped her and incited a need only he could quench.

Tomorrow, she thought, stepping out of his car after he opened her passenger door to find herself in his arms. She looked up to catch him gazing at her lovingly and couldn't help wrapping her arms around him and pulling him closer. When he kissed her in a way that only James could, the rest of her resolve to speak up faded into the recesses of her mind, to be replaced with a yearning to make love with him. At least one more time.

Together, they walked arm in arm through the darkened house without turning on a light, all the way to his bedroom, where they spent exquisite minutes undressing each other in between slow and extended kisses. By the time he carried her to his bed, she was so ready to make love with him, but still he lingered over kisses. Lingered over touches, in no hurry to rush things.

Tonight his actions were deliberate. Every kiss and every stroke of his hands tortured her with sensation after sensation. When he entered her, she couldn't contain her moan over how right it felt. He kept his rhythm slow, drawing out her pleasure one thrust and retreat at a time until she erupted, her love spilling out so much she almost blurted out the words. In the throes of the afterglow, she wrapped her arms around him and buried the need to hear those three little words in return.

She swallowed more disappointment when he kissed her forehead and said, "Goodnight, Sam. I was really proud of you today."

For a long while, Sam lay awake more confused than ever. Enfolded in James arms as he slept soundly next to her in the darkened room, she held her gaze on the ceiling, seeing only shadows that allowed her dissatisfaction to return full force. To make matters worse, her conversation with Charles wouldn't shut off in her mind. She squeezed her eyes shut to hold back tears of frustration.

It was getting harder and harder to keep her feelings inside. Unable to continue being so close to him without grabbing him and shaking him awake to have it out with him, she eased herself out of bed. In the dark, she padded her way to the living room and the huge window that overlooked the San Francisco Bay.

A full moon reflected off the water, its luminescence adding a lonely quality to the view. Lonely described how Sam felt. Damned lonely. She stood for a long while doing nothing but staring without seeing, her mind in too much turmoil for her to really appreciate the breathtaking beauty in front of her. This had been the biggest day of her life, so why did she feel so bad?

She let out a resigned sigh. She knew why. As much as she tried to pretend it didn't matter, it did matter. It mattered a hell of a lot. James still hadn't said he loved her and it hurt. It hurt so much, tearing a hole in her heart that wouldn't close.

What was she going to do?

She slowly shook her head, already knowing the answer. She should end things. Maybe even go back to Charles, who at least could promise her tomorrow. Because Sam had finally come to the realization that she needed the promise of tomorrow. She yearned for a future with a man who could commit. For children, and for someone who could give it all to her.

Face facts, Sam. Charles did offer her everything she always wanted—love in the form of security and someone to count on. Only, that didn't seem like enough either.

"Sam?" James' voice from behind startled her out of her thoughts. "What're you doing out here?"

She wiped at her tears before turning. "I couldn't sleep, and didn't want to wake you."

Moonlight provided enough illumination to allow her to note his concern as he nodded.

Then his gaze narrowed and he stepped closer. "Are you crying?

She shook her head and tried to keep from sniffling. "No." Blinking back her watery gaze, she smiled at him. By this point, he was an arm's length away and his attention was fixed on her face. His expression told her she hadn't gotten away with her lie, so she turned back to the view and sniffled. "Okay, you caught me. I'm crying."

"Why?"

She shrugged. "Why not?

"But I thought things were going really well."

Of course he did. He was happy enough to continue as is, when he wasn't the one who craved what she did. "I don't know, James. I just wonder if I'm not making a mistake."

"You promised to give me time." He wrapped his arms around her and pulled her to him. The back of her head nestled in that juncture between his shoulder and arm, and his heartbeat thumped in her ear. A steady *thump*, *thump*, *thump*. He was a warm and caring man, but he wasn't hers. Not completely. She wondered if he ever would be completely hers.

"Yeah, I know I did," she said, in response about her giving him time. She turned in his arms to face him. "But at what cost?"

"I care about you. You know I do."

He cared about Kate too. What if the past was repeating itself? Did she have years to waste for him to realize what they shared as Kate had? She sighed and slowly shook her head. No. She knew what she wanted and somehow she let passion sway her from her purpose and fell in love with the wrong man. She was her mother, all right. Vickie deserved more and so did she. "I can't do this anymore."

"Do what?" James kissed the side of her face.

"Wait until you figure it all out. It hurts too much."

"Shush. It's okay. We'll deal with it."

"How?" She leaned away from him. "I'll tell you how. You'll run."

"You're so sure?" His intense gaze gave her hope and more courage to ask for everything she yearned for.

"Can you tell me you love me? Right here, right now? And offer me some sort of commitment?"

"I do love you. Is it enough for a lifetime? Hell, I don't know." In the moonlight, his eyes didn't hide his turmoil. She watched several more emotions sweep over them, but in the end they revealed only frustration. "You knew going into this I had issues. We've only been together a couple of months. I need more time."

"Of course you do." She forced out a laugh. A harsh sound with no humor. "I could give you a year, and I doubt it would matter." She closed her eyes, hating the truth of what she'd just said, but seeing it for the first time. "We've been dancing around each other since my confession right after the basketball game at the center. I know you're petrified. Here's where I really scare the hell out of you. I love you. So much that I'm dying to spend the rest of my life with you. I want to bear your children. But I won't wait for empty promises. I've had that my whole life, and I decided long ago, I wanted more. I'm sorry, James. I've gotta go. I have a busy day tomorrow."

"Wait," James said, following her as she rushed around to find her clothes and start dressing. "Can't we talk about this?"

She tugged her sweater over her head and stopped to look at him. "Are you ready to offer commitment?"

He ran a hand through his hair and swore under his breath.

"I thought not," she said and resumed dressing. She grabbed her jeans and as she sat to put them on, she added, "Which means the answer is no. We're done talking." As soon as her shoes were on and tied, she found her purse and headed for his front door. She'd worry about the rest of her things later, when she could deal with it.

She rushed outside as fast as her legs would carry her. The entire time she ran toward her car, her heart was breaking. He didn't follow to stop her…just let her go. Actions spoke louder than words. Fear would prevent him from reaching for love. In that moment, Sam knew she was better off than James. She'd gone beyond her fears and conquered them. Nothing would diminish her love for him, but she needed to love herself more, especially if James couldn't love her enough.

~

His chest heavy, James stood immobile after she left him.

Go after her. She's offering you the chance of a lifetime.

He didn't move. He was such a selfish bastard, because he was too afraid to go after her, even though the answer seemed so simple.

Why not give her happily-ever-after?

He knew why. She was asking for more than his love and he was scared shitless to give it. He did love her. But he couldn't jump in…couldn't commit. Not yet. Nor was he about to hurt her further with his indecision. No. He was better off letting things cool, as he should have done weeks ago.

He never wanted anyone like he wanted her, but she didn't deserve eight years of misery like he gave Kate. She deserved someone who wasn't afraid to commit to her. Right now that wasn't him. He was beginning to doubt it ever would be him.

He started for his bedroom with a heavy heart. As James slipped in between the sheets, all he could think of was how empty the room seemed without Sam.

Chapter 15

Sam woke the next morning with a horrible headache. She had spent most of what was left of the night crying and thought seriously about not going in to work, but that would only prolong the inevitable.

She had to face James sometime. They were partners in the same firm, and they were both dealing with the McAlpin project. Fred McAlpin was James' client to begin with, and he wanted James' feedback in all the stages, so she had no choice but to buck up and work with him. Pretend the past few months hadn't happened.

You can do it, Sam. You're good at pretending and you've survived much worse.

Her mental cheerleading did nothing to slow the burning ache in her heart. Still, the inner pep talk pushed her on as she forced herself to shower and dress.

She pulled into her parking spot, grabbed her usual apple and Starbucks coffee, and headed inside. She stepped off the elevator and hurried past James' office, not stopping until she reached her own.

Finally behind the door, she heaved a sigh of relief over not having to deal with seeing him just yet. She'd have to face him sometime. She was just damned glad that time wasn't now. She wasn't exactly sure what she'd say or what she'd do. Something else to regret the morning after returning to her senses. She'd always known this day would come. Why hadn't she thought more about it? Right now, as well as dealing with a broken heart, she felt as foolish as her mother must have felt.

The week dragged and by Friday, Sam missed their working relationship more than anything. Too many times over the last few days, she'd wanted to run into James' office for advice or to bounce an idea off him, but stopped herself in the nick of time. As she left the office that afternoon, she decided to be the bigger person and reach out to him, even if it killed her.

Monday morning, Sam stepped off the elevator still filled with indecision, and saw James heading her way. Damn, he looked good. He was smiling and was staring straight at her as he continued walking toward her.

"Good morning, Sam," he said politely. "I trust you had a nice weekend?"

"Yes. Thanks. And you?" She mentally groaned. Listen to the two of them, she thought, as he threw out a stock answer. They might as well be strangers. Was it only a week ago that she made glorious love to him and now they acted as if that had never happened? He looked too attractive standing there, his smile sending the same signals to her brain. Her eyes drifted lower to those hands that had given her such pleasure. A streak of longing shot through her, one so strong, she knew at that moment she'd made a horrible mistake by giving up on him so easily when he'd been going in the right direction. "Well, I've got work to do." She had to escape. To think about how she could undo her mistake.

"Maybe we can have lunch sometime and talk?"

"That sounds nice."

"How about today?"

"I can't." She sighed, a little relieved to have an excuse to delay action. "I'm meeting a client for lunch. What about tomorrow?" She had no idea how she would go about getting things back to the way they were, so this would give her time to come up with a plan.

"Sure." His warm smile filled her with hope that things would work out. She started for her office, loving the sense of anticipation she hadn't felt in over a week.

~

James watched her go, happy to note she was at least speaking to him now. She'd seemed to want to keep her distance last week, so he'd honored that by staying away. More than anything, he wanted to hug her and say they could work things out, but he still hadn't dealt with his inner demons. As a result, their working relationship was now strained. He realized right then that he missed the easy friendship they shared before they ever got physical.

Making love with Sam in the first place had ruined things between them. As much as he missed her sexually, he was too afraid to go there again. Restarting the physical would be the selfish act of that bastard he didn't want to be. It was past time to be a better man. He *would not* cause her more unhappiness. She wanted commitment more than anything. He thought of Charles waiting in the wings for Sam to come to her senses, and somehow James knew he had to undo the damage he'd inflicted in their relationship. If he could get them back together, no matter how much he hated the thought, then at least one of them would be happy. Her happiness was most important at this point.

~

Sam strolled off the elevator the next day, her spirits buoyed with confidence for her lunch date with James. Yesterday, her projects had consumed her time at work, but once she'd made it home, she'd spent the evening thinking of what she'd say and how she'd go about apologizing to James for not giving him a chance. Excitement for what lay ahead kept the knot in her tummy tight. She could barely eat her apple, and coffee seemed to intensify the feeling.

Rushing into her office, she set the cup down on her desk before pacing back and forth. She glanced out the picture window as another glorious day greeted her. An omen of things to come, she thought. Damn. How was she going to wait until lunch? She wanted to shout her decision to the world. She stopped pacing as it hit her.

Why wait? Why not run in and tell James what was in her heart and that she'd give him all the time in the world. That was how she felt just then. Optimistic.

She turned and headed for his office, but the sound of angry voices stopped her. She never meant to eavesdrop, but hearing her name in the heated conversation had her stepping closer to listen more intently.

"I must be insane to even consider this meeting. Why would I listen to you about Samantha in the first place when you're the reason she's no longer happy with me?" she heard Charles say, recognizing his clipped tone. His office was nearby and it wasn't unusual for him to drop by, but she was surprised to hear his voice this morning. Since she'd kicked him out of her apartment after her first date with James, he hadn't stepped foot in their building. "Weren't there enough women in the world, you had to go after her? You should've left her alone."

"Pointing fingers won't help," James said.

"And why should I believe you want to help us get back together, when you're the reason we're apart?"

What? Sam's stare widened. Were they arguing over her? She

inched closer and concentrated harder.

~

James sighed and wanted to shout, "Who gave her the shove in my direction?" Instead, he said, "Look, I called you here to help you. If you had doubts about your relationship, you should've worked on them with Sam instead of asking for a break. If you had, this whole fiasco wouldn't have happened."

"Don't twist this around," Charles said. "I was only trying to make things better."

James swallowed the retort on the tip of his tongue and dug deep down for patience. "Then make them better, and talk to Sam. Apologize. Grovel. Let her see that you're willing to do whatever it takes to please her."

"I wouldn't have to do anything if you'd left her alone, like you should've done in the first place."

"Then read my lips. We're no longer seeing each other. Okay? I'm trying help you, buddy, only you're too dense to realize it." James broke off and was silent before he offered an audible sigh. "If you think she loves you, then quit blaming me and romance her. Let her know what she means to you. That's all she wants."

"I don't take advice from you, and I am blaming you. She trusted you and you took advantage of her. If not for you, we'd be engaged."

"You're so sure?" He couldn't forget Sam's admission that she was no good in the bedroom. At least she'd demand more of him now that he'd awakened that part of her. Of course, that didn't make this any easier.

"Yes," Charles yelled, yanking him back to their argument. "You had no business butting in—no business seducing her. Stay away from her. We could've worked things out if not for you. It's obvious she's enamored with you, spouting off about passion, but you couldn't keep your hands off her, could you?"

"Things happened." He'd just as soon punch the guy out as give him pointers on winning Sam back, but Charles was offering something he might never be able to offer, and that fact spurred him to finish what was quickly becoming a distasteful endeavor. "I won't say I shouldn't have acted more responsibly, but you're not listening. I'm trying to rectify my mistake."

Charles' answer was a brittle laugh. "Yeah, right."

"Do you love her?" James asked.

"Of course I love her."

"Then prove it. Don't let her get away. Fight for her."

Just then a noise from the door drew their attention and Sam barged in looking like a warrior on the verge of battle. "Where do you two get off deciding my future as if I was a piece of meat rather than a human being with a mind of my own?"

"Sam? I can see you're upset. You shouldn't be listening in on private conversations," Charles said, pushing his glasses higher on his nose. Bright spots of embarrassment touched his cheeks. He clearly hadn't expected her to overhear this conversation; for that matter, neither had James.

"It wasn't my intention, but it seems fitting, since you both seem to think you have some say over my life." She turned to James with a hurt look that made him feel lower than pond scum. "How could you? How could you sit there so coolly and tell Charles to fight for me? Why not take your own advice?"

"How much did you hear?" James cleared his throat to dislodge the lump of remorse growing. His calm voice only seemed to enrage her further.

"Enough to know you two are idiots," she spit out. "You might as well rip out my heart and stomp on it than try to pawn me off on Charles after all we've shared." She snared his gaze, hers deadly serious. "Listen and listen well because I'm only saying this one time." She then turned to Charles and focused the same glare on him. "I was honest with both of you and told you how I felt. I wanted more. Yet, neither of you listened to me, did you? Instead, you come here behind my back. You, blaming James for your stupidity?" she said to Charles. "Maybe we could've worked things out. But not anymore." Her intent focus moved to James as the hurt he'd inflicted erupted further. "And you! I was ready to give you more time. But I guess you don't need it. Now I wouldn't have either one of you on a silver platter."

She pivoted and stalked out of his office and probably out of his love life. For good, it seemed, judging by her blowup. Shit. How had he screwed this up?

~

This was too much, Sam thought, fighting tears and rushing for the safety of her office. She should be happy Charles was still interested, but she didn't want him. Not really. All she could focus on was

James' pep talk on how to win her back. Why? How could he? His comments had sliced her heart open.

Safely inside, she leaned against the closed door and struggled to keep from crying. James had disappointed her again. Why did he have to be such an idiot?

Is that how he really views our relationship? A mistake…a fiasco? Does he think he can just re-gift my love like it holds no value for him?

The minute she sat behind her desk, her tears flowed.

Why did loving him have to hurt so much? She had never felt such pain. Well, now she knew.

How could she work with him, day after day, knowing how he really felt? He didn't want to fight for her love. They could be so good together but he'd never allow it. She got that now.

A loud knock interrupted her misery. Her attention flew to the opening door. She mutely watched James slip inside and stand in front of the door he just closed.

"Did Charles leave?" she asked softly, after an uncomfortable moment of silence.

"Yes. I'd say he got your message."

She snorted. "He's just being Charles."

"I got your message too." James' eyes locked with hers, his intense gaze filled with remorse. His expression said everything, only it was too late. She had to look away.

"I never meant to hurt you," he said, after eyeing her thoughtfully for quite a while, when she purposefully wouldn't meet his gaze again. "You have to believe that."

"I thought you wanted time," she said on a sigh as she finally glanced up, allowing him to see the pain etched in her eyes.

"I did. But I wanted your happiness more."

"You have a strange way of showing it." She swiped at her cheek, brushing away a tear.

"I was trying to help."

"I can't help thinking you were trying to ease out of what we started."

"No, I—"

"Come on, James," she said, cutting him off. "Be honest. You were the one who wanted honesty. So let's be honest, shall we? You're scared to death of what you feel, and you're doing the only thing you can think of to destroy what we shared. Well, you've succeeded."

"That's not true. Last week you said you needed a commitment. I can't commit right now, but Charles can."

"A perfect solution to your dilemma, except for one glitch. I don't want Charles."

"He'd make a much better husband. You should give him a chance."

She offered a brittle laugh. "You don't get it. I don't want either one of you. I couldn't pick my parents, but I'm damn sure not going to pick a man who's already hurt me and one who'll only disappoint me further. Not anymore. I deserve someone who can love me totally, without reservations, and someone who isn't afraid of feelings. To accept less would be settling. I'd rather be alone than settle. I've come too far to turn back now." She wiped her tears, grabbed a Kleenex to blow her nose, and sniffed. She took a deep breath and offered a wan smile. "You want to know what saddens me the most? I feel like I've lost my best friend."

"I am your friend. I honestly think you should give Charles a chance. He'd make you happy. Happier than I ever could. You have to admit, I was only making you miserable."

"Then why get more involved with me?"

"Sam, I—"

"Don't," she warned, interrupting whatever excuse was on his tongue.

"What do you want from me?"

"Nothing now." She slowly shook her head, as she realized it was the truth. "Why couldn't you leave well enough alone when we returned from the wine country? Before that, I'd have been content with Charles."

"You know why. I never made any promises."

"Maybe not, but I hold you responsible for letting me fall more in love with you. I was perfectly happy without knowing what it could be like."

"What was it like?" He swallowed and she saw regret mirrored in his eyes.

"Heaven," she stated honestly, not adding that in a split second, heaven had turned to hell. A hell worse than anything she'd experienced as a child.

"I'm so sorry. I never meant to hurt you." His whispered tone conveyed his sorrow. She heard it as plain as day. Saw pain flash in his eyes. She wished more than anything they were two different people.

She grabbed her briefcase and purse and stood to leave. She had to get out of there or she would completely lose it.

"Where are you going?" he said to her departing back.

"I'm taking the day off."

"What about our meeting with McAlpin tomorrow?"

"I'll reschedule." She didn't look back as her heels clicked on the marble floor, marking time to her dignified retreat down the hall.

~

James allowed the best part of his life to walk out, wanting more than anything to stop her. Knowing that he couldn't give her what she needed, he let her go. When the elevator doors closed with finality, it hit him. No one had ever walked away from him before. He'd always been the one to do the walking. How ironic that Samantha Collins, the one woman he'd fallen in love with in such a short time, would be the person to leave. Leave before he got emotionally involved enough to feel the pain of rejection or the pain of loss. Just another fact he'd learned about himself in the last few minutes, and certainly not a pretty one.

He grunted disgustedly. *Has to be some sort of prophetic justice or karma.* That's what he got for being such a selfish bastard in the first place. She was right. He should never have let things go so far.

He started for his office, ignoring the sense of loss and praying their working relationship would survive his stupidity.

~

Sam rushed out of the building in record time and practically ran to her car. Seconds later she was driving toward her apartment.

The minute she made it inside, she grabbed her cell phone and called Mary Ann.

"Can you meet me for drinks and dinner? Early?" she asked, after a few minutes of small talk.

"Sure," Mary Ann replied. As a manufacturer's sales rep, her friend worked out of her condo and had a flexible schedule. Mary Ann would know what to do. Sam just didn't think she could face an empty apartment, after she finished the work she'd brought with her. Not tonight.

Shoving her sadness away, she sat at her drafting table to begin working on the few projects she'd let slip while focused so intently on the McAlpin project.

Four o'clock finally came and Sam headed out to her car. She turned over the ignition, backed out of the space, and sped away from the parking lot like an Indy race car driver. She pulled up to Mary Ann's condo, shaving off two minutes from the twenty-minute ride. Reaching for her bag, Sam pulled out her cell phone and texted Mary Ann to let her know she was parked outside.

Mary Ann didn't waste time and soon slid in next to her.

Sam shifted into reverse. "Where do you want to go?" She turned onto El Camino Real.

"How about Mexican? Ernesto's sounds good."

"I'm game." She didn't have to wait long until Mary Ann blurted out, "Okay, what's wrong? What happened?"

"What do you mean, what happened? Can't I just have a nice dinner with my friend without something happening?"

"No. You seldom leave work early. You and I rarely go out to dinner, especially during the week. Always lunch, which is okay. Don't get me wrong."

"I'm sorry. I guess I haven't been much of a friend lately."

"Don't say that. You've always been a friend. So, answer my question. Why are we going to dinner, when you're usually too busy working?"

"James and I broke up."

"What?" Of course Mary Ann was shocked speechless. Sam had given her play-by-play updates of her relationship with James during the past month. The last one had been the glowing account of the night he'd cooked for her. Sam hadn't mentioned leaving his house, though. Mary Ann would have chided her for expecting too much too soon, as her friend had already done during those few conversations where Sam had vented. Now that her fears had turned into reality and the worst had happened, it didn't matter.

Sam poured out her heart during the ten-minute drive, giving Mary Ann the abbreviated version. They would spend the rest of dinner going back over it in full detail, second by second.

The restaurant came into view and neither spoke as she parked. They hopped out of her Honda together.

Both ordered margaritas after being seated in a booth. Since Sam drove, she would limit herself to only one.

"I think you need to visit your mom," Mary Ann said, after they'd done exactly what Sam had predicted on the drive to the restaurant. While eating tacos and drinking margaritas, the two had dissected every detail of James and Sam's relationship.

Despite feeling so wretched, Sam laughed. "That's not going to happen." She fully planned on picking up a bottle of tequila on the way home, because right now one margarita wasn't nearly enough. The thought of getting drunk held a definite appeal, especially after hearing Mary Ann's suggestion.

"Sam, you need to come to terms with your past." Her friend turned to the waitress and lifted the folder with her credit card sticking out, indicating she wanted to pay. "You need to see Vickie. You need to forgive her. I don't think you're going to find happily-ever-after until you do."

"What good will seeing Vickie do?" She sighed. She'd ignored her mom's pleas to visit during the many *short* phone calls over the years. "And how can I forgive her when she's never going to change?"

"That's not true. She knows about your success and she's happy for you. She's proud of you."

"Oh?" Eyebrows lifted, she glanced at Mary Ann. "How do you know that?

"My mom. She and Vickie have become tight."

"They're friends?" The news would have knocked her off her perch if she hadn't been sitting in a booth. Sam waited until the waitress left with payment before adding, "I feel violated."

"Don't. She's changed. Your leaving changed her. Opened her eyes to her stupidity. She's really done a complete turnaround and tried to become someone you'd be proud of." Mary Ann smiled. "I've wanted to tell you, but I knew you wouldn't listen or you'd get pissed off and change the subject." Her hand covered Sam's and she squeezed. "She's even found someone who loves her. You know. She was always looking for love."

"Yeah." Sam knew all about looking for love in all the wrong places, as the song went. Vickie could have written the song and Sam had followed in her footsteps. Something she'd vowed never to do.

"Well, it's just an idea." Mary Ann broke off. A minute later she offered, "I'd even go with you. You know what they say about forgiveness being good for the soul. I think it's time to forgive

Vickie."

"I don't know. Let me think about it." She didn't need any more emotional shit to deal with and dealing with Vickie had always taken its toll. "I just don't know if I have the strength."

"Sure you do. You have the strength for anything." She hesitated. "I think you should give James another chance." Mary Ann held up a hand, cutting off her protest and added, "You should've given him more time to begin with. I mean, come on. You were expecting the impossible. It's only been a couple of months. No guy is going to commit so quickly, especially one like James."

Sam stared at her friend for a long moment, thinking about her logic, then shook her head. "You make it sound so easy. I'm not like you, Mar. I have too much baggage. I'm so afraid he'll disappoint me again. Like my mom's always done." Tears filled her eyes. Thankfully, the waitress interrupted again and she didn't have to say any more. "I just don't know if I could survive it again."

"Well, you don't have to decide tonight. Just think about what I said." Mary Ann signed the check, then stood. "Next dinner's on you. I expect it to be in weeks rather than months like this dinner was."

"Oh, Mar. I love you." Sam stood and wrapped her in a bear hug. "You're a good friend."

Once she dropped Mary Ann off at her condo, Sam wound her way back home, forgoing the tequila, and let herself into her apartment as her friend's suggestion about seeing Vickie lodged in her brain. Could she forgive her mom as Mary Ann suggested? Sam just didn't know. Giving James another chance seemed a sure road to more heartache. She doubted she had the capacity for either one right now.

As she got ready for bed, she wondered how she would survive the rest of the week when she and James worked so closely together. Heck, in a couple of weeks they would have to drive to Half Moon Bay to be at the property for the groundbreaking ceremony, so she couldn't avoid him for long. Why oh why had she ever gotten involved with him? She'd known going into it he had issues, so she had no one to blame but herself for the ensuing heartache.

The memory of their shared nights of lovemaking at his house barreled back and a tear streaked down her face. She wished she didn't love him. It would be much easier to go back to Charles if she didn't. And now she had no one.

~

The rest of the week went by in slow agony. She'd been fairly successful at avoiding James, since he seemed to be avoiding her as well. Like before, too many times during the week, she'd catch herself wanting to run into his office dying to bounce an idea off him for feedback, only to stop herself at the door.

On Monday, Sam, armed with her coffee and apple, exited the elevator and headed for her office and a drafting table full of work. She was no longer concerned with seeing James. She couldn't be. She had a job to do. Mary Ann was right about one thing. She was strong…she could face this head on. For nearly a week she'd gone back and forth. Flip-flopped so many times, the only thing she was sure of was that she had to live her life a day at a time. So what if she'd never have happily-ever-after with him. He'd never lied to her about his issues, which meant she could certainly work with him. Maybe she could even see her mother.

She sat on the stool and reached for her pencil.

A movement caught her attention and she looked up to see James leaning against the door frame, his usual confident manner evident in the pose.

"You're in early. I've missed seeing you."

"I've been busy." She offered a forced smile. "And I have lots to do. I got a little behind when I concentrated so much on McAlpin's building."

"The groundbreaking's set for next Monday morning." He met her gaze. "That is, if we're still driving together?"

She nodded. Taking two cars would be stupid. Besides, she needed to let him see she could handle her duties without pining away for his love.

"Are you okay?"

My heart is aching and he asks such a stupid question. What do you think, idiot? "Of course," she said, holding on to her plastic smile and lying through her teeth. "Why wouldn't I be okay?"

"I know you're still upset. I was hoping you'd have lunch with me. We need to talk."

He thinks talking will fix things. She eyed him, erasing all emotion from her face. She was dying to say yes, but spending any more time with him than necessary wouldn't be in her best interest. Not yet. She was still too raw from everything to be able to hold it together. If she caved now, she would be right back to where she'd been last week, when everything fell apart.

"Please? Talk to me. Give me a chance to make things right."

Why is this so hard? Ignore those pleading blue eyes and that beautiful, begging smile. She shook her head, breaking eye contact, and took a long, deep breath, stilling the desire to agree. "I don't think it's a good idea." She swiveled back around and concentrated on the blueprint on her drafting table. "Now if you'll excuse me, I have work to do."

You can handle working with him, Sam. Just pretend. Pretend you don't love him and that it doesn't matter that he'll never love you back enough to commit to a lifetime together.

For endless minutes, she felt his lurking presence. The entire time she couldn't breathe, could only pray he would leave, so she could quit pretending.

He finally sighed, then turned and walked away. Sam glanced up in time to see the defeated hunch of his retreating back.

A tear formed, trekked down the side of her face before she brushed it away. Eyeing the empty doorway, she wondered about Mary Ann's advice. Maybe her friend was right and she expected the impossible. That thought led to more of their conversation about fixing things from her past. Maybe if she came to terms with her mother, she could deal better with James.

~

Thursday morning, James kept an ear out for the elevator, hoping to waylay Sam when she arrived at the office.

The second he heard her voice, he jumped up. Then, he paused. Pushing a hand through his hair, he hoped she wouldn't continue giving him the cold shoulder. Every time he tried to strike up a conversation, she just smiled like he was a pest to be tolerated. Then, she would shake her head and walk away. Those encounters left him feeling totally unsure of himself. He shared something special with Samantha Collins and he'd carelessly tossed it aside like it meant nothing, when in reality, life held no meaning without her friendship. Color had disappeared from his life and he had no idea how to bring it back…no idea how to rectify his mistake.

He started for her office determined that she would at least talk to him.

"Hey, Collins." James stopped at her door, like a hundred other times, only today she didn't even bother to look up from her drafting table.

"I'm busy," she said in the same dismissive tone as earlier. "What do you want?"

What did he want? Hell, the answer was easy. He wanted her friendship again. He wanted to see her smile with invitation when he stood at her door. He wanted to look up from his desk and see her bounding through his door with enthusiasm, excited by an idea she had to share. What he wouldn't give for any one of those things.

He stared at Sam's hunched-over back as more memories assaulted him. Intense memories of the last time they'd been intimate played over and over in his mind. He couldn't shut off the images. How he missed her. Night after night. He couldn't sleep in his bed any longer. Her scent clung to it, no matter how many times he washed the sheets. So, he took to sleeping in his guest room…getting what little sleep he could because he'd spend half the night wanting her.

Misery. Pure, absolute, complete, and utter misery. That's what his life had become. The realization brought forth a surge of regret. He left her office shaking his head.

If only he could be different and give her what she needed.

~

Later that night, James parked his SUV outside Paul and Kate's house, remembering the last time he'd made the drive. Sam had been with him.

Wondering why he even bothered tonight, he sighed and climbed out of the car.

"Where's Sam?" Kate said laughingly, after opening the door right as he stepped onto the porch. She looked beyond his shoulder then sought his gaze for clarification. "I thought for sure you'd bring her tonight."

"I'm not her keeper." He mentally rolled his eyes. Of course, she'd ask. Why in the world would he think otherwise when Kate Morrison was the nosiest person he knew?

"Did she wise up? Give you the boot and go back to Charles?" she asked, her voice teasing. When he didn't return the laugh, she eyed him thoughtfully for a lengthy moment. "I was joking, but I can see it's not a laughing matter. Something happened, didn't it? You look like hell."

"Nice to see you too."

"Don't tell me you blew it with her." She shook her head, tsk-tsking, and stepped aside, letting him go ahead of her.

"Okay, I won't, but why do you assume I'm at fault? Maybe she blew it."

"I doubt it." She closed the door and turned back to him. "Anyone with half a brain could see you two were made for each other, and knowing you like I do, you probably couldn't handle that."

James schooled his face to show nothing of the torment her comment brought forth, staying silent, unwilling to let her know how close to the truth she'd hit.

"So, what happened?"

"News flash, Kate. I didn't drive all this way for the third degree." He knew he sounded surly and curt, but damn it all, she could just stuff her nosiness. He wasn't in the mood to be jovial right then, nor was he in the mood to confide his troubles.

"Whoa!" She put her hands up, forming a cross. "I'm not the enemy. Consider the subject dropped…for now. At least until you've had a few beers."

"Thank God for small favors," he muttered, saying louder, "I really could use a beer." He started down the hallway, without adding it'd take a dozen beers before he'd feel ready to discuss losing Sam. "Where's Nick?"

"Out back with Paul. I figured as long as the weather's cooperating, we could eat outside like we did last month." The phone rang. She nodded toward the sliding screen door. "Go on out while I get the phone. Then, I'll grab you a beer."

"Thanks," he said, rushing for the patio door and his nephew. When he spied the baby crawling toward him with a worshipful expression highlighting his cherubic face, his thoughts switched to something besides missing Sam for the first time in days. "Hey, big guy." He stepped onto the deck and bent down to pick up the child. "You gotta quit growing, kid. Every time I see you, you've sprouted another inch. Soon, you'll be too heavy to hold."

"He's definitely a bruiser," Paul said, rising. He grinned at James. "Where's Sam?"

James was saved from having to reply when Kate stepped out and said, "That was Dev on the phone. He and Judith are going to be late." She added, "And don't mention Sam. She's not with him."

James looked to the heavens for patience.

"Oh?" Paul's eyebrows shot up and though he didn't ask, the question definitely lurked in his eyes.

"You don't see her, do you?" James worked to still his annoyance. Why had he bothered coming tonight? He should have known Paul and Kate wouldn't let Sam's absence go unnoticed without prodding him for information as to why. His biggest mistake was bringing her here in the first place. What had he been thinking to do such a stupid thing? "We broke up. Okay? I'm sure you don't need a play-by-play account of what happened, so can we just drop it?"

Paul said, "I can drop it," at the same time Kate said, "I'd like the play by play."

He rolled his eyes and looked down at Nick, who was watching him intently. He cooed, "Come on, let's go get a beer, partner, and leave your nosy mother to wonder about my love life. She doesn't need to know everything."

Thankfully, both Kate and Paul skirted the subject of Sam, until Dev and Judith arrived.

James sighed and headed outside to help Paul with the burgers after Kate's, "Don't ask," when Judith glanced around, obviously looking for Sam.

She nodded. "Okay, I won't."

After taking the beer Kate handed him, Dev followed on his heels and said as he closed the sliding screen door, "I'm not as polite as Judith, so I'll ask. Where is she? You two seemed tight. Thought she might be the *one*."

James ignored the question, hoping he'd drop the subject.

"I can't believe you let her get away."

Irritation swept over him. "I didn't let her get away," he snarled, feeling much like a hungry junkyard dog having had his meaty bone taken away, and Dev's remark was a stick, poking at him, provoking him. "No one lets Sam do anything."

"Ah."

"Ah, what?"

"She dumped you, didn't she?"

"What is it with you guys? Can't anyone drink in peace without twenty questions?"

"Hey, why're you getting upset with me?" Dev put up his hands in mock surrender. "I was only making small talk."

"No, you weren't. You were rubbing it in, getting me back for all those times I was a thorn in your side. God knows I deserve it, but I'm not in the mood for shit tonight."

"Judith is four months along," Dev said. "And since I'm going to be a dad, I don't play such juvenile games anymore. I'm too happy."

"Yeah, right," he snorted unconvinced. "You sound like one of those religious nuts who've found the light."

"My point exactly. I have found the light. Judith. After committing my fair share of sins, I have no idea how I came to be so lucky to end up with her. I certainly didn't deserve her." Dev sat on the chair next to him and took a sip of beer, eyeing him thoughtfully. "Why don't you tell me what happened. Maybe I can help."

"Too late for that." James stood and headed inside, ending the discussion. No one could help him at this point.

Later, Judith and Kate were upstairs going through baby paraphernalia. Paul suggested one of their usual poker games.

"Take a look at my kid," Dev said, handing a picture to James.

James passed the picture to Paul without looking at it.

"I can't believe how clear ultrasounds are." Dev's satisfied grin took over half his face. "I've even got a DVD of him kicking."

"I remember when I first saw Nick on film," Paul replied. He shuffled a deck of cards and dealt. "All I cared about was making sure he had ten toes and ten fingers."

"I can understand now why Tom Cruise tried to buy one of those machines. Would be nice to see him at different stages." Dev picked up the cards in front of him and put them in order.

"You're sure it's a boy?" Paul placed the deck to the side and grabbed his cards.

"Wishful thinking. Although the nurse did say she'd be surprised if he turned out to be female after spotting the telling appendage. I'll be happy with either."

"Give me three. And do me a favor, will you? Talk about something besides babies." James threw down his cards, picking up the three Paul dealt. "That's all I've heard about since we sat down. You guys are worse than Kate and Judith."

"Why?" Dev tossed two cards toward Paul and nodded. "Two." Then he fixed a narrow-eyed gaze on James, clearly expecting a reply.

Why? You really want to know why? Because you guys are happy and I'm not, that's why. But James couldn't admit that. "It's not masculine, nor is it something I care to discuss, okay?"

After listening all evening to his best friend and brother go on and on about babies and due dates and ultrasounds, need clutched at his soul. To make matters worse, while observing Kate put a sleepy Nick to bed, his yearning grew. He hadn't even realized a family with Sam was something he wanted until that moment, which had made the simple task pure torture. He couldn't mention that either. The realization tore his insides in two, and the pain was worse than anything he could imagine. Much worse than what he'd glimpsed in Aunt Chloe's eyes because he was experiencing it. Here he'd run, fearful of feeling and inflicting pain, when all running had done was make the pain excruciating in the end. On both sides.

"Times have changed. Men today can participate with their wives when she's expecting. Dealer takes four." Paul dealt himself four cards and exchanged them. He picked them up and perused his new cards speculatively. "I was Kate's coach in the delivery room. Watching Nick being born was an incredible experience."

"Yeah. I was going to ask you about that Lamaze shit."

"I'm out." James gave up all pretense of enjoying himself and slapped his cards on the table. "You two are acting like old ladies. You're men, for Christ's sake. Act like it."

"You just wait." Paul's voice filled his head as he pushed away from the table and stood.

He sighed. He could wait, but waiting wouldn't do a damn bit of good. Why was he obsessing about kids and family? He knew why. He might never have a chance to experience parenthood with Sam. Watching everyone around him move on to the next phase of life without him made him feel lost and even more alone.

"I'm out of here," he said. He had to escape or he'd lose it.

He climbed into his SUV with one thought. He missed Sam. The pain of not having her in his life was a million times worse than any pain he tried to avoid.

No way he could let her go without a fight, he thought, remembering her words. Unfortunately, others she'd voiced came back to haunt him because they also held a ring of truth. He *had* tried to ease out of their relationship. He'd been too wrapped up in avoiding pain to realize his stupidity in offering to help Charles. What had he been thinking?

For the millionth time in days, he silently blasted himself. *Fool, fool, fool, fool, fool. No one could be as big a fool as you, not to see what you had with her. And what a bigger fool to let her slip out of your grasp. A billion times more so than Charles had been.*

At that moment, he finally admitted the truth. He loved her more than life itself. He now wanted to shout it out, but given her cool demeanor toward him, he doubted she'd listen.

Damn. He'd really messed things up with his fears. Hopefully, he could fix them. She was working on a project with him, so she couldn't keep avoiding him. Somehow, some way, he'd win back her love. He had to, he suddenly realized, because he wasn't just fighting for love. He was fighting for his life.

Chapter 16

Sam wiped her sweaty palms on her jeans and fixed her gaze on the house she'd left all those years ago as Mary Ann's Nissan Murano edged to a stop at the curb. She recognized little but the address in the tiny bungalow she'd shared with her mom for over a year, one of their longer stays in the same place. That Vickie still lived here spoke volumes in regard to stability and change.

"Amazing. Vickie planted roses." Someone had also recently added a fresh coat of paint. The property looked as good as it could, considering the area. She glanced beyond the yard and noted other houses on the street appeared more neat and trim than the run-down places in her memory. "Look, real grass," she added, eyeing an array of color from several red, yellow, and pink bushes outlining a lush green area that had once been bare dirt.

"Told you she's changed."

"I guess." The only plants Vickie grew back then were weeds, and even those died in the dry spring and summer months. Her focus swung back to the surrounding houses. "Neighborhood's improved."

Mary Ann shifted into park and killed the engine before her gaze followed Sam's. "The Bay Area's sky-high prices over the years have helped. Now, this area is considered a starter neighborhood. Lots of young professionals like the proximity."

Sam nodded. It made sense, considering Union City was close to three major northern California cities: San Jose, San Francisco, and Oakland.

"Mom's even thinking of selling and moving to Sacramento or further north, where prices are a little cheaper."

"Really? Times *have* changed," she said. "Fifteen years ago, your parents would never think of selling." The Murphys' house, on the next block, was less than two miles from both sets of grandparents. Despite the neighborhood being a little rough, the Murphys were comfortable here, having lived in the same house for as long as she could remember.

"Someone offered her eight hundred thousand. Can you believe it? That's almost a million dollars. For our little *old* house."

"Damn," she blew out. Times had changed. "Must be true about what realtors say about location, location, location." Vickie also liked the area for its location, but her mom didn't own. She rented. Or bartered her services. *No. Don't go there, Sam.* Even though she mentally shook her head, the memory of Vickie and the landlord caught in the act filled her mind. Her mom had promised no more men just weeks before that, when Sam had first threatened to leave. Sam had been too tired of the lies to endure any further disappointment, especially after interrupting such a scene. It didn't help that Vickie had sworn she and the landlord were more than friends. To Sam's ears, it just sounded like another excuse.

Uncertainty filled her and suddenly she wasn't sure if she truly possessed the courage to face her mom after all this time. Desperation had led Vickie to her downfall, one with severe consequences because Sam had simply left and had never returned. Until now. Even more disconcerting, considering her recent experiences of the last month, she could no longer view her past through the eyes of an angry teen.

Too bad the view from an adult perspective revealed more truth than she was ready to accept. This was all James' fault, she reasoned. If he hadn't kissed her and awoken her to certain realities in life, then she would have been content to marry Charles. Then she would never have had to confront Vickie, which really meant owning up to her own imperfections. Sam got that now. She also understood that as much as she'd tried to be perfect, she wasn't. No one was. Everyone made mistakes, including…no, *especially* her.

Sam had to rectify the mistake of expecting her mother to be perfect. The truth was as plain as the roses in front of her. She pushed aside past transgressions, both hers and her mom's, and glanced at Mary Ann, biting her lip.

"Do you think she's home?" She hadn't called for two reasons. First, to provide an out in case she lost her nerve, and second, she wanted to catch Vickie off guard with no chance to prepare for a meeting. That way Sam could gauge her honest response. The mom in her memory had a tendency to twist the truth to her advantage. As vulnerable as Sam felt right then, she didn't want to get caught up in lies or have to wade through excuses. Doing so wouldn't solve a damned thing.

"I think so. Let me find out." Mary Ann reached behind the seat for her big purse, or what could pass for a small suitcase.

Her friend had always carried everything with her…just in case. She could probably spend a weekend in Tahoe and not have to pack a thing if she took along her purse. Smiling at the thought, Sam watched her pull her cell phone out and start texting. As best friends, they were as different as night and day. Sam hated texting, thought of it as a big time-waster, so she rarely did it. Unlike Mary Ann, who lived to text and typed faster with two fingers than most admin assistants did using both hands.

"My mom says they get together on Saturdays for coffee," Mary Ann said. The little device beeped as she sent her message. A second beep sounded and she clicked the screen. "Yep. Mom says Vickie's expecting her any time now, so she's definitely home." She stashed the phone into her bag and set it aside. Then, she gripped her knee, squeezed reassuringly, and offered a warm smile. "Don't worry." Her positive tone added to her encouragement. "This'll work out. You'll see. She *has* changed."

"What do I say to her?" For that matter, she couldn't imagine what her mom would say in return. It's not like they left on the best of terms.

"Say hi and give her a hug."

Sam's smile turned wistful. Easy for Mary Ann to suggest. The image of a drunken Vickie yelling at her to go and ranting about her high and mighty standards, filled her head. Sam had shot back just as loudly something about how her mom would never understand why standards were so important when she had none. She'd slammed the door to Vickie's, "You walk out that door, don't ever return. I'm better off without an uptight bitch of a daughter who thinks she knows it all." Sam sobered, as it suddenly dawned on her why she'd never done this before now. She had no clue as to how to go about reuniting. She had no clue how she would react, either.

"I guess we should go in." She was dying to give forgiveness a fair try, but didn't really believe it would work. She and Vickie were just too different. Sam exhaled a large sigh, pulled the handle, and shoved against the door. "I'm procrastinating at this point."

On the front porch, Sam felt her heart race as she rang the bell.

She brushed at her jeans, trying to remain calm, then held her breath when the door shot open and a laughing Vickie, who looked ten times better than on their last meeting, halted, too stunned to speak. After a long hesitation, during which her expression skipped from disbelief to wonder to understanding to joy in a matter of seconds, ending in a warm smile and misty eyes, she said, "Oh my God." Her dangling gold hoop earrings danced as her head shook in evident glee.

Sam didn't have a chance to say anything before her mom had her wrapped in a huge bear hug, and her shoulders shook. Not with laughter as Sam first thought, but from sobs. Vickie sobbed loudly into her shoulder, hugging her tightly as if she'd never let her go.

"My baby." Vickie finally released Sam to wipe her eyes, which only made her look like a raccoon. Fresh tears streaked down her face, ruining makeup that had always been important to Vickie, but right now she was oblivious. Her tearful gaze was full of happiness as she said, "You've come back to me."

Sam cleared her throat and swallowed a lump the size of a grapefruit. She blinked at the tears forming, surprised that she was actually crying too. She hadn't expected to shed any tears over this reunion. Yet, here she was practically bawling like a hungry baby. She sniffed. "Hi, Mom." She brushed away the few tears that had escaped and smiled, her eyes brimming. "You look good."

"So do you." Vickie's gaze flew to Mary Ann, who stood off to the side, remaining quiet. "Thank you so much for bringing her home. You don't know how happy this makes me." Her attention returned to Sam and she then grabbed her hands and held them up, inspecting her from head to toe. "Just look at you. You're beautiful." Vickie was always the beautiful one and even in her mid-forties, her beauty hadn't faded. She still had her hourglass figure and she hadn't toned down her style one bit, still wore body-hugging jeans and a low-cut top. Yet on her it somehow worked. "I hear you're successful. Got a big job in San Mateo as an architect." She let go of one hand and turned, her other hand pulling her further into the room. "I'm still waiting tables. It pays the rent and I like the regular customers."

As Sam walked, she glanced around. The place was clean, not that it had ever been dirty, just barren and lacking charm. They never had the money to spend on frivolous items like decorator pillows or throw rugs. Whose fault was that? No. Both had changed and Sam wasn't one to dwell on what-ifs. But damn it all, as she looked around and noted how cozy everything looked, she so wished things had been different. If they had been, then maybe she wouldn't be so screwed up right now, which would mean she would be the type of person who could give James more time. As it was, it seemed she was still protecting her heart and, reflexive action or not, she just didn't know how to take the protective cover off.

"I knew you'd do something with all your talent. Always drawing, in a world of your own. Even when you were a baby, I never could figure out what to do with you," Vickie said, now half-dragging her into the kitchen. "Don't laugh, but I always thought I'd taken home the wrong kid because you were nothing like me, even from the get-go."

Sam heard those same words too many times in her past and they elicited more memories, buried deep that rose to the surface and collided with the not-so-nice ones she'd never been able to forget. She realized just then that not all of her past was ugly. There were a few good times interspersed with all the bad, with most of the negative occurring after Sam turned thirteen, so those were what she remembered the most. Nights where they watched old movies and ate popcorn and drank hot chocolate or dressing up for Halloween in like costumes. Vickie had a creative streak too, but hers was for the avant-garde and different. Sam never appreciated that aspect because it set her more apart from her peers and she only wanted to be like everyone else—like all of those girls whose lives she assumed were perfect, but now knew couldn't be true.

"You seemed so put together, as if you were born older and wiser than the rest of us," her mom's voice droned on, drawing Sam out of her thoughts. They neared the kitchen table and Vickie pulled out a chair then guided her to sit. "I have coffee. Or soft drinks?"

"Coffee's fine." It would give her something to do with her hands, along with something to focus on other than her sick thoughts.

Her mom nodded then turned to Mary Ann, who'd plopped into a chair across from Sam. "How about you, sweetie?"

"Coffee'll work for me too." Mary Ann smiled. Sam couldn't mistake the look that passed between her best friend and her mother. Vickie's was grateful and Mary Ann's was satisfied.

"I must look atrocious." Vickie patted her hair, then walked over to the sink and tore off a paper towel. After wetting it, she wiped the remnants of her makeup off her face.

Seconds later, she filled three cups, served Mary Ann first, then Sam, before joining them at the table. "You knew your own mind all those years ago and I couldn't change it, which is probably a good thing." After taking a sip of coffee, she glanced up. "I guess you still do. Anyway, you'll have to meet Bob. Well, you've met him before." She cleared her throat and looked down, as a pink flush rose up her face. Yeah, Sam had met him and all of his naked splendor. "But now we're married." Vickie's smile burst out and all embarrassment vanished. She actually beamed when she made eye contact and said, "Can you believe it? Last year we tied the knot," sticking out her left hand to show off a small diamond in a gold band featured on her third finger. "Been happy for three years."

Vickie pushed a strand of hair behind her ear and lowered her gaze again, now appearing more nervous than embarrassed as she studied the tile floor intently. She added in a soft voice, "I kicked him out after you left and did a little soul-searching. Hated you for a long while, until I realized you were right and I was wasting my life with losers. Bob wasn't a loser, but if I hadn't have kicked him out, we'd never have come this far." She finally glanced up at Sam again. "I wanted to invite you to the wedding. I even called you, but then I chickened out and hung up the phone before you answered." Vickie made clucking noises, "Bwk, bwk, bwk, bwk," and waved her hands under her armpits. "Big chicken. That's me."

The burst of laughter that rose from Sam's chest felt natural and somewhat freeing, yanking her back mentally fifteen years. Her mom had always had a weird sense of humor, except that during their last months together she'd been too angry to appreciate it.

Hell, if only things had been different and Vickie had found Bob a year or two earlier.

"It's taken me a lifetime to return, so you're not the only chicken in the family." Her smile turned sad as she added, honestly, "I seem to have grown a few feathers."

"Well, we won't talk about that." Smiling, Vickie inhaled deeply and her focus returned to her mug. Then, she looked up allowing their gazes to reconnect so that Sam could see in the depths of her mother's brown eyes, so like her own, that Vickie didn't want anything to mar this reunion. "We can talk about it later," she said, her tone adding to the conclusion. "Right now is a time for celebrating. After all, we've both taken big steps in rectifying our past and we're grabbing hold of our future. I only pray we'll grow closer as time goes by."

Vickie's hand inched across the table to cover hers. "Oh, baby, I'm so glad you stopped by. You don't know what this means to me. I love you. I've always loved you. Just never had a very good way of showing it." Her grip tightened. "Can you ever forgive me? It's taken me years to realize how stupid I was, but you have to understand, I was just a naïve kid myself when I had you. I didn't grow up until you walked out that door. By then it was too late."

"Oh, Momma." Suddenly all those years, while not forgotten, because you just can't forget stuff like that, were at least pushed to the side for a time and an overwhelming feeling of understanding and love took over the place where hurt had lingered for too long. Sam got up and went around the table to give her mom a heartfelt hug. "I love you too." For the first time in over twelve years, she actually felt love in her heart for her mother. As Mary Ann had said, it was damned freeing, because love, it seemed, trumped anger and hurt every time.

She glanced at Mary Ann and noted tears streaming down her friend's face. She mouthed over her mother's shoulder, "Thanks. I owe you."

Maybe there was something to be said for forgiveness after all.

~

Later that night, lying in bed, Sam mentally reviewed all that had happened in the past twenty-four hours. Her visit with her mom had filled her with renewed hope that some sort of a relationship could exist between them. Maybe not mother and daughter. After all, Sam had to face facts. Her mom had never been mother of the year, but she wasn't all bad either. Vickie had redeeming qualities and the two of them were blood.

Funny, she'd always thought of Vickie as lazy or never wanting anything better. Now, she realized that was too easy an answer. In reality, her mom had merely accepted the horror of her life and hadn't been strong enough to fight it. Sam grasped the full extent of that revelation earlier while the two spent the afternoon talking.

Yep, she thought, staring into the darkened room. Maybe she

could take another chance on James. Her conversation with Mary Ann on the drive home infiltrated her thoughts just then.

Now that she'd solved the problem of her relationship with Vickie, Mary Ann urged her to work on her relationship with James. Mary Ann seemed to believe James loved her and if Sam had only given him more time in the first place, things would have work out. Easy for Mary Ann to say, when she didn't possess all of Sam's baggage. Yet, also according to her friend, she wasn't that needy kid anymore. She could count on herself now. No one—including James—could give her what she needed to give herself.

It all made sense.

He seemed to want some type of relationship—one that included more than friendship. On the other hand, what if he needed as many chances as Vickie? Her mom had disappointed her time and time again before Sam finally left home. Earlier, Sam voiced those concerns to Mary Ann. She doubted she possessed the stamina to endure any more disappointments in life, especially if they involved her heart and James. Mary Ann only shook her head and said something about how nothing worthwhile in life came easy, and that the only reason James had the power to hurt her was because she loved him.

"We're all human," Mary Ann said. "We all make mistakes that need forgiveness, especially men like James." Then Mary Ann went for the jugular of common sense. "Forgiveness is freeing and anything can be forgiven. It's the holding on to the grievance that amplifies the pain inside. You forgave your mother, right?" Sam could only agree, to which Mary Ann added, "Look how that turned out."

Sam sighed in the dark. If only she weren't a coward. Admittedly, she was too afraid of what would happen if she dropped her guard.

She hit the pillow, wishing for the hundredth time she'd never kissed the man to begin with.

The moment the thought was out, she discarded it as false. James had taught her much and she would never regret their affair. A few months with him had been the experience of a lifetime.

What she really wanted was a crystal ball to see into the future, then she'd know what to do. Her after-dinner conversation with Kate flashed and added more indecision into the mix. Kate told her to follow her heart. Yet, right now, her heart was too damned scared to lead her anywhere.

Chapter 17

At seven a.m. the following Monday morning, James opened the passenger door of his SUV.

A frisson of pleasure made Sam pause for a second at seeing her usual *venti* cup of Starbucks coffee resting in the cup holder.

She snatched the apple, before sitting inside and grinned. "Thanks."

"You already know my take on rituals."

"Yeah." She noted his shirt, recognizing the same pale blue fabric. "You're wearing your lucky shirt, I see."

"Today is another important day, so of course I had to wear it." His grin was infectious and instantly, the old James, the James she'd come to love as a friend, was back.

"Damn right." She returned his grin, as a band around her heart loosened. "I completely understand." Her grin relaxed into a soft smile as she turned to look out the window. He wasn't the enemy. Memories of all they'd shared encompassed her and she yearned to go back in time.

"I miss our friendship," she said truthfully, after remaining silent for several miles. She kept her eyes on the passing scenery, too much of a coward to meet his gaze.

"So do I."

The regret in the simple statement caused her to risk a glance at him. She glimpsed the same regret in his eyes when their stares connected. She offered a sad smile. "Since I'm being open, I should also say I miss bouncing ideas off you. So many times over the past weeks, I've wanted to rush into your office."

"Why didn't you?" He held her gaze for a brief moment, then shifted his focus back on the road.

"You know why." She grinned, feeling suddenly lightheaded, and thankful he had to keep his eyes on traffic. His intense gaze did what it always did. Grabbed her heart with a soul-searing need that scared her.

"Yeah, I guess I do. My actions weren't exactly that of a true friend, were they?" He heaved a wistful sigh. "But you have to understand. I was so immersed in our affair, friendship took a vacation." He glanced at her once again and total candor spilled from that intense gaze. "I *do* love you, Sam." He returned his attention to driving. "I'm sorry I hurt you. You don't know how much. If I could go back to that day and undo it, I would."

"I know." She had no defenses against such honest emotion that pummeled her guard and dragged her obscured feelings closer to the edge of her mental precipice. Mary Ann's remarks resurfaced and she realized their significance.

"Have I got a chance?"

She understood what he was asking. Did she have the guts to grab on to love? "I don't know. I need more time." Geez, listen to her! She took a deep breath and tried not to think about how she was asking for basically the same thing he'd asked for before she jumped ship.

"How much time?"

"I don't know—enough to figure out what I want."

"Uh-uh. You can't attack me for my indecision and then use the same ruse. Try again. "

She smiled and the air she was holding in came out in one long sigh at his shrewdness. "Before we went to Sonoma, I had a clear picture of what I wanted. Now I have no clue. How could I when I've only dated two men in my entire life?"

"I see." He nodded, appearing to accept the statement. Then, his lips pursed into a thin line. He slowly shook his head and grunted. "Pretty lame excuse, if you ask me."

"No, it's not," she defended. "You have to admit, my experiences are limited. What if there's someone out there who's more suited for me?" He didn't need to know she agreed with his assessment. Dating anyone else did seem a lame excuse to avoid facing the truth. So, why was she still running?

"There isn't." Smug confidence was present in every syllable as well as every cell in his body.

She laughed. His audacity was so like him and such a big part of his charm. "Just like that," she said, snapping her fingers. "You're so sure?"

"Yes. It's the only thing I *am* sure of. Unlike you, I have dated. Too many women not to know by now what's what with us." His self-assured grin spread, showing more conviction, only she didn't see how it was possible. His eyes flashed genuine warmth, heated her insides, and made her realize when he looked at her with such intensity she wanted to forgive him anything. "I just figured out something else. Since I know what I want, I can back off. Wait until you finally realize it too. We were real, Sam. Doesn't get any better."

She returned his smile, ready to concede, wishing he didn't know her so well.

Suddenly, images of her past flashed like a neon sign warning her heart to beware. Uncertainty swamped her. "I still need time," she murmured, refocusing on the passing cars outside her window. She really needed that crystal ball.

Neither spoke for the rest of their ride, but the silence hummed with an underlying awareness. Sam heaved a sigh of relief that he seemed to be honoring his promise. He was backing off. For now.

Thankfully, they were close to Half Moon Bay. Sam was never so happy to see their exit up ahead. She needed a break from his proximity. She couldn't think when he was this close.

Within minutes, he pulled into the gravel driveway and parked. Both stepped out of the car together and headed toward the group of people near a couple of bulldozers and other heavy trucks.

An hour later, amid all the mucky-mucks and press, Sam cut the ribbon. She and James, along with the builder, dug the first three shovels of dirt, which signified the highlight of the groundbreaking ceremony. She handed the shovel over to one of the workers as two reporters from the local news approached for an interview. For the next two hours, both she and James did their part, giving the firm more exposure.

Finally, the hoopla was over. The day was a huge success. McAlpin was happy. So much so that he invited them to a late leisurely lunch. Sam had no more time during the crazy day to obsess or even think about what James had said earlier.

Now, on the drive back to San Mateo, their conversation infiltrated her thoughts.

Neither spoke. James seemed to be as lost in his thoughts as she was in hers.

They exited Highway 92 and he glanced over. "The day's pretty much done." It was now ten to four. "Want to get a drink at the Pit Stop?" His attention went back to the road and his shoulders lifted in a careless shrug. "We need to celebrate. It's not every day the firm of Morrison, Morgan, Stone and Collins gets two segments on the local news."

"Sure." Sam sighed. It was stupid at this point to pretend she didn't want to be with him. "A drink sounds nice." Still, her heart raced. What if Mary Ann was wrong?

Both remained silent as he guided the car into the parking lot. Sam stared straight ahead, completely aware of his energy. A trace of his aftershave wafted under her nose. Memories of the last time she smelled the scent filled her, eliciting more memories of their last night together. The same night she'd run out of his house.

It dawned on her that she was still running. Here she blamed James for everything and she owned part of the problem. Mary Ann was right. She *had* let her expectations destroy what they'd built in a couple of months.

Thankfully, her thoughts faded when he jerked to a stop. The second he turned off the ignition, she practically leapt out of the car.

"So, what've you been up to?" Sam asked in as nonchalant a voice as she could muster, meeting him at the back of the SUV. It was a silly question, but nerves kept her brain from functioning normally and coming up with a better one. Hopefully, alcohol would dull those nerves so she could finally relax.

"Just working." He pointed to the entrance and smiled. "Shall we?" Before she knew what he was about to do, he grabbed her hand. He looked straight into her eyes and said in a low voice, "I didn't lie earlier. I have missed you, Sam."

Sam swallowed hard, wishing she didn't find him so attractive. Wishing she could ignore the heat she caught in his gaze. Holding his hand, she followed him into the bar as indecision gripped her. *No. Remember Mar's advice.* She threw her shoulders back and lifted her head higher. She could do this. It was only drinks. So what if it might lead to dinner and then a night spent together. Sam needed to let go of the past and move forward. She needed to grab on to love as Mary Ann had said and not worry about what-ifs.

~

Five minutes into happy hour meant they lingered only seconds for a table in the fairly empty bar, as patrons began trickling in. They sat and waited for service.

James asked a few questions about Sam's other projects. In between ordering and receiving drinks, she answered along with asking a few questions of her own about his projects.

He finished speaking of his latest problem and reached for her hand. He laced fingers, no longer concerned with his promise. It was time to let her know exactly what was in his heart. "I missed this," he said candidly. "I miss sharing our lives, maybe even more than I miss making love."

Sam nodded. "I know what you mean." She smiled. "I miss waking up with you." Her attention then went to their intertwined fingers.

Though heartened, James wasn't entirely sure how to respond. He watched her roll a paper napkin up, then unroll it with her free hand. A definite sign of nerves in his opinion, so he was unwilling to say something that might ruin the truce they seemed to be forming.

"I went to see my mother," she said, ending the long silence.

Her statement shocked him. His focus drifted to her face. "Really?" he asked, with eyebrows raised. "How'd that go?"

"Better than I expected." She offered a tremulous smile, but still wouldn't meet his gaze as she recounted her day, ending with, "I forgave her for being human." She cleared her throat and brushed a strand of hair behind her ears. "According to Mary Ann, forgiveness is freeing and anything can be forgiven. It appears she was right." She hesitated, then looked right at him. The seriousness in her tone matched the earnestness in her eyes. "I was hoping we could forgive each other."

Elation filled James. "Works for me." He smiled. "I've done a lot of thinking since that morning," he said minutes later. "You were right about me not bothering to fight for you. But you were dead wrong about the reason. You *are* mine, Sam, just as I'm yours. You can date a thousand guys and never find what we had. We belong together. You know it and I know it. I won't deny I was petrified by what I felt. What petrifies me more is living a life without you in it."

Her brow furrowed in confusion. "I don't understand."

Of course she didn't. Why would she believe he could declare himself so effortlessly when he'd always avoided the subject? Well, no more. "Then, allow me to make myself very clear," he said in a louder, more distinct voice. "Commitment. You say you want it, then prove it. Marry me." He snared her gaze, gauging her reaction. "I've shocked you." That was an understatement. "I'm asking you to be my wife. Right here, right now, make a decision."

"Wow." Sam continued staring at him, her eyes huge.

Seconds ticked by.

"I'm waiting."

"You don't give a girl much notice," she offered, in an obvious attempt to stall for more time. "What if—"

"You've had plenty of notice and you damn well know it," he said, unwilling to listen to any excuses. When she silently kept her cautious gaze on him, his smile broadened and his heart melted on the spot. "Admit it, Sam. You're just as petrified as I am, so let's be petrified together. I miss you…in my bed…in my life. I love you. I'll always love you. I'm not perfect, so I can't promise never to make mistakes, but I can promise to keep at it until I get it right."

Just then the place exploded with noise when those around them started whistling and clapping. James' attention returned to his surroundings along with Sam's. His proposal had caught the notice of every person around them.

~

Sam wanted to crawl into a hole, but not James. He only chuckled. Then his grin spread. He stood and bowed, nodding to the onlookers, before aiming that sexy gaze in her direction.

"They're rooting for me. So, what do you say?"

Like always, his crinkled oceanic gaze carried her away to never-never land and she knew in that exact moment what her heart craved. *Him.* She laughed as love infiltrated her soul, shoving out the last of her indecision.

"I say yes. Catch me and make me the happiest woman alive." Then she jumped up and threw herself into his arms, knowing without a doubt, she'd forgiven him. More than that. She couldn't live another moment without telling him how she felt.

"Oh, James. I love you too," she murmured, right before her lips found his.

The long and soulful kiss pulled another round of applause from those around them. James lifted his head and grinned. He glanced at her and winked. "I think we'd better wait till we get home to finish this kiss. Otherwise these people will get more of a show than they bargained for."

He adjusted her against his hip in order to reach for his wallet. He pulled out enough to cover the tab and a generous tip, then readjusted her so that he could carry her. Giggling, she wrapped her arms tighter around him while he started out of the bar. She nuzzled his neck, as more love than she thought she possessed engulfed her heart. How had she ever thought she could live without him?

In the privacy of the parking lot, out of view of any of the rowdy customers, James slowed, then inched his head closer to hers. "You've made me the happiest man on the planet. I love you. I'll always love you. I can't live without you."

Before he could lower his head the rest of the way, she placed a stilling hand on his mouth and said with all the emotion pouring out of her heart, "I love you too. I'll need a lifetime to show you how much."

"A lifetime works." He grinned, then sealed the promise with a kiss.

About the Author

Sandy Loyd was born and raised in Salt Lake City, Utah. Wanderlust hit early on and she has lived a varied life since then. She joined the Army to see the world and to get an education. Living and training in four states and Germany during the three-year stint provided a cultural education. She graduated from Arizona State University with a BS in Marketing and landed a job in San Francisco that involved extensive travel throughout the United States. She's always considered San Francisco a US treasure that few other cities worldwide can compare. She's since married and moved on from her single days, but she still misses the city's diversity and beauty.

She now lives in Kentucky and 'retired' from sales after twenty years to become a stay at home mom when her son kept asking why she had to be gone all the time. She filled her days with volunteering, ending up as a PTA President in her son's elementary school. When her son moved on to Middle School, boredom set in. She wanted to be around when he came home from school, so she began to write to fill in the time. And she's been writing ever since.

James, the third story in the California series, is set in the Bay Area, as are the first two in the series Winter Interlude and Promises, Promises. They're fun stories of crazy friends who, like single people everywhere, are seeking that someone special to share their lives with among thousands of eligible candidates.

Made in United States
North Haven, CT
07 March 2023

33709708R00117